Caitli...,

# THE CURSE OF DOLL ISLAND

OCEAN

It was great meeting you
at the 2019 GCLS CON!

Stay away from islands
with Dolls!
    "

Ocea

OCEAN'S EDGE PUBLISHING

AND SO IT BEGINS...

**The Curse of Doll Island**

**By Ocean**

CUBA 1732

Night of the Curse of the Damned

"Do they know they are to die tonight?" he asked, his face and voice stone cold with seriousness.

His worried gaze bounced between the goat and the two women who lay on the bottom of the canoe.

He was the younger of the two men she'd chosen to assist her yet he was still only a boy. His chest was brown, beautiful, smooth and hairless like a girl's. Only the shadow of light fuzz decorated his chin. His hand rested reassuringly on the goat's head, gently rubbing the velvety short nubs in an unsuccessful attempt to quiet the frantic bleating. The animal struggled fiercely to get away, and in its distress, the young goat had bitten its tongue. A thin trail of blood dripped from the agitated animal's mouth. As the burgundy fluid snaked toward its chest, it left a dark shimmering stain down the side of its throat. The young goat's golden eyes, with their horizontal black center, were flared open, round and wide with terror. They stood out in sharp contrast against the obsidian black of the distressed animal's skin.

"Shush." The word seethed through the Mambo's teeth as if she herself were a snake, hissing the command. The man shot a glare at the boy with a fierce intensity that communicated a grave mistake had been made by speaking. Both he and the boy froze, not daring to move as their gaze fixated on the old woman, their eyes wide and filled with fright like those of the goat.

The boy prayed as he held his breath and waited to see if the high priestess would cast a spell on him. If she did choose to perform an incantation, he wondered if the curse would turn him into stone, a snake, or worse. She knew of curses that could turn a person into a being who walked the earth for eternity in human form but whose *gros-bon-ange* – who's soul – had been removed.

When the Mambo returned her attention toward the two figurines she was working on, her two assistants relaxed their shoulders and resumed breathing.

The woman studied the dolls intensely while the blade of her knife carved expertly and the blocks of wax took shape. Two small, human figures appeared to come to life under the magic of her skillful hands. Her concentration was fierce, and she took great care in the precision of every movement of the knife to ensure the accuracy of each detail.

The man and the boy waited, silently, patiently, watching as the sun set beyond the distant horizon behind them and the moon rose above the skyline in front of them. From where they sat, in a tiny boat at the edge of the island, there was nothing but waves on three out of the four directions. Behind them was a white sandy beach lined by a lush tropical forest. At this time of night, nothing moved but the waves, so their gazes fell on the woman's hands as she worked, and they waited.

The boy's own hands continued to smooth along the top of the goat's head and down its throat. It was his way of trying to calm the agitated animal and also an endeavor to satisfy his own restlessness. They were both young and afraid, he and the goat. Both stood on similar wobbly legs with boney knees that struggled to keep balance as the double-hulled canoe gently rocked side-to-side. The boy wondered if the goat knew it had been selected to be the *l'kabrit*–the holy sacrifice – and if it did know, was it afraid or was it proud to have been selected for such an honor? But he dared not speak again, choosing instead to remain quiet and keep his thoughts and questions to himself. His curiosity would have to wait to be satisfied. He'd ask the man later, when they were alone.

The sound of waves rhythmically splashing against the side of the boat, then crashing onto the beach were the only noises on this otherwise still night. As if the world knew what was about to happen, animals, people, and even the weather, remained still out of either respect or fear. It was a chilled, unnerving silence.

The man possessed more patience than the boy. He'd been on these trips before. Many times. It was his job to be patient. To wait without complaint or comment until the Mambo was ready. That's the way it was. When she gave the command, he would row. The boy would help, as much as he could, of course. But the man knew it was because of his own wide shoulders and thick, massive muscles bulging beneath the tight, dark skin of his back, that they'd get where they needed to go. And safely return. This is the reason he'd been selected to be the Mambo's assistant. He was the largest man on the island, and he was aware and appreciative of the honor it was to have been chosen to serve her.

He watched with quiet respect and wondered if the rumors were true. That she was the daughter of Diablesse.

She was certainly beautiful enough. Even though the years had robbed her of the attractiveness of youth, she regained the elegant kind of beauty that accompanied power and confidence. Legend had it Diablesse had been an exquisite woman, but because she'd made deals with the devil, she'd been turned into a demon. If it was true that this Mambo was Diablesse's daughter...

*Could be,* he thought as he stared at the symbol positioned at the center of the necklace that hung around her neck. Surrounded by teeth and bones, most of them human, the center piece was a V-shaped symbol of a woman's punta: the symbol of Diablesse. He glanced at the leather bindings wrapping her feet. Had her feet been bare, he'd know for sure. But they were hidden, swathed tightly in leather. As they always were. The rumor in the village had long been that one of her feet was identical to a cow's hoof. The sign of the demon. He watched wordlessly, not daring to speak. He was fearful that if he interrupted her in any way, one of his bones or teeth would end up on her necklace along with the remnants of her past enemies.

*The boy is lucky,* he thought. *He is young. He will learn.*

When the Mambo was done, she held the dolls up, one in each hand, to admire her work. They were beautifully and intricately carved. The light of the moon reflected off each of the delicate etches and the tiny figures sparkled and glistened.

*Magic,* the boy thought as he stared consumed with awe.

Each face and body was different in its shape and proportion, but it was undeniable who the figures were intentionally made to resemble.

The man and the boy studied the faces of the dolls with a combination of admiration and fear. Their gaze slid from the miniature figurines to what lay next to their bare, brown feet.

Two women lay sprawled across the bottom of the canoe. Their bodies were contorted with limbs twisted in unnatural positions. But there was no mistaking it. They matched in extraordinary detail, the two wax dolls that the Mambo now clutched in each palm.

Prologue cont.

# TO THE ISLAND

T hough the women appeared to be in a deep sleep, the man and boy were both well aware it was not the type of sleep that brings rest. They'd witnessed before what happened to a person under the spell after having been given a drink from the "vine of the dead," and they knew what the inevitable outcome would be. The women's minds were now being filled with horrible nightmares of demons and death. When they awoke, they would try to spit out the demons but instead, their insides, a combination of black, green and red would violently project from every orifice, signally the beginning of the trail to death. The Mambo would make sure they finished their journey.

The man studied the two women and his heart ached with sympathy. They were beautiful as they slept at the bottom of his boat. He wondered why they would risk such a fate and tempt the demons by doing wrong to the Mambo. He also wondered which bone or tooth from each the

Mambo would choose to be the newest addition to her abundant necklace.

*No matter to me,* he thought. All that mattered was he do his job tonight, do it well and return the Mambo back to the island tomorrow. Then he could get on with his life. Until she summoned him the next time.

The Mambo climbed cautiously to the front of the canoe. The years had taken their toll, and she moved slowly, yet gracefully. The boy wondered why she didn't use her magic to make herself young again. Another question he'd ask the man later.

She turned her back to the occupants of the boat, carefully placed the two carved figurines on a pillow at her feet, sat and began chanting. Her hands beat rhythmically on the small ceremonial drum she'd brought with her. This was the man's cue to begin. Without hesitation, he jumped into the black water. His feet sank into the cool, silty mud as he pushed the canoe away from shore as his father had taught him to do as a young boy. He guided the boat toward the sea as his ancestors had done for hundreds of years before he was born.

He directed the boat until the cool, salty water splashed his nipples and with a final push, hoisted himself up onto the craft as it silently drifted from the island. The boy sat, cautiously clutching the side of the canoe with one hand while the other arm wrapped tightly around the neck of the goat. He did his best to stabilize the animal as they swayed with the waves. Though the trip would be rocky, the boy was confident the two large bamboo logs that extended from each side of the boat would provide balance and prevent it from tipping over. It was his responsibility to make sure the goat made it to the island. He was well aware of the seriousness of the task that'd been assigned to him and was mindful to remain vigilant.

The man's skin sparkled as drops of sea water trailed down his skin, reflecting the dull moonlight that peeked through a thin layer of gray misty clouds. He gripped and tugged on the ropes. As if on cue, the wind picked up. The heavy sail flapped as it unfurled and rose up the solitary mast that impaled the center of the small vessel. As he secured the cow skin sail, it made a flapping sound as it fluttered in the night breeze. *That's a good sign*, he thought. *A good sign from the Voodoo spirit Bacossou who controls the wind.* The gusts at his back would help with his paddling. *The Mambo must have arranged for the wind to be here tonight.* For that, he was grateful.

As he settled into the back of the boat and adjusted the oars, the greenish-yellow eyes of several crocodiles, as they slithered from the land and into the water, caught his attention. On another night, they would've been a cause for concern but not tonight. Even the man-eaters were aware of the Mambo's powers. They'd leave the occupants of the boat alone and search instead for food not involved with bad magic.

The moon had risen to the right, and the sun had set to the left. He placed the nose of the canoe straight ahead between the two, adjusted the sail and, as the Mambo's soft chants and drum beats created a rhythm for him to follow, began to row. His thoughts drifted to what he knew was about to take place tonight, and he said a silent prayer for the souls of the goat and the women.

Prologue cont.

## THE SACRED CEREMONY

~

The man leapt from the boat, thankful for the relief the cool water gave to his over-heated body. He tugged the craft toward the shore, then dragged it up onto the sandy beach. His back, chest and arms ached from hours of rowing. He grunted as he strained to yank the canoe and the occupants with it, out of the water. When the boat was securely tied to the base of a massive palm tree, he raised a large, thick hand toward the Mambo to aid her in climbing out of the vessel. She wavered slightly when she stood, but firmly gripped his dense wrist and allowed him to assist her. Even though the night air was hot and moist, the thin fingers that clung to him were chilled like an eel. He stared at her hand. Disturbing thoughts raced through his mind, images of the kinds of magic that the hand may have performed. In horror, he watched as goosebumps rose on his arm in the area where their skin met.

Once on land, she squared her shoulders, stood tall and surveyed her surroundings. The man understood what she searched for. She was looking for the best place to perform the ceremony. She needed to find a *poto mitan*, a sacred tree. Her gaze took note of the stars and location of the moon. She closed her eyes to better determine from which direction the wind came. Slowly, mindfully, she walked the beach, carefully considering each of the many large palm trees that towered over her. Finally, she stopped in front of a particular tree, closed her eyes and placed her forehead and palms against it. Her lips were moving though the man could not hear what she was saying. She remained there for a few moments, appearing to merge her energy with that of the tree. When she stepped away, she wasted no time setting up the ceremonial circle around it. The man could tell by the puzzled look on the boy's face that he wondered what she was doing. Once, the boy opened his mouth to speak but quickly pressed his lips tightly together when the man pressed a finger against his own lips. He'd explain to the youth later.

Many years ago, the first time he'd gone on a trip like this, the Mambo had shared with him the details of what she did and why she was doing it. It'd been the first time she'd ever spoken to him and he'd not asked to have it explained, she'd just started talking. It was also the last time she'd ever spoken to him. Since that night, he'd been on many trips such as this with her. Always to a different island. Usually with just one other passenger in the boat. Usually, a male. This was the first time the Mambo's target was a woman. And not just one, but two. It was not his place to ask.

The man and boy watched from a distance as she drew a sacred design in the sand. She created the large symbol by pouring blessed flour made from the dried and crushed bones of others who had betrayed her.

When the man gave him a nod, the boy struggled to lift the goat off the boat and carry it onto land. The goat resisted and bleated, but the boy held it firmly and led it to the outside border of the ceremonial circle. He tied the panicked animal securely to the base of the tree with the other end of the thick rope that tightly encircled its neck. Parts of the rope were stained pink from where the goat's blood had dripped from its injured tongue.

They were both tired, the boy and the goat. One would soon sleep and one soon die.

One at a time, the man hoisted each unconscious woman over his shoulder and carried her to land. He lay the women down, gently and respectfully onto the soft, white sand in the center of the ceremonial circle that the Mambo had made for this purpose. The women had stirred during the journey, thrashing and calling out incoherently, but had not awakened enough to comprehend what was happening to them. They would never fully awaken.

The Mambo snapped instructions to the boy to gather firewood, which he dutifully did. Next to the bodies of the women, she methodically built an enormous bonfire. Once the fire blazed, she paced the circumference of the circle, chanting and rattling her *asson*. The shells, stones, and bones clattered inside the small skull attached to the end of the handle she gripped. The rhythm of the rattling matched her chants perfectly.

When she was ready, she indicated for the boy to bring the goat. He held the animal's body as tightly as he could, comforting the terrified creature who, as if sensing what was about to happen, struggled and bleated, begging to be spared. They both trembled uncontrollably as they stepped over the line drawn in the sand. The skin on the boy's flesh turned icy the moment he entered the circle, and he said two silent prayers. The first to Guede Nimbo, the spirit of the dead, asking that the animal's passing be swift and painless and that his little friend be given peace in the afterlife. The second prayer was to the Laos, the Gods of his departed family, thanking them for keeping him safe on this journey so far. For more good luck, he kissed the *paquet congo* hanging around his neck. It had been given to him by his grandmother to ward off bad spirits. He then knelt beside the doomed animal and with quivering hands, held its head as steady as he could.

The Mambo stripped naked and rubbed herself with a mixture of habanero peppers and dark rum. She drank the holy *kimanga* potion. This would connect her to her Gods before beginning the sacred dance. Within moments, possessed by the spirits and foaming at the mouth, she reached for the handle of the knife that lay in the center of the circle. With the skull rattle in one hand and the knife in the other, she danced. The long, thin blade sparkled in the moonlight with a magic the boy had never seen before. He watched, as if in a trance, mesmerized. When the slice of the silver blade slipped across the tender skin of the goat's throat, it was done so swiftly and expertly that it surprised both the goat and the boy. Maroon blood spurted. Both the Mambo and the boy were sprayed as the sacred liquid spouted into the bowl that had been brought specifically to capture it. Instantly, the goat fell limp in the boy's arms.

The Mambo dropped the rattle and the knife, grasped the bowl of foaming, red blood, and faced the two recumbent women. She chanted words that were foreign to the boy, but they flowed with an intense fury.

*"Dooha bangoo bahaba mozzubee. Witchabak nosquito. Witchabak morang zee chagga!"*

Her voice escalated in tone, intensity and volume, until reaching a powerful crescendo. Though he didn't understand what she was saying, he did recognize the *petro zemi* that had rolled in, summoned by the Mambo for the ceremony. Enormous black clouds covered the sky, bringing with them fierce gusts of wind, sheets of rain, and magical lightning. A crack pierced the air, and the boy dropped the body of the goat and pressed the palms of his hands to cover his ears. A bolt of lightning crashed from the dark skies, striking the ground where the Mambo had drawn the circumference of the circle with the holy flour. The ground shook, and the boy screamed. Instantaneously, the circle ignited and a red and orange flame burst alive as it whooshed around the circle, enclosing the boy, goat, women, and Mambo inside a ring of fire.

The boy crawled backward like a crab, away from the bloody corpse of the goat and froze in terror, trapped by the wall of fire. The man, fearful to enter the ceremonious circle, reached through the flames, wrapped a large hand firmly around the boy's thin arm and yanked him away. It was not meant for the child to die there today and their job was done. It would be bad juju to stay and witness the rest of the sacred ceremony. Whatever the Mambo intended to do to the two women was her business and hers alone. Besides, he was ready to drink the flask of whiskey he'd been given as part of his payment from the Mambo. His services would be needed no more tonight, not until the morning when he would row the boy and the Mambo back to the island.

The boy had trouble walking, partly because of the sand and partly because his fear had traumatized his brain. His muscles were weak. The man, with a firm grip on the boy's arm above the elbow, led him, as he would have guided a young bull by the nose, away from the fire and toward the forest.

"But the Mambo. She will burn?" the boy protested.

"No. She will not burn." The man answered in a confident voice as they left the beach and made their way toward the jungle. They settled in protected from the wind and rain by the lush foliage but far enough so the Mambo's incantations were muffled chants.

When they stopped, the man plunked himself down in an area surrounded by the protection of large, twisted roots of the mangrove trees. The boy followed suit and sat leaning against a nearby tree trunk. He pulled his knees to his chest and wrapped his arms around his bent legs. It was then he noticed the splattering of blood from the goat that covered him. He closed his eyes and murmured another prayer to the Gods asking them to take care of his little friend.

The man unwrapped the thin rope that tied the piece of cork in one end of the flask that had been made from a goat's bladder. He raised the pouch to his mouth, and drank. A pained smile curved his thick lips as the liquid burned his mouth and lit a fire inside him as it trickled down his throat. Soon the aches in his muscles and in his mind would be gone. It was a magic potion of the good kind. Mambo's good magic. He passed the flask to the boy who took a cautious sip but forcefully coughed most of it on to the ground. The man's laugh was long and deep throated. He took back the flask from the boy who continued to expel the dark liquid onto the sand.

When he'd finished, the boy sat still, not speaking. His chin rested on the tops of his knees. He stared straight ahead and although his body did not move, his mind was busy like a monkey. It didn't take long for the man's hand to drop. The empty flask fell into the sandy earth, his eyes rolled up behind his eyelids and his torso drooped sideways against the tree. His jaw dropped, and his snores competed with the thunder that hovered over the beach.

The boy jumped up and ran in the direction of the coastline. Barefoot, he ran swiftly and silently through the forest, guided by what little light the rising moon cast as it peeked from behind the dark clouds drifting past.

Nearby, the cracking of a branch caught his attention, and he spun around. To his horror, there stood Guede Nimbo, the God of Death, who guards the eternal gates where a soul must pass on their way to the underworld. He was tall, taller than the man who had rowed them there, and darker than a shadow. His eyes blazed a fiery red. He stood, solid as a mountain, and the boy knew he was there waiting for the three newest souls to join him. When their gaze met, the boy shivered. He'd heard that if a person looked into the eyes of Guede Nimbo, this is what would happen. First, cold creeps through your veins. Next, your muscles freeze and, unable to breathe, you die. It was then that Guede Nimbo could steal your soul.

The boy forced himself to break the gaze, turned and ran, but continued to glance over his shoulder. Fortunately, he was not followed, and he attributed his luck to the souls of the women and the goat that the Guedo Nimbo was here to collect. He also thanked Laos and his ancestors for protecting him.

By the time he'd reached the beach, the rain poured cruelly down on everything in sight, including the Mambo who remained, naked and dancing wildly in the circle. The fire in the center as well as the burning edge of the loop continued to flare. Why the torrential rain hadn't put it out, the boy did not know. *"Mambo's magic,"* he decided. *"There is much that cannot be explained."*

Her brown skin was beautiful and shimmered with the mixture of sweat, rain, and elixir beneath the occasional flash of lightning and the glimmer of moonlight. For the second time tonight, he was mesmerized as he watched her prance, chant, and shake the rattles she grasped in both hands. The women were on their hands and knees and vomiting violently. The non-human sound they made as they tried to spit out the demons was only occasionally smothered by a crash of thunder that followed the bright, sputtering flashes of lightning. He wondered what the women had done to bring the wrath of the Mambo down on them and pitied them. He wasn't sure what the Mambo planned to do to them, but one thing he did know for certain. Their souls would forever be restless. The Mambo would make sure of that.

*It's a shame,* he thought. *They were both so beautiful.*

He crouched low, squatting on his heels, mindful to remain hidden behind the thick, prickly vines and knotted tree roots. His lips moved in another silent prayer to his Laos Gods, this time asking them to forgive him for being unable to resist watching the sacred ceremony. And he begged them to protect him from any bad juju that this recklessness might cause.

His body still shook from having seen the Guede Nimbo. He glanced to make sure it had not changed its mind to come for him. He hoped the God of death was not there for him today but kissed the paquet congo that hung from his neck, just in case.

The heart inside his rib cage banged as if demanding to be let out and he hoped the Mambo would be too occupied to hear it. He inhaled deeply, held his breath and peered through the thick brown roots that his small body hid behind. Reaching with both hands, he separated the tall, wet, green weeds to get a better view, swiping at a large intricately woven, silver spiderweb that spread before him. A furry black spider the size of his palm with two yellow spots on its back that looked like eyes, scampered off the web and onto a vine. He watched it long enough to be confident it headed in a direction away from him.

He then turned his attention toward the beach and waited for the souls of the doomed women to appear.

## A THREE-HOUR CRUISE

"And now ladies and gentlemen, we're approaching the infamous Doll Island." The guide stood at the bow of the boat and pointed with outstretched hand. Spread before him, a crowd of tourists adorned in colorful, flowery printed shirts, donning straw hats and sunglasses, stood 'oohing' and 'aahing'. His voice boomed over the many loud speakers strategically located throughout the boat.

"Legend has it, in the early 1700s a Shaman cast a spell on two women and banished them to live on this island for eternity. Their spirits were horrifically removed from their bodies and transferred into two wax dolls. As the story goes, two men rowed the boat from Cuba to this island and back again the next day. One of the men, who was actually still only a boy at the time, allegedly witnessed the event and the story has been passed down from generation to generation. The boy claimed to have observed the ceremony called '*The Curse of the Damned*.'"

Rosie leaned forward against the guardrail. The dense crowd of eager lookers tightly surrounded her as people struggled to get in a good position to view the island. Parents pushed the shorter, younger children toward the front of the crowd. A pair of twins elbowed her thighs in an effort to get in front first. A mom with an infant strapped to her chest repeatedly leaned against her, accompanied by repeated and insincere, "excuse me's." To her left, a teenage boy and girl, arms, legs and tongues entwined in a romantic pretzel, were pushed by the crowd into her. The old cliché of sardines squeezed together in a can came to mind. The combined odor of suntan oil and dirty diapers, along with the rocking of the vessel, had caused her stomach to act up. She checked her phone again for the time. The next two hours of this three-hour cruise couldn't come fast enough. Why she'd decided to take a boat tour was beyond her at this moment.

It was early afternoon and the blazing Florida sun beat down. She was reminded of a country song she'd heard once, something about frying an egg on the hood of a pickup truck. Although most of the tourists looked silly in their floppy wide-brimmed straw hats, she kind of wished she had one right now. She was afraid the top of her head would be tomato red by the time the boat returned to Key West.

From her oversized beach bag, she pulled out a spray bottle of suntan lotion. The label read *15 SPF.* Gently, her fingertips patted her forehead, tip of her nose, and tops of her ears. She wished she'd brought a higher SPF.

The tour guide continued. "You'll see as we approach closer, the island is now filled with dolls. No one knows how all these dolls got to the island, but it is rumored that each doll represents a person whose spirit has been trapped inside. It's said that they come alive at night, returning to the form of an immobile toy with the first light of the sun's rays in the morning."

As the boat approached the shore of the small island, exclamations rose from the crowd. "Ooh", "Ah", "Oh my God, they're so creepy."

Rosie squinted but couldn't make out the details of what was on the island. The land stuck out of the middle of the ocean and was covered in thick green foliage, much of it decorated with brightly colored flowers. She recognized the coconut and palm trees, but there were many other tropical trees that were unfamiliar to her. A huge network of lush vines crisscrossed through the foliage. High cliffs towered out from the tops of the trees. There was a lot of white rock. Coral she guessed. And beaches. The island's coast was a combination of large coral rocks and sandy white beaches.

She could make out that there were small forms dotting the beach, bushes and trees, and guessed the forms were dolls. But, at this distance, they were mere blurry blobs to her.

*This was a dumb idea,* she thought as she crossed her arms and held them tightly against her nauseated, grumbling stomach.

She decided that sitting in the air-conditioned café below deck might help. Picking up the oversized beach bag at her feet, she turned to head toward the stairs that led to the bottom level of the boat. But before she took a step, she literally bumped into a person standing inches behind her.

"Excuse me," she mumbled and took a side-step in an attempt to walk around the human blockade. The body, however, took a matching step in the same direction, thwarting her escape.

"Care to look?" At the same time the calm voice spoke, a camera appeared in front of Rosie's face.

She glanced up at a woman who towered several inches over her. The first thing she noticed was a pair of phenomenally large, wide lips perched directly in front of her line of vision. The freshly tanned skin surrounding the lips glowed an attractive combination of light red and brown. The woman's short, windblown, tussled hair was bleach blonde white, and she had a solid, square jaw. The camera was lifted and hovered between them, cutting short Rosie's mental inventory.

"Um, no thanks." The mumble escaped her lips as Rosie searched for an exit from what had become a claustrophobic crowd.

"Ah come on, you have to see them. It's really quite fascinating. You can't have come all this way and not see the haunted dolls." The woman's smile stretched wider, forming a rectangular opening that exposed beautiful teeth. The first two things Rosie usually noticed about a woman were her teeth and eyes. This woman's eyes, however, were hidden behind the multi-colored lens of sporty sunglasses.

Rosie hesitated.

"Go on. It doesn't bite." The camera was inched closer to her face. "I promise, you won't regret it. Here. It's a camera, but it also acts as binoculars."

"Ok, um, thank you." Rosie took the camera, removed her own glasses, placed them on the top of her head, and pressed the round eyepiece against the orb of her eye. The island in front of her, and everything on it, remained blurry, only larger.

"I can't see anything. It's all blurry," she said, handing the camera back to the woman.

"You have to adjust it to your eyes." The woman moved to stand behind Rosie, reached over her shoulder, and cradled her own hands over Rosie's. She lifted the camera and gently placed it in front of Rosie's eyes.

"Here. Let me show you." The voice was spoken directly into Rosie's right ear. The sensation of breath on her earlobe caused a shiver to run from Rosie's neck down her spine as if someone had run the tip of a feather over her skin. The woman flipped a lever and a second lens popped out, so the camera now had two eye lenses like a pair of binoculars.

"Both lens work independently to adjust to each of your eyes. Here, with this finger, you move this dial." The index finger of the woman's left hand rested on top of Rosie's. Slowly, she guided Rosie's finger to the dial, then moved it left and right several times. "See?"

The images in Rosie's left eye gradually came into and out of focus and she nodded. At first, all she saw was the leaves at the top of the trees. When she lowered the scope of field and scanned, images of dolls scattered throughout the trees and bushes flashed before her. She jumped and sipped a quick inhale.

"Oh my! Yes, I do see them!" she exclaimed.

"See? I told you, you wouldn't be disappointed."

She scoured the landscape. There were hundreds of dolls, maybe thousands. A variety of sizes and shapes. Dolls dangled from trees. They were perched in bushes, entangled in vines. They lay abandoned on the beach. Many were missing body parts. Some were naked. Most were gruesomely distorted. All were filthy.

"It's very creepy. There are so many of them. They're haunting. What are they doing there? How did they all get there?"

"That's the mystery of Doll Island. Ok, now, let's adjust the other eye, so you can get a good look," the woman said. She remained behind Rosie, and now leaned in, pressing her body lightly against Rosie's. Whether the crowd forced this, or the woman moved closer of her own accord, Rosie couldn't tell.

*"Is this what it's like to be hit on?"* she wondered. If it was, she wasn't sure if she liked it or not.

With her right hand, the stranger guided Rosie's right thumb and index finger to the edge of the round eyepiece and slowly started to twist. "This is how you do it. Go slow. Mm, hmm. Yes, like that. How's that for you? Is that ok?"

Both their thumbs and forefingers moved in unison, slowly, toggling the lens back and forth.

Rosie swallowed. "Um, yes," she muttered as the images in front of her right eye moved into and out of focus. "Yes. That's good. Like that. Right there." Her attention had drifted from what was before her eyes. She was now focused on the fact a woman she'd never met before was standing behind her, pressing into her back, with arms around her shoulders, and had hands on top of her own. All that combined with the absurdity of the conversation made her uneasy. She fought to stifle a giggle.

*What the heck do I do?* she thought. It'd been over a year since another woman had been this close to her and the sudden proximity of a stranger's body was unsettling.

"Now that you have the focus part down, here's how you zoom." The woman gently guided Rosie's fingers to the far, larger end of the camera, and squeezing Rosie's hands with her own, began rotating both their wrists. As the end of the lens turned, the images zoomed closer and farther away.

"Ok, got it," Rosie said. She turned her head to glance at the camera-giver and was caught by surprise when the woman's face was directly over her right shoulder. She gasped a quick inhale and with it, caught a whiff of the woman's scent. It was a mixture of earthy, spicy, peppery and not at all unpleasant.

"Oh, yeah, ok," the woman lowered her hands and leaned back as much as the crowd would allow.

Rosie returned her attention to the island and zoomed in on a doll that hung from a tree branch. It was twisted, mangled and smeared with dirty, dark streaks. A solitary eye peered back at her. The other socket was a black, empty hole. Half its head was bald with neat rows of holes where the hair had previously been plugged in. Several small tufts remained. The other half of the head was covered in a tangle of matted and stained hair with remnants indicating that previously it had been blonde. The dress was torn and scattered with holes. One foot dangled bare while the other retained a solitary dirty, red shoe. Despite the warmth of the afternoon Florida sun, a chill flashed down Rosie's spine. She shivered as if an ice cube had been placed at the nape of her neck.

Slowly, she moved her head and along with it the camera until another doll came into her line of vision. It lay, naked, face down on the ground. A flock of seagulls were scattered on the beach and one waddled up to the doll. It began pecking at the back of the head and each time the bird's beak picked at the scraggly hair, the body twitched.

Beside it lay another plastic figure, in a crawling position. This doll had only one leg. The missing appendage lay abandoned several feet away in the sand. It appeared as if the toy had been intentionally positioned to look as if it were crawling to retrieve its leg.

Nearby, entangled in the low bushes that separated the edge of the beach from the forest rested a ballerina doll. She wore what remained of pink tights and a tutu. Her neck was bent in a grotesque position as if it had been snapped. She gazed upward toward a single arm lifted overhead. Where the second arm should have been was simply a dark, gaping hole.

A branch draped over the ballerina and from it dangled a large doll's head, suspended by a mass of tangled hair. The breeze from the sea caused the head to swing gently back and forth. The eyes were closed, and the lower part of the jaw was gone. It reminded Rosie of something from the cover of a nature magazine advertising a skull missing its lower mandible. The doll's cheeks were painted scarlet and its top lip was bright crimson.

Another doll sat as if resting peacefully perched against the base of a nearby tree trunk. It wore a frilly pink dress.

One eye was open and one closed. It had no nose and looked like its face had been smashed in. Where the nose should've been, instead, a jagged black hole decorated the center of the head. A small, orange striped snake slithered out of the gaping crack. The camera had zoomed in enough for Rosie to see the reptile's forked tongue flicker as it tested the air.

She scoured the beach scene a final time then lowered the camera and returned it to the woman. Her head shook as she replaced her own glasses. "Here, I've seen enough. It's disturbing. It's like the scene of a massacre without the blood." She turned her back to the island and faced the sea.

The woman took the camera and held it to her own eyes. "Holy crap!"

"What?" Rosie's attention snapped. "What did you see?"

"No. It's your vision. You're blinder than a bat with glaucoma," the woman said while adjusting the focus.

"Ha. Ha. Very funny," Rosie crossed her arms. "Not."

The woman lowered the camera. "Oh, come on, it was funny. Bat with glaucoma?"

"Pfft," Rosie spat and with her arms still crossed in front of her chest, rubbed her own upper arms as she snuck a glance in the direction of the island.

"This was a dumb idea," she said.

"What was a dumb idea?"

"Taking this tour. I'd asked the concierge at the hotel what would be a fun, touristy thing to do. She suggested," she counted the list off on her fingers, "either go for a parasail ride, join the jet-ski tour around the island, sign up for a sunset cruise dinner, or take this tour to Doll Island."

"Those all sound like fun. Parasailing looks awesome." The woman had not stopped studying the island.

"Awesome? Sure. If you call being strapped to a parachute and yanked by a speeding boat while you float a thousand feet in the air, with the threat of falling into shark-infested waters awesome. No thanks. Sounds more like torture. Not my idea of fun."

"Sounds like a blast. I'd do it," the woman said, her attention was still captivated by the island and she kept the camera pressed tightly to her face. Rosie took the opportunity to scrutinize her. She was strong, athletic, with a handsomely beautiful face and a matching ruggedly solid body. Suddenly, Rosie felt small and frail in comparison. The woman's short, unruly, hair and scar running along the bottom of her chin contributed to her wild, untamed appearance. She wore an oversized, colorful linen shirt and baggy jeans. On her feet were flat, black sneakers. A small day pack hung off her shoulders.

Two women in their mid-20's stood a few feet away from them. They repeatedly stared, leaned toward each other, whispered and giggled.

*What's their problem?* Rosie thought, and she checked to make sure the wind hadn't blown her dress up.

"Well then, how about the jet-ski tour?" the stranger asked.

"Jet-ski tour? Forget about it. Ninety minutes flying through the ocean, bumping over waves, wind, cold water?" Rosie batted away the idea with her hand as if flicking away a mosquito.

The woman lowered the camera and faced Rosie, her voice matching the enthusiasm that was evident on her face. "One of the locals was telling me about that jet-ski tour last night. It sounds great. You get to jet-ski completely around the island of Key West. It's a ninety-minute tour. There's a lot of history around here. They take you out to an island where Blackbeard used to hang out." Her voice picked up speed. "And they take you past where the Navy used to hide submarines in the '60s during the Cuban missile crisis. Oh, and there's a part of the island that supposedly is haunted.

No animals will go there. If you take an animal near there, they freak out and run away."

"Oh great. A ninety-minute nightmare is more what it sounds like to me." Rosie shuttered. "Again, what if you fall into the ocean? Sharks? Hello."

The woman let out a hearty laugh. "You're funny. No shark would want you. Too skinny."

Rosie made what her friends called, 'Rosie's annoyed face' by twisting her mouth to the side and fluttering her eyes up into their sockets.

"Ok then," the woman continued, "how about the romantic cruise? That sounds relaxing. I'm guessing not too many people have fallen overboard from a sunset cruise boat."

"Are you serious? Go alone? On a romance cruise, surrounded by kissy-faced vacationing couples?" Rosie shook her head. "No way."

"So I guess you chose the lesser of four evils. This isn't so bad, is it?"

"Humph. I've had better."

"You got to meet me." The woman lowered the camera and lifted her sunglasses to the top of her head, revealing the most gorgeous pair of kaleidoscope blue-green eyes Rosie had ever seen. She tried not to stare but couldn't help herself. She inhaled and the only words that came to mind were, *"Oh. My,"* which she stifled. The woman's eyes were the same color as the crystal-clear water they floated on. And if the color wasn't spectacular enough, they were speckled with tiny golden flecks reminding Rosie of specks of gold she'd seen floating in a bottle of tequila once.

*Those eyes,* she thought. *I could get lost staring into them.*

She broke her gaze away and turned to face the island, when she noticed a group of young lesbians, staring at them. Again, accompanied by much whispering and giggling.

*Are they checking me out?* That was doubtful. Plain-Jane Rosie, no one ever noticed her. She glanced at the attractive woman standing beside her.

Suddenly her stomach rumbled, and it reminded her, the seasickness hadn't really left. She'd simply forgotten about it. But it had returned and with a vengeance.

"I just want to go back to Key West, finish this day and go home," she said.

"So, you're here on vacation? By yourself?"

"Yeah, to both."

"Doesn't sound like you had much fun."

"Nah. Yeah. It's ok. My own fault for not getting out and doing more. I thought it was a good idea to come here, alone, force myself to be adventurous, try something new. Get outside my comfort zone and all that crap, but now I'm here, and it hasn't been much fun. I'm not exactly the adventurous type. Mostly I stayed in my hotel room and read. I could've done that at home and saved a lot of money. I'm ready to go home."

"When do you leave?"

"In the morning."

"In the morning? It's a shame you wasted a vacation and didn't have a good time. Maybe we can change that." The stranger turned to face Rosie, replaced her sunglasses, and leaned her weight on an elbow against the railing. Her movements were smooth and unforced and reminded Rosie of someone who was comfortable with their body and confident in their personality. Something she'd always admired but definitely was not herself.

"Slim chance of that," Rosie muttered.

"What percent?"

"What do you mean, what percent?"

"I mean, what percent chance is there of that happening?"

A quick chuckle escaped from Rosie. "Like a ten percent chance."

"Ten percent, huh? That high? That's better than I'd thought." She gave Rosie a friendly shoulder punch. "Oh, come on. I'm not that bad, am I? Do you think we could up the percentage to fifteen?"

One side of Rosie's lips curled as she tried to hide a smile.

"Forgive me for not introducing myself." The woman stood, stepped away from the railing and extended a palm. "I'm Devin. Devin Fitzroy.

Rosie reached for the hand. It was warm, large, and strong yet still soft. "Hi Devin. I'm Roslyn. Roslyn Moorea, but everyone calls me Rosie. Nice to meet you. Are you here on vacation too?"

"Yeah, I guess. Kinda I mean, I was working, but we finished yesterday, so I'm on vacation for a few days."

A young girl who stood toward the front of the crowd, raised her hand and shyly asked the tour guide, "Excuse me, but why did the Shaman guy cast a spell on the two women?"

The guide's response thundered over the loudspeakers. "The young lady here wants to know why the Shaman who, by the way, was a woman, not a man, but why the Shaman cast a spell on the women. Legend has it, one of the two women had been the Shaman's lover, and she'd cheated on her with the other woman. Their names were Ria and Naomi. The Shaman, determined to get revenge, carved two wax voodoo dolls in the likenesses of the women, drugged them, brought them here and cast a spell on them. Those were the first two dolls. Rumor has it the original two wax dolls still haunt the island though I've never seen them. As you can see, there are now many more. No one has been able to figure out where they come from, how they got on the island, or why they're here. It's one of the Florida Key's greatest mysteries."

The boat had slowed and now cruised along following the edge of the beach. From this distance, details of the dolls were clearly visible.

From the crowd rose a variety of comments and questions.

*"Holy shit, that's creepy."*

*"There are freakin' dolls everywhere."*

*"What the heck is this place?"*

*"How did they get there and why are they in such rough shape?"*

*"What happened to them?"*

*"Do you think they're haunted?"*

The guide paused, allowing the stunned spectators time for discussion among themselves. As the boat sluggishly maneuvered around the circumference of the island, the guide cleared his throat and began speaking. The crowd of eager onlookers, mesmerized by the haunting images that drifted before them, grew eerily quiet.

"Many locals, some who are friends of mine, insist that this little two-by-three square mile piece of rock in the middle of the Atlantic Ocean is haunted. They swear they've been by the island after sunset and have seen with their own eyes the dolls come to life."

A collective, low groan rose from the tourists on the boat.

As if on cue, the guide waited for the moan to cease then resumed. "And, there the human's soul remains for eternity. They come alive at night and you can hear the tortured souls as they moan, walk and crawl around the island. It's worse than being dead. At least in death, you can find peace. And that, ladies and gentlemen, is the reason we don't let you get off the boat to walk among the dolls of Doll Island. The risk is too great."

A nervous laugh emanated from the crowd.

"Boo!" Devin clutched Rosie's waist. "Look! One's crawling!"

"Ah!" Rosie jumped and grasped her heart. Her glasses flew off her head and skidded across the floor of the boat.

"Darn!" she muttered as she bent down and picked up the frames in one hand and a lens in another. She struggled to reinsert the misplaced lens.

"I'm sorry. I'll pay to get them repaired." Devin hovered over her.

Rosie turned her back while she fidgeted with the frames. "No, it's ok. Happens all the time. They're insured. I'll take care of it when I get home." She pressed the lens back into the frame but when she placed the glasses on her face, it instantly popped out. She caught it mid-air, sighed and allowed her hands to flop against her hips. "I knew this was a dumb idea."

"Oh, come on," Devin planted a gentle elbow into Rosie's side. "It's all in good fun."

"This island gives me the creeps. I want to get away from here, the sooner the better."

"What? You don't believe all this hocus pocus, do you?"

"No of course not." Rosie had reinserted the displaced lens and was testing its stability.

"I mean, obviously it's all a marketing ploy," Devin said. "It makes a great story to sell these boat trips, Doll Island t-shirts, coffee mugs. Just another way for the locals to make a buck off the tourists."

Her voice mimicked the tour guide's booming proclamation. "Hurry, hurry. Step right up. Come and see the one and only haunted Doll Island. Oh and while you're at it, don't forget to get your official Doll Island t-shirt!"

Rosie fidgeted with her glasses as she gazed toward the island.

"I don't know," she said. "Some of my family members live outside Miami and I've heard this story many times. It wasn't one of my relatives that was involved, but everyone in the community has known about Doll Island for generations. The story hasn't changed. You have to admit, it's kinda creepy."

"I think it's a good story. But that's all. A story. Someone, one of the locals, goes out to the island at night, adds a few dolls and moves the ones out there around a bit. For dramatic affect."

"You don't believe it?"

"Nope." Devin shook her head. "Not for a single, solitary, Barbie-minute."

Rosie didn't respond.

"Wait." Devin pointed at Rosie. "What? You do? You believe it, don't you?"

"Humph," Rosie had replaced her glasses, but they tilted slightly, and she re-adjusted them. "I don't plan to ever find out if it's real or not."

"Hey. Let me take a shot of you," Devin toyed with the controls on the camera.

"Oh no, thanks. I'm not very good at taking photos. I—"

"Ah come on. I bet you don't even have one picture of yourself here on vacation, do you?"

Rosie shrugged.

"It'll be painless, I promise," Devin pressed the eyepiece to her eye. "Ok, look at me. Smile. No, I mean a real smile. Not a fake one. That's better. Ah-ha! Got it!" She studied the photo first then held the LCD screen toward Rosie. "Look. See? I told you it'd be painless."

Rosie had to admit that it was a good picture of her.

Devin fidgeted with the camera again. "What's your number? I'll text the picture to you."

Rosie started, "201... Ah-ha, ok–" She waggled a finger toward Devin. "I see what you did there. That's pretty slick."

"What?" Devin held her palms out. She was feigning a serious face but the hint of a smile crept in. "I don't know what you're talking about." She was having a hard time containing her laughter.

Rosie shook her head.

"Oh, come on. You can't blame a girl for trying, can you?" Devin said.

The boat was filled with tourists of all sizes, shapes, ages and genders, and the straight couples had paid them no attention. The children's concentration was riveted on the island. But repeatedly Rosie caught the lesbians staring at them, whispering and sneaking fleeting glances.

*What could they possibly be captivated by?* Certainly, the two of them were not an unusual sight here in Key West, two women talking to each other. It's not as if either of them were freaky. It was an odd sensation, catching women staring. Something that had never happened to her before, and she found it unsettling though Devin didn't seem to notice or care.

"So, what do you say," Devin said. "Let me make it up to you, about the broken glasses, and take you to lunch."

"No thanks. My stomach won't be able to handle food for a while. I'm not very good with boats. Like I said, this was a dumb idea. In fact, I think I'll go sit downstairs, in the shade, for the rest of the trip back." She bent down and reached for the rope handles of her beach bag.

Devin pushed away from the railing and removed her sunglasses.

"You're leaving me?"

Rosie avoided eye contact and chuckled. "Yes, I guess I am. It was nice to meet you. Ah, thanks for letting me look through your camera."

"That's it? Just like that?" Devin's face deflated. The playful exuberance that had previously decorated it disappeared, replaced by a blank stare of questioning confusion.

Rosie repeated and snapped her fingers. "That's it. Just like that."

Devin shrugged, placed her forearms back on the rail and stared toward the island. Her enthusiastic voice had disintegrated. "Ok, fine. Nice to meet you too. Enjoy the rest of your vacation."

Rosie turned and walked, swaying side-to-side like a drunk along with the unsteady movement of the boat, and headed toward the door that led to the lower level. Her thoughts weren't focused on the island, her stomach, or getting back to Key West. Instead, her mind was swirling about a nervousness that seemed as much a part of her as her skin. Something that had haunted her throughout her entire life.

*Why hadn't she accepted the invitation for lunch? What was she afraid of?*

She had no answers, but alarms were going off in her gut and her gut never failed her. Whenever she felt anxious about something, she was wise to listen. Every time she hadn't followed her gut, she'd ended up regretting it. Like last winter when she was going on a ski vacation with her friends to the mountains, and a storm was predicted. She'd had the same nervous fluttering in her stomach then and wanted to cancel but her friends had teased her so much, she gave in and went anyway. She ended up getting a flat tire on the way and the storm turned out to be a lot worse than they'd originally thought. She was stuck in her car on the side of the road for three hours waiting for a tow truck to help. She could've died out there. To top it all off, she got a bad cold from that weekend.

*And I don't even ski!*

Like her mother used to always say, *"better safe than sorry."*

As she stepped over the door jamb, the boat turned the corner. The ground beneath her feet moved to the left, sending her body swerving to the right and into a wall. She clutched at the doorway before stepping over and into the stairwell. Clinging to the rail, she walked hand over hand toward the lounge. As the engine kicked in and the boat picked up speed, they maneuvered away from Doll Island. From somewhere in the middle of the crowd, a young child's voice whined.

"But mommy. I'm NOT pretending! The doll DID wave to me. She winked and then waved."

## JIMBO AND THE GREEN MERMAID

I t seemed to take forever for the boat to get back to Key
West. There was a second forever as they waited for the
crew to tie up to the dock. Then a third forever while standing, waiting for the Captain to announce that the passengers
were cleared to depart. As the crowd shuffled tediously
single file off the boat's ramp, Rosie's physical and mental
annoyance increased as the crowd of strangers surrounding
her closed in tighter. They were all anxious to get off the
boat and back onto land. Apparently, most of them thought
that pushing their way toward the front of the crowd would
help speed things along. Her sense of claustrophobia grew as
she waited, jammed by a sea of bodies, to depart. The smells
and sounds of strangers in too close proximity bothered her,
a disturbing mix of suntan lotion and body odor, wafted
through the air. And, even though the boat had stopped
moving, her stomach still reacted as if the ocean rocked
beneath her.

In the midst of all the chaos, from behind, a soft voice
whispered into her ear. "The offer for lunch still stands."

The instantaneous tingle that scampered up her spine

surprised Rosie. Her upper lip twitched involuntarily as she fought a smile. "No thanks. I'll pass," she said without bothering to look.

"Pass?" Devin gently took hold of Rosie's arm and attempted to turn her. "But why?"

The crowd had stopped moving, and the assembly of sweaty bodies, wedged like cattle on a ramp, annoyed Rosie. She realized her frustration was evident in her tone but didn't care. She decided she didn't need or want to explain herself to a complete stranger. Her head swung around to peer over her shoulder and her words snapped.

"I don't need a reason. I just don't feel like it. I want to go back to the hotel."

"By yourself?"

"By myself."

"Wow. Well, ah, ok, then, where's your hotel? I'll walk you there."

The crowd started to move again, and they all scuffled forward taking tiny steps. Rosie tugged her arm away from Devin's grip and turned back to face the front of the boat.

"I can make it back by myself, thank you."

"Well, all righty then. I guess I'll just walk to my hotel by myself then too."

When they were finally off the ramp and onto the street, the crowd dispersed. As soon as she was no longer compressed against strangers, Rosie's shoulders relaxed. She inhaled deeply, released a long exhale and walked briskly in the direction of her hotel.

A familiar voice trailed directly behind her. "Oh gee, we happen to be walking in the same direction. Imagine that."

Again, Rosie fought it, but the corners of her lips moved, threatening a soft smile.

"Come on, what is it?" Devin placed a palm on Rosie's shoulder, stopping her in her tracks.

Rosie turned to face her and placed her hands on her hips. "What is what?"

Devin slid her sunglasses onto the top of her head. Her short, windblown hair scattered in multiple directions. Again, Rosie found herself gazing into a pair of eyes that somehow had the magical ability to make her thoughts and words disappear.

"What is it about me you don't like?" Devin's fingertips tapped against her own chest.

"I, ah," Rosie searched for words. "I never said I didn't like you," she said then resumed walking.

Devin skipped in front of her, walking backward as she talked. "Well then, why won't you have lunch with me?"

As they progressed down Key West's crowded Duval Street, Rosie again noticed that they'd caught the attention of most of the lesbians. Straight couples wouldn't look twice. Young kids paid no attention. The elderly didn't glance. But practically every lesbian between the ages of 22 and 62 stared.

Rosie stopped abruptly. "What's the matter? Haven't you ever been scorned before?"

All emotion dropped from Devin's face and the muscles in her neck pulled her head backward, away from Rosie.

"Scorned?" Rosie repeated and leaned forward. "You do know what scorned means, don't you? Rejected."

With the word, Devin's head pulled back again, like a turtle retreating further into its shell.

"You haven't, have you?" Rosie chuckled. "If it wasn't sad, it'd be funny."

Devin recovered from the momentary shock and her head returned to its normal position over her shoulders. "Ah come on. Give me a chance. I'm not asking you to marry me. It's only lunch."

Rosie exhaled and her posture slumped. "Ok, listen. It's not you, it's me."

Devin crossed her arms and allowed her eyes to roll up in their sockets. "Oh boy, last time I heard that one, I fell off my dinosaur."

"Cute." Rosie tilted her head and pursed her lips tightly together. "No, I mean it. First, I'm not feeling well. Maybe it was the boat ride, seasickness, or the island. It kinda creeped me out."

"Fine. That's valid. And second?"

"What?"

"You said 'first', so I'm assuming there's a 'second' that's about to follow."

"Oh right, second, I ah. I can't explain it."

"Try."

"I can't…"

They'd stopped outside the Green Mermaid. The doors of the restaurant were opened wide. Jovial music and laughter floated from inside.

Devin glanced longingly at the cheerful activity then back to Rosie.

"Rosie. Come on. You were on the boat three hours. You're probably dehydrated. Let's pop in here for some water and something to eat. I have an idea of something that'll help with the seasickness. It'll be fun and you'll feel better, I promise."

Rosie peered inside the Green Mermaid and hesitated.

"Come on," Devin encouraged. "I don't bite. Promise."

Rosie stood firm. "You sure do promise a lot."

Devin flashed a smile, bookended by two charming dimples. "Yeah, but I keep my promises. Come on. It's the last day of your vacation. You admitted you didn't enjoy yourself. Come have a beer with me. What's the worst that can happen?"

"I don't even like beer," Rosie said.

"Piña colada? Shirley Temple?"

This time, Rosie couldn't stifle a laugh. It slipped out unimpeded.

"Ok," she relented, "but just one."

Devin wiggled her hips and swung her arms in an enthusiastic dance, which caused even more nearby sets of eyes to study them.

They entered the restaurant and after they'd adjusted to the dark interior, Devin pointed toward two empty seats at the bar.

A female bartender greeted them by flipping a couple of Green Mermaid napkins in front of them.

"Good afternoon ladies. Welcome to the Green Mermaid. What'll be your pleasure? The regular for you, dear?" She directed the last question to Devin.

"No Jill. We'll have two Jumpin' Joe's Gator Killers," Devin said.

The bartender turned two tall, silver shaker glasses upright onto the bar and reached for two liquor bottles from the well below.

"I'm perfectly capable of ordering for myself," Rosie flashed a flat palm toward the bartender then hung her bag on the hook under the bar.

The bartender raised a single eyebrow, paused with the liquor bottles hovering over the glasses, and waited.

Devin placed a hand on Rosie's forearm. "Just try a sip. If you don't like it, you can order whatever you'd like. I think it'll be good for you. It's a secret, magical concoction created by the owner of this fine establishment, designed to cure motion sickness, hangovers, headaches, nausea, ingrown toenails, or simply bad moods."

Rosie's mouth twisted.

"Not that you're in a bad mood mind you." Again, the

charming smile and dimples flashed. "Just a sip?" Devin's hand made a drinking motion.

Rosie relented. "Ok. Fine. But just one sip. If I don't like it, I'm not drinking it."

"Deal." Devin gave the bartender a nod. Immediately and simultaneously white liquid flowed from four bottles, two in each hand. She'd overturned them and they hovered over the shaker glasses. It was a well-rehearsed and perfectly executed performance as fruit and ice were spun, air borne prior to landing in the drink.

Devin wiggled out of her knapsack and hung it on the hook under the bar beside Rosie's bag before settling comfortably into her bar stool.

"So, I take it you're a regular here?" Rosie asked.

"Oh, I've been here a few times." Devin's attention was focused on watching the bartender shake the mixture then pour the foaming liquid into two tall Green Mermaid glasses. A straw was plopped into each drink and a glass filled with a raspberry colored cocktail was slid in front of each of them.

"Cheers!" Devin exclaimed as the rims of the glasses clinked. Each woman rose the beverage to their lips.

Devin studied Rosie's face and when the hint of a smile lifted Rosie's lips, she smiled too.

"I knew you'd like it."

"What's in it?" Rosie asked as she stirred the drink with her straw.

"If I told you, it wouldn't be a secret, now would it?" Devin said. "But I will tell you, part of what gives it the healing properties is ginger-ale and mint. So, see? It's not all that bad for you."

Two young women passed by them, paused, and after a couple minutes of private conversation and giggling, took a step closer.

"Hi Shane," one of them said. She spoke in a shy, nervous

voice that young women who have recently exited their teen years often have. The other clung to the back of her friend's shirt and pressed against her as if they were Velcroed together.

Devin acknowledged them with a polite nod and a flip of a few fingers. The two walked away, giggling and clutching the other as if they needed each other to stand.

Rosie narrowed her eyes.

*Ah-ha!* she thought. *Her name's not Devin. It's Shane. The little lying creep. I knew there was something fishy about her.*

She swiveled on the bar stool and faced the woman who sat beside her, happily drinking her beverage.

"Ok, let's get to the bottom of this. Why does everyone keep staring at us, I mean you? And why did they call you Shane?"

Devin's lips pressed tightly together as she swallowed the sip and slowly replaced her glass onto the bar.

"It's nothing. Just forget it. Tell me, what do you do?"

"Oh no." Rosie waggled a finger in front of Devin's face. "You're not going to change the subject. You're going to tell me what's going on. I'm not getting a good feeling about this. About you."

Devin swiveled on the bar stool to face her. "Ok, listen. I'll answer your questions but first, we're having such a nice time. Is it ok if I tell you later after we've gotten to get to know each other a little better?"

"Gotten to know each other a little better? Are you out of your mind? There'll be no getting to know each other a little better if you don't tell me who you are. And, why everyone keeps staring at you and why those girls called you Shane when you told me your name is Devin."

Devin sighed, swiveled back to face the bar, and cradled her glass. "Fair enough." She turned her head to glance over her shoulder and stared directly into Rosie's eyes. Rosie had never been hypnotized before but the thought occurred to her that those amazing aquamarine orbs might be casting a spell on her this very moment. And if they were, she didn't care. She wondered if her own eyes turned into those spiraling circles, like what happens in the cartoons when a character has been clobbered over the head.

A mischievous grin erupted on Devin's face. "I might as well tell you. I'm a famous psychic. I can read people's minds, tell your fortune, foresee the future, read your palm, talk to the dead. All of it." She rotated her bar stool back, so she was facing Rosie. Their knees touched.

"No way. Get out. For real?" Rosie said.

"For real."

"Prove it."

"No problem. What do you want me to say about you?"

"What do I do?"

Devin closed her eyes and concentrated. "You're a librarian."

Rosie laughed. "Wrong!"

"But I'm close right? I mean it has something to do with books."

"Maybe."

"Ok, let me try again. You need to understand, when the spirits talk to me, they talk in symbols. It's not as if they whisper the message in my ear. Sometimes it's difficult to decipher what they're telling me. Hold on." Again, she closed her eyes and concentrated.

"They're telling me you're either a teacher or an accountant that lives in New Jersey."

"Well, not exactly, but close enough I guess." Rosie shrugged and stirred her drink.

"Ok, then. Spill it. What do you do?" Devin asked.

Reluctantly, Rosie acquiesced. "I work with deaf children. I teach them how to read."

Devin pointed at her. "Ah-ha! I was right! I said teacher. And New Jersey?"

"Yes," Rosie swiveled her bar stool back to face the bar. "My accent must have given it away. But I'm still skeptical."

"You should be," Devin said.

"I should be?"

"Yeah, I'm not a psychic."

"How did you guess what I did and where I was from?"

"Let's see. Area code 201."

"Darn!" Rosie pressed a palm against her own forehead.

"Conservative hair style, woven into a neat braid. Tortoise-shell glasses. Pale skin, no tan. Cute, conservative sun dress. Fashionable flip-flops. Tasteful jewelry. Shy, introvert. You have a librarian, accountant look."

Rosie peered down at her outfit. "Oh goodness, I didn't realize I was that much of a stereotype."

"The kicker was the ten percent chance of me making your day better. No one talks in numbers unless they work with them or teach them. But there's a hint, no wait, two hints, that tips me off that you have a touch of wildness in you. You just don't want others to know."

Rosie adjusted in her seat. "Oh really? Do tell…"

"One, your flip-flops aren't plain. They're decorated with," she wiggled her fingers, "those sparkly things."

"They're called sequins. And that makes me wild?"

"Yep. And two, the tiny tattoo on the inside of your ankle. I can't make out what it is, but it tells me you have a wild side that's waiting to burst forth."

Rosie's face dropped. "Not hardly." She changed the subject. "Ok Ms. Smartypants, now I get to guess what you do."

"Fair enough. But you'll never guess. Go."

"Let's see… disheveled hair, bleached blonde highlights. Tan." She glanced to the floor. "Those flat black sneakers, I don't know the name of the brand but they're very trendy. All the cool kids wear them."

A smug smile erupted on Devin's face. "Of course they do. They're—" she pointed to a red devil's tail logo on the side of her sneaker.

"What's that?" Rosie asked.

"You don't know what it is?" Devin's face drooped.

"It looks like a devil's tail," Rosie said.

"Ok, never mind, keep going."

"Wild shirt, baggy jeans."

"Yep, you pretty much described me."

"I'm guessing you're a musician. You play in a band. That's why all the young girls recognize you."

Devin swung her head, "Nope."

"Am I close?"

Again, her head motioned side-to-side. "Nope, can't play any musical instrument."

"Hmm... ok. Let me think." She studied Devin's features. "A crazy artist?"

Devin laughed. "Crazy. You might've got that right, but an artist? Nope. You only get one more try."

"Who made up those rules?"

"I did."

"Oh. So you're the bossy type. Let me think, you're a chef?"

"Nope, you lose. I win."

"Bossy and competitive. Give me a hint."

Devin leapt off the bar stool and stood with her body turned sideways and bent her knees to lower her center of gravity. Her left foot was in front of the right and her arms floated to her sides as if balancing on a tight rope.

Rosie clapped her hands, "A surfer! You're a surfer!"

Devin bounced back onto her bar stool. "Close enough. A skateboarder."

"A skateboarder? Who's a skateboarder?"

"I am."

"A skateboarder as in for fun?"

"No. A professional skateboarder."

"A professional skateboarder?"

Devin flashed a hand signal of a closed fist with an extended thumb and pinky finger. She beamed when she said, "Yep." Rosie wasn't sure what the gesture meant exactly but she'd seen surfers flip it to each other when she'd visited the shore.

"No way," she laughed. "You're lying to me again."

"No, I'm not. Skate to My Heart." With a finger, she crossed her heart.

Rosie felt her face scrunch and she blurted, "Huh?" Immediately, she made a conscious effort to undo the scrunched-face look. She hated it when she made those faces. It always made her look like a pumpkin someone left out a month after Halloween.

"Skate to My Heart." Devin pointed repeatedly to her own face with both hands.

Rosie searched Devin's expression, hoping for a clue of what she was talking about.

"Skate to My Heart," Devin repeated. "The movie."

"What movie?"

"What movie? Last year! It was the most popular chick flick going. You must have seen it."

"No sorry. I don't watch movies."

"Don't watch movies? Oh, come on. Every lesbian saw 'Skate to My Heart'."

"Sorry," Rosie shook her head.

Devin's face assumed the same blank expression she'd had earlier when Rosie had rejected her. The look reminded Rosie of the face of a pancake in the children's story she read to the kids at school. She fought back a laugh.

"And you don't recognize this brand?" Devin pointed to the same red devil's tail logo on the back pocket of her jeans that decorated her sneakers.

"Nope," Rosie said.

"That's 'Devin's Devils'. It's my brand." She indicated toward the crowded restaurant. "Half the girls in here are wearing something from my line."

Rosie glanced around the bar. "You said earlier you were working. Were you here filming another movie?"

Devin's previous jubilant smile was gone, replaced by a more somber expression. "Well, yes and no. Yes, we finished filming a couple days ago. We were at Disney. I do some amazing skating around the park. But I came here because I'm thinking of getting into producing, making my own movie. It'll be my first one. I came here to get away and, well, try to figure things out. Life stuff."

"Yeah, me too. Get away. Figure things out. Life stuff."

A man sat beside Rosie. He was unshaven. His clothes were torn and dirty. A pair of tattered sneakers, held together with silver duct tape, barely remained on his feet. Rosie inhaled and her nose wrinkled.

The bartender ambled in front of him, crossed her arms, tilted her head and asked, "You got money Jim?"

"Of course, I got money Jill." The man's voice was deep and garbled.

The bartender tapped a fingernail on the bar. "Let me see it."

He leaned back on his bar stool and rummaged through one pocket then another. The bartender crossed her arms and nodded as if each head tilt was counting down a second.

Devin spoke up. "I'll buy this man a drink."

The bartender's tongue rolled along inside her cheek and she shrugged. "The usual Jimbo?"

He nodded. "Thank you kindly ma'am," he said as he

tipped the rim of his weathered, stained and torn hat toward Devin.

"My pleasure."

"Where y'all from?" He spoke slow and with a southern accent.

"New Jersey," Rosie said.

"L.A.," Devin pointed to herself.

The bartender slid a frosty mug toward the man and he lifted, then tipped the rim of his hat, toward the women. "Well, you're a nice couple. God bless," and he again reached to tip his worn cap in their direction.

A warmth flushed Rosie's cheeks. "Oh, we're not a–"

The man pointed a grungy finger toward Devin. "Hey, ain't you that skateboarding chick?"

Devin nodded.

"Good movie. I seen it. Cheers." The rims of the three glasses touched, and the man took a healthy chug, smacked his lips and released a low hum. "Damn, that first sip is always the sweetest, ain't it?"

"Are you a local?" Devin asked him.

"Yep, born and raised here," he spoke but his eyes never left the mug. They remained fixated on it as if he were admiring an item of beauty. "I'm a street person and mighty proud of it."

"A street person? Is that difficult? I mean, how do you get by? Food, drink, sleep?" Rosie asked.

"Oh, it's easy. There's a bunch of us. We get plenty of food from the tourists and the locals. They leave leftovers out for us. We earn our money down at Mallory Square at sunset, doing little things for the tourists. You know, juggling, magic tricks, jokes, making babies laugh, whatever it takes to make a dime. As long as you're respectful, the cops'll mostly leave you alone. I get to meet plenty of nice folks. Like you two. It's not a bad life at all. We get along just fine. My name's Jimbo, by the way, and yours?"

He turned and faced them. One of his eyes was permanently squinted shut. The other, his good eye, was propped open wider than what appeared to be normal. It was scattered with tiny red veins and had a wild, crazed look about it.

"Devin." Devin reached across Rosie and shook the man's hand. It was large, dirty and dwarfed hers.

"Rosie," Rosie said before reluctantly grasping the extended palm with her own fingertips.

After a half hour of the three of them talking and laughing, Devin placed her arm around Rosie's shoulder and leaned in toward Jimbo.

Lowering her voice, she said, "Ok Jimbo, now tell us the truth, and no bullshit. Doll Island. What's the scam? Locals go out to the island and plant dolls. A tourist trap, right?"

Jimbo chewed his bottom lip. He stared into his mug, drumming his fingers against the glass as he thought. When he raised his gaze, he scanned right and then left as if checking to make sure no one was listening. He held up his beer and before taking the final swig said, "If you'd be so kind as to order another, ol' Jimbo will share with you a secret about Doll Island."

Devin waved the bartender over and motioned for another round of drinks. Rosie was still trying to decide whether she even wanted to know what the secret of Doll Island was when Jimbo began speaking.

# THE SECRET OF DOLL ISLAND

The drinks were delivered, and the three huddled together, creating their own private space amid the noise and activity of the busy bar that surrounded them. Jimbo lowered his voice as if he were about to share the mightiest secret in history. His thick eyebrows, like two dark, hairy caterpillars that had been resting on his forehead, lowered as he narrowed his eyes. As he spoke, his large, dirt stained hands moved and accentuated his words.

"Ok, you took the tour, so you heard the story. Hundreds of years ago, in Cuba, the Shaman, or witch doctor, they're basically the same thing. So anyway, this witch doctor's girl-friend cheats on her, see? So the Shaman, she gets all pissed off, and she takes the two women, the one that used to be her girlfriend and the woman she cheated on her with, to the island. That's the island we now call, 'Doll Island.' And it was there she performed a secret, sacred ceremony. And she placed a curse on them. The curse she cast on them is called, 'The Curse of the Damned'. It's called, 'The Curse of the Damned' because the curse traps your soul into the body of a doll and there it remains, damned for eternity."

He held eye contact with each of them with his good eye as if to make sure his words had sunk in. When he was sure they had, he sat back with a satisfied smile and reached for his beer.

Devin and Rosie exchanged glances.

"That's it?" Rosie said.

"That's it," he replied.

"That's no secret," Devin sat back. "They told us the same story on the boat."

Jimbo's mug was on its way to his mouth and he paused it mid-air for a moment before solemnly replacing it back on the bar.

"Ah, Doll Island has lots of secrets. You ladies want another?"

Devin's head nodded vigorously while Rosie's shook in the opposite direction.

He narrowed his good eye and leaned closer to the women. The three curled toward each other again. With Jimbo on her left and Devin on her right, Rosie was squeezed in the middle.

"It's real," he whispered. A tiny bit of spittle drooled down his lip, and he licked it.

"I don't believe you," Devin straightened up and leaned back on her bar stool.

Rosie's head swiveled to her right and left as the conversation between Devin and Jimbo unfolded.

"Don't matter to me if you believe me or not. It's true."

"How do you know? Have you seen it with your own eyes, uh, eye?"

"No fuckin' way would you catch me near the island after sunset." He waggled a scruffy finger with its dirt encrusted fingernail. "But I know people who have. People who don't lie. Them Cubans, when it comes to black magic, voodoo, witch doctors and all that shit, they don't mess with making up stories. That shit's holy territory. It's bad karma to lie about it. I know a guy, his parents are from Cuba. He's a direct relative of the boy who witnessed the original curse ceremony. The same story's been told from generation to generation for centuries."

"How did so many dolls get on the island if it only started with the two that were cursed?" Devin asked.

"Now that, young lady, is a very good question. Ain't nobody I know has an answer to. But there are people that live right here in this town," he tapped the bar several times, "people I know. They've been by the island at night, and they heard the screams and seen some scary shit with their own eyes. Dolls walking, crawling. Like something out of a fucking Stephen King movie."

Devin shook her head as he spoke. "I still don't believe it. I think it's made up hype, a tourist trap."

"I'm telling you the truth. Us street people, we may be homeless, but we're honorable. That's the one thing we got going for us. Ask anyone. Hey Jill," he called to the bartender. When she glanced his way, he rolled a finger toward himself. She answered by holding up a single finger toward the customer she was talking with and approached Jimbo, giving him a reverse nod by lifting her nose in his direction.

"Are we street people honorable or not?" he asked.

"Absolutely. That you are." She gave him a fist bump, then returned to the customer to finish the conversation she'd been having.

Jimbo slapped the bar then turned back to face Rosie and Devin.

"I told you. Now, you listen to me. And you listen good. If you go out there at night, after sunset, you can see them dolls come alive." He gave a hard look to Devin first then Rosie, staring directly into their eyes. He shook an unkept finger at them. "But don't blame me if you don't come back."

"This is creeping me out," Rosie reached for her bag. "I've had enough and got to get going."

"Me too," Devin said. "Jimbo, it was nice to meet you. Thanks for the story. It's a good one, but you really didn't tell us a secret my friend."

They paid the bill and were about to leave when Jimbo grabbed Devin's arm. Their eyes met, and he said, "It's real. That's the first secret. There's more. If you buy one more beer, I'll tell you another."

"Sorry dude but no deal." Devin slapped Jimbo on the back. "You have a nice night."

Jimbo shrugged and turned to face the couple sitting on the other side of him.

"Where ya'll from?" Rosie heard him say as they turned to leave.

She squinted as they re-entered the afternoon air. The humidity was thick, and it felt as if she'd walked into a spiderweb of moisture. The sun shone brightly, but occasionally a cloud drifted by, throwing huge shadows that drifted lazily along the street with them as they walked.

"I hope I don't have nightmares," Rosie said as they maneuvered through a crowded Duval Street, dodging groups of tourists as they headed toward their hotels. "It's a creepy story."

"Yeah, it is kinda creepy. But it's only a story," Devin said. "I mean, seriously, dolls coming alive? That's the kind of thing you'd see in a movie at Halloween." They walked by Santiago's Sub Shop and she stopped. "I'm starving. How about you? That smells amazing. Come on. I promised you lunch. Let's get a sandwich."

"Nah, I'll eat at the hotel." No sooner had she spoken than her stomach growled. The menu posted on the window caught her attention.

"Ah, come on Rosie." Devin tugged gently at her bag.

"You've had a fun afternoon, right? Admit it. The best time you've had since you've been here, right?"

Rosie struggled for words. "Well, um."

"Say, 'yes Devin, it's been a wonderful afternoon.'"

Devin's eyes twinkled like they were enchanted and this time, Rosie couldn't keep her smile hidden.

"Yes, Devin, it's been a wonderful afternoon, but—"

A hand shot up and covered her mouth. "No buts," Devin said. "Come on, my treat. Let's get a sandwich and eat it down by the docks." She clutched Rosie's hand and led her into the sub shop.

They left with two sandwiches, a large bag of chips and a bottle of red wine.

"Those sandwiches are huge. One could last me a week," Rosie said as she watched Devin stuff the newly acquired food and drink into her backpack.

"Maybe I'll be able to convince you to extend your vacation." The more Devin smiled, the deeper her dimples grew. She hoisted the knapsack up and onto her back. Once it was in position, she yanked on the two front straps, securing it tightly to her torso. At the end of a raised arm, a finger pointed in the direction she intended to go and she began walking.

"Not a chance of that," Rosie said as she stepped into pace beside Devin. "I can't wait to get home to my quiet little life and my girl."

Devin stopped and spun to face Rosie. "Your girl?" Her eyebrows arched high on her forehead.

Rosie giggled. "Yes, my girl. Itchy."

"You call your girlfriend Itchy?"

"No, silly. She's a Chihuahua. A rescue. The cutest little thing. She only weighs five pounds. She's so little and nervous. When I saw her, she reminded me of myself. I couldn't leave her at the shelter. She was so scared, sad and lonely."

They started walking again.

"And that's like you?" Devin asked.

"Yes, in many ways, it is."

"So, tell me about your quiet little life. What's it like?"

"It's actually quite boring."

"Tell me. I love boring."

"Well, I get up at six, feed and play with Itchy. Have breakfast, shower, go to work. I told you, I help deaf children learn to read. I teach from 8:30-3:30, and when I get home, I usually read or knit—"

"You knit?"

"Yes, I knit. My grandmother taught me. I love it. It's very relaxing. I make little hats and mittens for babies at the women's shelter. Look." She swung the bag off her shoulder, unzipped it and pulled out a half-finished light pink blanket. Two large knitting needles were interwoven with the yarn. "Well, this is actually crocheted, not knit, but it's similar. I've been working on this for months. It's a gift for the woman who runs the women's shelter."

Devin reached for the yarn and rubbed it between her fingers. "Wow, I never met anyone that actually knits before. That's pretty awesome." She ran her fingertips along one of the two large knitting needles. "Those needles, yikes. Are they big enough? I mean, in college I threw javelins that were shorter."

Rosie chuckled as she replaced the blanket, yarn and needles back into the bag, zipped it closed and slipped her arm through the rope handles, adjusting it up onto her shoulder. "Yeah, they are kinda big, aren't they? See? I told you I was boring. Who else goes on vacation and carries knitting around with them?"

"Besides a grandma?"

Rosie's face drooped. "A grandma?"

"Oh come on. I'm kidding. Really, I think it's wonderful. Tell me more."

"There's no more to tell. I go home, make dinner—"

"You cook?"

"Yes, I cook."

"Wow. That's awesomeness extreme. Nobody I know actually cooks. I mean, microwave yesterday's pizza, maybe."

"Then, after dinner, I read or knit. That's it, I go to bed and do it again the next day."

"Don't you ever socialize?"

"Oh sure, on the weekends, I'll hang out sometimes with friends. We'll either talk about books we're reading, or we'll all get together and knit. And Sunday mornings I go to the pottery studio. I spend an hour teaching children with physical or mental handicaps to either make things out of clay, or paint things, like cups, plates. It's so rewarding to see how happy they are when they take home something they've made. After the class, I'll spend a few hours on my own projects. It's amazing to work with the clay." She caught herself. "I'm sorry, I'm probably boring you."

"It sounds wonderful. I'd like to try it sometime."

"Try what?"

"Knitting. Or making pottery. I mean, since you teach kids with handicaps, I'm guessing you could teach me, right?"

"Really? Would you?" Rosie glanced sideways at Devin. "Nah. You're messing with me."

"No, I mean it. It sounds wonderful. And, no girlfriend?"

As they walked, Rosie contemplated a fingernail, then began picking at it. "I did have a girlfriend, until about a year ago. She broke up with me. She um, said I was too boring, and she wanted more excitement in her life."

"Damn, that's hard."

"Yeah, it was hard, but, you know, she was the wild type.

We never were meant to be together," she shrugged. "It's ok now. You get used to it, being alone I mean. Kinda." She stopped picking at the fingernail and allowed both hands to fall by her sides.

"Why did you come here to Key West, all the way from New Jersey, for vacation?"

"My friends talked me into it. They said I needed to get out of my routine, meet new people, do something fun. They said, 'Rosie, go somewhere fun for your birthday this year. Treat yourself. You deserve it. Go on a little adventure.' So, at a weak moment, with the encouragement of my friends and after too much red wine, I thought it was a good idea. I booked a flight and a room. The next morning, I regretted it but I'd booked non-refundable options. So, here I am."

"Then it was to be your destiny." They'd reached the docks and Devin pointed toward the end of one of the long wooden walkways. "Let's go that way. So, this is a birthday celebration?"

"Yes, it was my birthday yesterday."

"Happy belated birthday. Sorry I missed it. But we'll celebrate today. My birthday was last week. So, you're a Virgo too?"

"Yes. I'm a typical Virgo. I guess. So, they tell me. Not that I believe in all that."

"I don't believe in it either, but I'm not a typical anything."

As they walked toward the end of the dock, they passed several boats tied to the pier. When they got to the second to the last boat in the row, Devin stopped. She held her palm out toward the boat.

"What?" Rosie asked.

"Get in," Devin nodded toward the boat.

"Get in?" Rosie glanced around. There were no other people on the dock.

"Is this your boat?" she asked.

"Get in," Devin repeated, this time a mischievous smile spread across her face.

Rosie didn't move. "Are we going to eat on the boat?"

"What is it with all the questions?" Devin placed one foot on the back landing of the boat and left the other on the dock. With her legs straddled wide, she reached a hand toward Rosie. "Come on. Give me your hand. I'll help you get on. Let's go have a picnic."

Rosie remained immobile on the dock.

"Come on Rosie, I'm not going to kidnap you. It'll be fun. You told me a little about you, I want to tell you about me. I'll talk while I drive."

Rosie scrutinized menacing clouds that sluggishly glided overhead. "What if it rains? It's been raining every day about this time."

"It rains every day here, but only for a short time. Then the sun comes out again. Besides, a little rain never killed anyone yet that I know of. Of course, there's always a first time." She chuckled. "Come on. We won't be gone long. We're not heading out for a three-hour tour to Gilligan's Island. Though you'd make a great Mary Anne."

"And who would you be? Gilligan?"

Devin smiled. "I'm a wonderful combination of Gilligan's fun, the professor's brains, and the millionaire's money."

"Gee, all that and humble too. Amazing."

"Yes, it is, isn't it? Come on, we're wasting time if you want to get back before the storm hits."

Cautiously, Rosie took Devin's hand and allowed herself to be assisted into the boat. It was a good-sized boat, not that Rosie knew anything about boats, but she felt safe enough on it. A large black engine with "150" hung off the back. There were four individual seats and a bench for sitting. A small door in the middle of the windshield where you could climb up onto the front part of the boat, was securely shut.

"You can sit here," Devin pointed to the plush, white, leather seat next to the Captain's chair. "You'll be the copilot."

Rosie placed her bag in front of the seat. "What does a copilot have to do?"

"Just sit and look pretty," Devin winked then gracefully jumped back onto the dock, skillfully untied the boat from the metal cleats and pushed it away with her foot. The boat gently rocked with the undulating waves beneath them. Rosie's anxiety spiked, and she raised herself from the seat. The boat slowly drifted from the dock and her heart rate increased as the thought that Devin was pushing her out to sea alone flashed through her mind. But, before she could speak, Devin elegantly leapt from the dock and landed on the back ramp of the boat. She hoisted up the round, rubber bumpers that hung off the sides then scampered to stand behind the steering wheel. With Devin back on board, Rosie released a long exhale and lowered herself back into her seat.

Devin laughed "What? Did you really think I'd shove you off and let you drift away?"

Rosie averted her gaze. "No. Well, yes. Maybe."

"You are the nervous type, aren't you? I'd never do that to you."

"Have you forgotten? I don't even know you. You could be a psycho killer. I'm going off to have a picnic with a lesbian Ted Bundy and they'll never find my body."

Devin reached for the key that was tucked in the ignition and the engine sputtered to life. She slowly pushed the throttle forward and the boat leisurely motored away from the dock.

"Good point," she said. "Yet, I suppose I could say the same thing."

"Ha," Rosie snickered. "Not likely."

"What do you mean?"

"I'm not exactly the serial killer type."

"And you're suggesting I am?"

"You have to admit, out of the two of us, you are the more likely candidate."

A hearty chuckle escaped from Devin. "You have a point there."

They were far enough away from the dock now for Devin to give the boat a little more gas and they picked up speed as she leaned into the throttle.

"Shouldn't we put on life jackets?" Rosie asked as she removed a light sweatshirt out of her bag and wiggled into it.

"If you'd like to, go ahead." Devin stood in a wide-stance, authoritatively gripping the steering wheel while surveying all directions, monitoring the choppy water that spread before them. She indicated with a toss of her head. "They're under the seat cushion of the bench."

"Are you going to wear one?"

"Nah, we're not going out that far."

"Do you have enough gas?"

"Yes, we have enough gas. Stop worrying. We're going to be fine."

To Rosie, Devin seemed to be a woman that was experienced, confident and sure of herself. Rosie allowed herself to relax as the land drifted away and they headed toward open water.

"So, tell me about you. Who are you, anyway?" she said.

"Who am I? Whoa, now that's a heavy question." Devin raised her voice to be heard above the noise of the engine. "I don't think I've figured out yet who I am."

"Well then why don't you start by telling me about your past? Like what you've done. All I know is you were in a movie."

Devin eased the throttle, leaning forward into it and the front of the boat elevated as it picked up speed. Rosie held firmly onto the dash in front of her to keep from bouncing out of the seat. The air smelled of fresh salty sea and the temperature dropped significantly. The wind pushed Rosie's glasses against her face. She took them off and placed them into her bag. Her eyes teared from the rushing wind and she squinted. Between the wind, tears and lack of glasses, her view was blurred.

"My father is Frederick Fitzroy." Devin tossed a glance in Rosie's direction.

"Is that name supposed to mean something to me?" Rosie yelled back.

Devin did a double take. "You never heard of him?"

"Nope. Never." Rosie peered through narrowed eyes attempting to see through the wind and tears, hoping to make sense of where they were headed.

"You sure you live in New Jersey and not under a rock?" Devin spoke in loud, short sentences.

"Funny," Rosie said. "Not. Go on."

"Well, anyway. My dad is a famous Hollywood producer. He makes movies. Like, 'The Lion's Roar' and 'Over The Moon'. Those are his most famous. Certainly, you heard of those?" Again, she allowed her eyes to leave the water and glanced at Rosie.

Rosie shook her head. "Nope."

The front of the boat slapped against a large wave and for a few seconds, they were airborne, surrounded by a salty spray. Rosie screamed. Although she was holding on to the dash board, the upward momentum of the boat lifted her when it rose and when it crashed back down, her bottom collided with the seat.

"Ow!" she yelled.

"Sorry," Devin shouted. "I didn't see that one coming." She pulled back on the throttle and the boat responded by imme-diately slowing down.

Rosie's sundress had blown up around her waist and she

pulled it down, grateful that it was her habit to wear running tights under these light summer dresses. She rubbed her lower back.

With the decrease in speed, the noise of the engine softened and Devin's voice returned to a more normal pitch.

"Wow," Devin said. "I didn't realize anyone existed that hasn't heard of my dad. Well, they were just silly little multi-million-dollar movies anyway. He got me into acting when I was young. The first movie I did was, 'The Littlest Cowgirl'. Let me guess, you never heard of it?"

Again Rosie's shaking head was her answer.

"I can't believe it. And I thought every little girl our age wanted to be me."

"Sorry to burst your self-importance bubble." Rosie was still rubbing her back.

"Goes to show. You learn something new every day. So, anyway, I was five years old, and in the movie, I got to ride this gigantic black horse and did all kinds of amazing things. Like had India–I mean, Native Americans chasing me with flaming arrows, rode a horse over a raging waterfall, you know, all the normal cowboy stuff. But I was only a little kid. It was quite a popular movie and the beginning of my career."

"Did you do all your own stunts?"

"Nah, I mean, I was only five. My dad was extremely protective of me. I had stunt doubles for most of the action parts. I did get to rope a calf once though. It took me about a dozen tries to get the rope around its neck. And they had to have a few stage hands hold its legs out of the camera's view so it'd stay still. That's about the most action I had."

"And now you're a professional skateboarder?"

"Yeah. I mean, I compete in skateboarding and, because I'm so good at it, my dad made a movie about me last year. It's called, 'Skate To My Heart'."

"What's it about?"

"It's about a skateboarder girl: me, of course. And I get into all kinds of trouble, with local gangs, the cops, etc. I'm in love with the girl of my dreams see? Of course, she's a good girl that wants nothing to do with me. But, in the end, my charming charisma overcomes her resistance and I win her heart. We live happily ever after. It's been a big hit in the lesbian community and actually crossed over to mainstream."

"No wonder all those girls were checking you out today."

Devin nodded and shrugged. "Yeah, I guess I'm pretty recognizable. You get used to it."

The sun was mid-way through its descent as they approached an island. Devin lowered the throttle even further, and the boat slowed to a quiet crawl. She removed her sneakers and socks.

"What are you doing?" Rosie asked.

"I'm bringing us on shore."

"We're going to a deserted island?"

"Yeah. You wanted a fun adventure, right?"

Rosie's finger swiped back and forth like the pendulum of a metronome. "No, no, no. I never said I wanted a fun adventure. My friends insisted I go on an adventure. I never said I wanted one."

"Too late," Devin said. "We're here."

Rosie fumbled to remove her glasses from her bag and place them back on her face.

The first thing she looked at was Devin. With wind tussled hair and a lightly sun-burned face, she was intensely attractive. A pleasant rush flowed through Rosie, one she hadn't experienced in years. It was like the warmth of the Key West sun combined with the excitement of Christmas all merged together inside her.

The second thing she noticed was the sandy beach, large

rocks and dense green foliage of the tropical island looming large directly behind Devin.

But it was the third thing she saw that caused her heart rate to spike and flooded her with a sensation of ice water being injected directly into her veins.

*Dolls.*

## A MEMORABLE FIRST DATE

"No." Rosie bolted upright and stood, waving her palms toward Devin. "Oh, no, no, no. No. You did not bring me to a haunted island at sunset with an approaching thunderstorm on its way. Tell me this is a sick joke."

Devin jumped through the small window of the windshield and tossed an anchor over the railing off the front of the boat. As it splashed through the waves, she scampered to the back of the boat. With a coiled rope clutched in her fist, she was poised to jump into the water.

"Come on Rosie. Don't be such a worry-Wanda. We'll have a nice little picnic and when you go home tomorrow, you can tell everyone that you had a fabulous adventure on a haunted island with a famous movie star. We'll take a few selfies. You can post them on your MySelfies page. Your friends will be jealous. It'll be fun. And besides, both the storm and sunset are two hours away, at least."

She jumped overboard, and the splash sprayed Rosie. As she tried to wipe the drops of sea water off the lens of her glasses using the hem of her dress, Rosie licked the briny moisture from her lips. The waves lapped against Devin's knees, soaking the bottoms of her jeans.

"Shit, this water's cold," she said as she walked toward the beach, pulling the boat behind her.

Anxiety and panic escalated in Rosie's chest. "I don't care about any stupid selfie. I'm not even on MySelfies. I really don't want to do this."

Devin continued to make her way toward the beach. "You don't have a MySelfies page? How could you not have a MySelfies page? Everyone has one. I thought it was like the law or something."

Rosie surveyed the island. Devin was headed toward a small sandy beach. Behind the beach, huge globs of dark moss and tangled vines covered the trees and bushes. Dolls of all sizes and shapes dangled from branches like grotesque Christmas tree ornaments. Several lay on the sand, either having been discarded there or having fallen from the trees.

"Devin. No. We are not doing this. I'm serious. You get back in this boat right now and take me away from this disgusting place."

Devin laughed and kept walking, pulling the boat behind her.

Rosie raised her voice and tried to make it as authoritative as she could. It cracked. "I'm not kidding. Get back in the boat or I'll drive the darn thing away myself and leave you here."

"I have the key," Devin yelled over her shoulder.

"This is not funny." Each time she spoke, Rosie heard the level of panic in her own voice rise.

"Please. Devin, I'm begging you. I get terrible anxiety attacks and I'm getting the sense one is coming on. I get extremely nervous, easily. Please. Come back in the boat and let's go. I'll have a picnic with you anywhere but here."

Devin had made it to the beach and, hand over hand, pulled the rope and along with it, the boat, toward her. Rosie gripped the back of the chair as, inch by inch, the island got closer.

She kept her eyes focused on Devin, refusing to let them wander over what she consciously resisted looking at. What she knew would terrify her. But as the beach grew nearer, she couldn't keep her eyes from surveying what was behind Devin.

*The dolls.*

Dolls were everywhere. They hung awkwardly from the trees and bushes. Many had twisted limbs and distorted faces. Some were missing arms. Some were legless. Many had no bodies and only a head remained, suspended by hair or stuck on a branch. All had smudges of filthy streaks of gray or black dirt covering their skin and clothes. Outfits were tattered or absent. Hair was matted or missing. Like a battlefield after a slaughter, disfigured and abandoned bodies were scattered everywhere. The only thing missing was the blood.

Panic flooded Rosie as the tiny hairs on the back of her neck bristled and an icy chill raced through her core. Her mouth was suddenly parched and her tongue felt thick, making speaking difficult. She sensed herself begin to hyperventilate and noticed her breaths were shallow and quick.

"Devin. I can't do this. I'm totally not kidding. You're freaking me out. You have to get me out of here."

"Calm down. Everything is going to be fine. This'll be a fun adventure, you'll see. I won't let anything bad happen to you. I promise. You'll thank me for this one day."

Devin hoisted the bow of the boat up onto the sand and tied the rope securely around the base of a coconut tree before wading back into the water. When she reached the boat, she effortlessly heaved herself back into it. "Come on, let's eat. I'm starving."

"How can you be so nonchalant?" Rosie's attention was focused on a doll tangled with a vine around its neck, dangling as if it hung from a noose. Its head tilted awkwardly to one side.

"Easy," Devin said as she flipped back the top cushion of the bench and surveyed the contents of the storage space below. "They're just dolls." When she spotted what she was looking for she reached in, pulled out a blanket and shook the sand off it. "Here. This'll work fine. Come on." She grabbed her backpack. "Let's go," she said before hopping back into the knee-deep water.

"You're not hearing me. I'm not going on that island," Rosie pointed toward the beach.

"Oh, I heard you. I'm ignoring you."

"No way are you getting me on that island." Rosie crossed her arms, sat on the bench and crossed her legs.

"Ok, fine. Stay here then. I'll hike to the other side of the island and—"

"What?" Rosie jumped up. "And leave me here? Alone? Are you crazy? You can't do that."

"Watch me." Devin turned and continued talking as she waded through the water toward land. "I've got the food and the wine. You can stay, or you can come, whatever you want."

"Wait!" Rosie snatched off her flip-flops, placed them in her bag, tossed it over her shoulder and cautiously climbed down the short ladder that hung off the back of the boat. Tentatively, she lowered herself into the water.

"Ack! It's cold," she screamed.

"It's the Atlantic Ocean honey," Devin yelled as she strolled away from Rosie down the sandy beach.

"Wait," Rosie yelled as she waddled through the ankle-deep water. Carefully, she'd scrutinized the ground beneath the crystal-clear waves before daintily taking the next step to avoid treading on anything.

When she got to the beach, she ran after Devin. As soon as she'd caught up to her, she punched her on the arm.

"Ow. What's that for?" Devin rubbed her bicep.

"For taking me here and for threatening to leave me alone." She slapped at something that was biting her on the neck and surveyed the nearby trees and bushes. Numerous sets of eyes from dolls stared at them. "This is the creepiest place on the planet. It's incomprehensible that you brought me here."

"I never would've left you. I figured you'd come. But you have to admit. It's the best first date ever," Devin joked as they walked along the beach.

"Oh, this is most definitely not a first date."

"Looks like a date to me."

"In order to qualify as a," Rosie struck the air with two fingers of both hands, "date, two parties need to enter into a mutual understanding that it is, indeed, a date. I never agreed to a date with you on a haunted island. This is more like a kidnapping. Plus, to call it a first date, presumes there will be a second, and we most certainly will not be having one of those."

"You sound like one of my father's attorneys. Anyway, you did agree to go on a picnic with me," Devin said.

"A picnic. Yes. Haunted island. No."

As they followed the coast, the sandy beach turned rocky. Cautiously, they made their way over the slippery, seaweed-covered rocks. Rosie noticed that her heart rate and breathing had returned to normal. She still felt slightly anxious but something about Devin had a calming effect on her.

"Where are we going?" She slapped at something that had nibbled her neck. "The bugs are horrible here."

Devin pointed ahead. "There, around the corner. It'll be a better view of the sunset."

"What sunset?" Rosie looked to the sky. "It's cloudy and about to rain."

"Sometimes a passing storm provides the most brilliant sunset as the sun creeps through the clouds."

"The only thing that creeps on this island are the dolls. Besides, shouldn't we keep an eye on the boat?"

"You are a little worry bird, aren't you? The boat will be fine. There's no one around. Come on, we're almost there."

When they turned the corner, another small sandy beach spread before them.

"See!" Devin said as she removed her back pack. "The perfect spot for a picnic."

She stood in the center of the beach, shook the blanket and laid it on the ground. Rosie plopped down onto it and Devin sat beside her. They faced toward the water, but Rosie repeatedly glanced over both shoulders, continuously looking at the dolls that hung from the trees and bushes surrounding them.

Devin reached into her backpack and removed a maroon, velvet bag. From it, she took out the camera.

"This baby," Devin stroked it as if it were the head of a prized thoroughbred, "goes everywhere I go now." She peered through the viewfinder, fiddled with buttons and began snapping photos of the dolls. "It's one of my hobbies. I make movies. This little camera is nothing short of amazing."

"What's so amazing about it?" Rosie asked but her attention was fixated on a doll laying on the beach nearby. Its long, scraggly hair fanned over the sand and its blue eyes stared up toward the sky. A crab crawled over its face, stopping long enough to pick something out of the doll's eye and eat it.

Rosie shuddered.

"Well, for one," Devin gazed lovingly at the camera as she spoke, "my father gave it to me as a gift for my birthday last week. That in itself is miraculous. It's the first nice thing he's done for me in almost twenty years."

"Twenty years? That's odd. Why the first nice thing in twenty years?" Rosie forced her attention away from the doll's face and toward Devin.

Devin shook her head as her fingers caressed the camera. "Ah, forgettaboutit. Ancient history, water over the damn dam. So, anyway, back to the camera. This little jewel is unlike anything you've ever seen before. It does stuff you can't even begin to imagine."

Rosie studied the square block of black metal Devin cradled. "It looks like a regular camera to me."

"Looks can be deceiving." Devin said. "Sometimes the most incredible things are hidden inside plain packages. You have to discover what is beyond the obvious. Look deeper to find what is truly magnificent." She paused as if contemplating what she'd said before continuing. "So anyway, about the camera. For starters, it takes awesome videos, slow-mo, freeze frame, macros and zoom, of course. It's incredible with night shots." She stood, zoomed in and snapped photos of several dolls. "But that's not what I like most about it. The amazing thing about this camera..." She pulled the lens away from her eye, then replaced it and focused the lens toward Rosie, "is what it can do with light."

"Light?"

"Yes. Light." Enthusiasm covered Devin's face reminding Rosie of a four-year-old on Christmas morning.

Devin's voice pitched with excitement. "You know how

light basically has three waves, right? Red, green and blue." She paused, waiting for an answer.

"Well, yeah, I mean, I guess." Rosie tucked her legs underneath her and kept a vigilant watch for any movement on the beach or woods around them. "It's a vaguely familiar concept from having heard it at some point in my education but I can't say I understand it."

"Well," Devin pointed to the camera. "The amazing thing about this baby is it not only picks up the three waves of light but it can also detect polarized light, ultraviolet rays, etc. Basically, every wave length on the spectrum. And the beautiful part is, by tuning some of them out, it allows you to see only the ones you select."

"And this is awesome because?"

Devin had returned to taking pictures of the dolls, intensely adjusting knobs before and after each shot.

"Because, well, I have this theory..." Her voice trailed off as she propped down in the sand on her knees and angled the camera skyward, zooming in on a doll hanging above them.

"They're so creepy. I can't even stand looking at them." A bug crawled along Rosie's leg. She let out a soft groan, slapped at it, then brushed it off the blanket. "It seems like they're all staring at us."

"Maybe they recognize me from 'Skate to My Heart'." Devin laughed at her joke. "Listen, don't worry about them." She sat back down on the blanket and crossed her legs. "Imagine they're nothing but a bunch of plastic and cloth. Nothing more than this blanket or," she pulled the wine bottle out of the bag, "this bottle. They're simply inanimate objects someone has placed here. They're not alive. Never have been. Never will be."

"That may be but you have to admit, the spook-factor is huge," Rosie said. "Doesn't it skeeze you out, just a little?"

"Nope. It's called having fun. It's an adventure." Devin carefully placed the camera on top of the velvet bag. "Is this the first adventure you've ever been on in your life?"

Rosie shrugged. "Maybe."

"It is, isn't it? It's the first adventure you've ever been on. Girl, you need me in your life to teach you how to live a little. How to have some fun."

A noise from behind them startled Rosie, and she jumped. "What was that?"

They both turned in time to see a small chimp scamper into the forest and disappear.

"A chimp!" Devin jumped up. "That was a chimp! Darn, I'd loved to have got a picture of it." She scanned the trees but when there was no more movement, she sat back down.

"Ready for a picnic?" Devin unzipped one of the pockets of her backpack and removed a small, red pocket knife. It had a variety of multiple sized blades. She flipped out a cork screw. "Pretty handy, huh?"

"You carry a whatever-you-call-it knife around with you?"

"Of course, doesn't every good butch carry a Swiss Army Knife? You know, the Swiss actually make these babies. They invented them to give to soldiers in World War II. They come in handy. You should always carry one." Devin lowered her voice and leaned in closer to Rosie. "What if you were ever stranded on a deserted island and chased by haunted dolls? What would you do without a Swiss Army Knife?"

Rosie glanced over her right then left shoulder. "Don't even say that. It's not funny."

A jovial laugh escaped from Devin as she twisted the corkscrew into the cork at the top of the wine bottle.

"It's so humid here," Rosie peeled off her sweatshirt then fanned herself. "It's like the air is made of water. And it smells." She wrinkled her nose. "It smells like a combination of something's rotting and mold."

Devin inhaled. "Yeah, that pretty much describes it."

"Aren't you hot in those jeans?"

Devin popped the cork from the wine bottle. She poured a half glass of wine into two plastic cups and handed one of them to Rosie.

"Yeah, a little. But you get used to it. Skaters don't wear shorts."

"What? Not cool?"

"Something like that. Bon Appétit.," Devin raised her glass and the rims of their glasses touched.

Rosie took a sip but hadn't swallowed it when she spotted a fuzzy black dot with long legs moving across the blanket. Each of the thin hairy legs moved slow and robotic, one at a time. She gulped, screamed, leapt up, grabbed a rock, and repeatedly pummeled the spider.

"Hey!" Devin protested. "You didn't have to kill it. It wasn't even headed your way. Next time let me gently remove it from your immediate environment and let it go about its business. It didn't ask to be born a spider, you know."

"Well, I didn't ask it to come onto my blanket," Rosie replied. She carefully surveyed the blanket before sitting back down on it. An insect landed on her shoulder and she slapped it away, grimacing at the squashed black remnant left on her hand. "Ack," she groaned as she wiped it on the blanket. "There are way too many things that crawl and with wings on this island for me. I swear, if I get West Nile virus, leptospirosis, malaria, or, or... mad cow or anything from this little adventure as you call it, you'll never hear the end of it from me."

Devin handed Rosie a wrapped sandwich, plate and napkin. "Oh, come on. This is the kind of trip that creates memories that'll last a lifetime. Here, let's take a selfie. Hold this." Devin handed her glass of wine to Rosie and reached for her camera. She stood, searched the surrounding ground and walked toward a chunk of driftwood. She lifted it onto her shoulder, brought it back, and set it in the sand at the edge of the blanket. As she set up the camera on the wood, she explained. "I'm setting the timer. I'll have ten seconds to get in position. It'll beep three seconds before the shot. Got it?"

Rosie nodded.

"Ready?" Devin pressed the button on the camera, ran onto the blanket, and took her glass of wine from Rosie. She wrapped her arm around Rosie and just before the camera beeped, she tickled Rosie's armpit.

"AH!" Rosie blurted a giggle as the shutter clicked.

Devin jumped up, ran to the camera and studied the photo. "Perfect!" she said. "I captured the rare and elusive smile."

Rosie stuck out her tongue. Devin returned to the blanket and showed Rosie the picture. "Great pic, huh?" It was a wonderful photo of the two of them, both laughing on a blanket on a beach. In the background was a variety of dense, green tropical foliage. Directly between and behind them, a doll's face hung, staring menacingly into the camera. A distorted smile twisted its lips.

Rosie pivoted and stared at the doll. It was stuck between two branches in the tree behind them. There was, however, no smile on its face. The lips were frozen open as if mid-scream.

"Devin. The doll!" Rosie said.

"What about it?" Devin's attention was focused elsewhere. She was scrolling through photos on the camera.

"In the picture, its smiling, but look," she turned toward

the doll. "That's not a smile." She stood and walked backward, distancing herself from the toy.

"What? No. Let me check." Devin scrolled through the photos until she came to the one of the two of them. "No. That's only how the light is hitting it. It's an optical illusion. It's not smiling. Look." She tilted the camera toward Rosie but Rosie didn't budge. "Your mind's playing tricks on you Rosie. Here, sit down and finish our picnic."

"Get rid of that disturbing piece of plastic first."

Devin laughed, reached up and disentangled the doll from the tree. She walked toward the water and threw it like a football. The doll tumbled through the air, arms, legs, hair and dress flailing until it landed with a splash several feet away. For a few seconds, it floated on top of the waves but slowly it sunk and soon had disappeared from view.

"There, happy now?" Devin slapped the sand off her hands before reseating herself on the blanket. Rosie followed her but kept watching where the doll had submerged.

"Do the same thing to another hundred of them, then maybe," Rosie said. "So, tell me more about growing up. What was it like having a rich and famous Hollywood dad?"

"Oh, as I'm sure you can imagine, all the normal millionaire's daughter stuff. Riding lessons, motocross racing, jet-ski competitions, skiing in the Alps in the winter, sailing in the Caribbean in the summer. Surfing in Hawaii. Vacations in London, Paris, all the normal stuff kids do."

"No way. Are you serious? That's amazing. Lucky you."

Devin nodded but the smile left her face and she focused her gaze on her sandwich. "Yeah, lucky, I guess." She shrugged and took a bite.

"What's the matter? You don't seem very happy about it."

Devin shook her head as if shaking off a thought. "Huh, oh, no. I am. I mean, I should be. It was a wonderful childhood. I live an exceptionally privileged life and I appreciate it. Really, I do. But sometimes, I wonder what it would be like to have had a normal childhood. One with a mom and dad at home, doing, you know, normal stuff."

"Sounds like my childhood and trust me, it's pretty boring," Rosie said. "But you did have a mom and a dad, right?"

"Yes, of course I did, but my dad was never home. He was always on the set. And my mom…" she paused and took another bite of her sandwich, pensively chewing it before continuing. "My mom was, well, let's just say she was absent in her own way as well. So basically, butlers and nannies raised me."

Rosie pulled a piece of bread away from her sandwich and played with it. "Sometimes I wonder, if I'd had a little more action in my life, like you did, if I wouldn't be so afraid and nervous all the time. I mean, you seem so confident and brave." She placed the piece of bread into her mouth.

"Yeah, that I am. Fearless Fitzroy they call me. That's part of my marketable charm."

"I would love to be brave and fearless. Everything makes me nervous. I think it was my mom's fault."

"Isn't it always the mom's fault?"

"Yeah, right? Anyway, my mom was super overprotective. She was always saying, 'Don't do that Rosie, you'll get hurt,' or 'Be careful Rosie, you'll catch a cold'. Or, 'You're not strong enough to do that Rosie'. Her voice still echoes in my brain every time I try something new. I hear her warning me to be careful and telling me I can't do it."

"What would she say about you being here with me right now?"

"She'd have a complete melt down." Rosie reached for the bag of chips. "And out of all the activities you did, you like skateboarding the best?"

"Yeah. There's something about it that's very freeing.

When I'm on my board, it's like the rest of the world ceases to exist. It's just me and my board." She stared off into the distance as if watching something that gave her great pleasure. "It's like, when I skate, it's as if I can fly. Like the world belongs to me. There's a power. A freedom." She snapped back to reality. "It's hard to explain. Do you know what I'm talking about? Does that ever happen to you?"

"Yes, I think so. That's how I feel when I'm at the potter's wheel. It's like the world disappears. When I'm creating a pot, and my hands are molding it, it's almost like you become one with it. You merge with it. As your hands shape it and make it into whatever you want, you get into a rhythm, and it's just you and the clay. By guiding it with your fingertips or your palms." Her hands massaged the air. "It's like you're bringing something to life that didn't exist before. It's, it's, I know it must sound silly, but during those moments, nothing else matters. It's amazing."

"Exactly," Devin said. "That's how I feel about my board. And, when I was younger, in my early teens before I could drive, when I'd be out skateboarding with a bunch of the guys in L.A., none of them knew or cared who I was. They had no idea who my dad was, or that I was," she held up two fingers and swiped the air, 'The Littlest Cowgirl'. And even if they had known, they wouldn't have cared. Either I could skate or I couldn't. Simple as that." A smile spread across her face. "And I could. I was damn good at it. And then there's the thrill. It's dangerous of course, so I get an adrenaline rush."

"That's amazing," Rosie said. "I'm happy for you. That you have excitement in your life. I have," she stifled a laugh with the tips of her fingers, "knitting. It sounds so lame after hearing how thrill-seeking your life is. The extent of my adventure is to be brave and use a different sized needle."

"No, hey, it's not lame," Devin said. "You're probably very

good at it. You make stuff for babies. And you work with deaf children and teach handicapped kids how to work with clay and paint. You give them joy. It's all great stuff. Important stuff that means something. The world needs more people like you."

Rosie's cheeks grew warm. "But you make movies. I mean, you actually make movies. Do you know how amazing that is? You reach thousands of people."

"Yeah, but it doesn't *mean* anything. Nothing I've ever done has ever *meant* anything."

"Oh, I'm sure your movies have meant something to someone."

"Nah. I'll tell you a secret, but you have to promise not to tell anyone."

"Cross my heart." Rosie's hands mimicked her words. "But you better make the thousands of dolls that are listening promise too."

Devin laughed. "They can listen. As long as they don't talk. My dream is–"

A flash of a lightning bolt zipped through the air followed by a deep rumble of a distant thunder clap. They both searched the sky at the same time. Thick black clouds rolled past them at an alarming speed.

Devin leapt up. "Those clouds don't seem like they want to play nice. We'd better finish up here and get going." She began picking up items that were spread over the blanket and stuffing them into her backpack.

"Fine with me." Rosie rolled the remainder of her sandwich in the white paper wrap and handed it to Devin to place in the backpack.

"We can finish this picnic and discussion when we get back to Key West." Devin firmly pressed the cork back into the wine bottle. They brushed sand off themselves. Rosie picked up and shook the blanket, and they made their way back toward the boat.

Devin was the first to turn the corner. She stopped in her tracks, spun, and faced Rosie. Her eyes and mouth both flipped wide open.

"What? What is it?" asked Rosie.

"It's the boat," Devin's eyes looked like they were about to pop out of their sockets and the next two words from her mouth caused Rosie's heartbeat to soar.

"It's gone!"

# FUNNY. NOT FUNNY

"Gone? You're kidding!" Rosie pushed Devin aside and bolted around her to see for herself.

The boat gently bobbed in the water. Exactly as they'd left it.

Devin held her stomach and bent over as she laughed. "You should've seen your face. Oh my God. It was priceless. I wish I'd snapped a photo."

Rosie's neck and face warmed as a combination of embarrassment and anger flooded her. She pushed Devin who stumbled back and fell into the sand.

Rosie's jaw tightened as she tried to think of an insult to throw at Devin.

"You're a real jerk, you know that. A real jerk. I about had a heart attack."

"I'm sorry, but I couldn't resist," Devin had difficulty getting the words out through the laughter. She stood and swiped at the sand on her pants. "Ah come on. It was just a harmless prank. Lighten up. It was funny."

As angry as Rosie was, Devin's laughter was contagious,

and she fought to suppress the smile that threatened to curl her lips. Instead, she stomped toward the boat. "Let's go."

Once onboard, after the blanket was put away and the anchor pulled in, they each sat in their respective chairs. Thunder grumbled in the distance and they repeatedly tossed glances skyward.

"You ready Captain?" Devin asked. An enthusiastic smile parted her lips.

"Ready Gilligan," Rosie replied with the extended thumb and pinky finger gesture that Devin had used earlier.

Devin threw her head back and released an enthusiastic laugh, holding her stomach as her shoulders bounced. Still laughing, she reached into one of her front pockets. The smile fell from her face. She searched another pocket. Then another. All traces of merriment were gone. Rosie watched as she slapped at every pocket. Then Devin's jaw dropped. She stared at Rosie with wide, rounded eyes.

"The key!"

## FROM BAD TO WORSE

Those two simple words caused an immediate flood of panic to rise throughout Rosie's body. Despite the warm afternoon air, a chill crawled over her as if a thousand tiny spiders crept over her skin.

"What do you mean, 'the key'?" she asked, fearing that she knew but hoping she didn't.

"I mean, I don't have the key." Devin continued to whack at her pockets. Her face was frozen in a look of alarm.

"Devin, please tell me you're kidding," Rosie said. A gust of wind blew a few strands of stray hair across her face and she swiped them away.

Devin thrust her hand deep into her front pocket. When she pulled it out, a metal key dangled from her fingers.

"Kidding!" she shouted as the expression of fear was instantly replaced by the playful grin Rosie had become familiar with.

"You're a major brat!" Rosie jumped out of her chair and slapped Devin on the back.

"Ow. Quit hitting me. Oh, come on. I'm playing with you.

I'm an actor, remember? You can't blame me for practicing my art."

"Practice on someone else. That wasn't funny. My heart can't take any more of this. Now start this stupid boat and get me out of here."

A few drops of rain fell as the thunder clasps grew louder and more frequent. The light had faded as sunset closed in and the clouds grew thicker and darker. The air carried the clean, crisp scent that signals an approaching rain storm.

Devin was still chuckling when she put the key into the ignition and turned it.

With the sound of a click, followed by silence, her laughter stopped short.

She turned the key again.

Again, nothing. She glared at the ignition.

"Oh, shit," she mumbled.

"Devin. I'm serious. You have to stop this. It's really not funny anymore."

Devin's face resembled the same expression as moments ago but this time, the color in her cheeks had disappeared.

"Rosie. I'm not kidding." Her voice picked up speed. "I can't imagine what's wrong. I mean. There's nothing…" Her head and shoulders swiveled as she surveyed the boat and area surrounding it. They had started to drift from the island. Repeatedly she turned the key in the ignition, each time with a harder, firmer, and more desperate turn. But every time she twisted it, the only sound Rosie heard was a soft click.

"Are we out of gas?" she asked.

"No, we have plenty. It's not that. We're not getting anything. No spark. Nothing. It's like it went dead. I can't…"

"What could it be?"

"I have no idea."

Devin pulled her phone out of a pocket and dialed a number. She ran her fingers through her hair as she pressed it to an ear. After several moments, she stared at it then let her hand drop. "Damn. I was afraid of that."

"What?"

"We're out of range. No service. Try yours."

Rosie fished through her bag. When she found her phone, she studied it. "It says 'no service'," she said but tried dialing anyway. She placed the phone to her own ear, then slowly lowered it while shaking her head.

"Doesn't your boat have a radio?" she asked.

Devin surveyed the instrument panel. "There's no radio on this boat."

Rosie dropped back onto the seat. "Oh no. What are we going to do?" She searched the horizon for signs of other boats.

The wind had picked up, and the waves had increased in size and intensity. They now splashed against the side of the boat, occasionally spraying them with cool sea water. The rocking motion had become more exaggerated. They both stood with wide stances, legs splayed and their weight shifting side-to-side with each movement.

"I haven't figured it out yet, but I'll think of something." She grabbed one of the oars and began paddling. Slowly the boat drifted back toward the island.

"You better think of something. I knew I shouldn't have listened to you. Every time I do anything I'm uncomfortable with, something horrible happens. I can't believe I allowed you to get me into this situation."

"Ok, now don't panic. We're going to get through this. What's the worst that could possibly happen? We spend the night on the island and are rescued in the morning by the cruise ship."

Rosie jumped to her feet. "What? A night on that island? Are you crazy?" Her voice rose an octave, and the words unfurled tainted with annoyance. "Spend the night on that island? There's no way I'm spending a night on a creepy, haunted, clump of deserted moldy land in the middle of the ocean." She pointed toward the horizon. "I'll swim back to Key West first."

Devin's eyebrows lifted. "Sharks?"

"Damn it Devin." Rosie stomped a bare foot.

"I know. I don't blame you for being angry. Try to relax. I'll think of something. I got us into this and I'll get us out of it. I've never gotten myself into a situation yet that I couldn't get myself out of."

"Yet." Rosie placed her hands on her hips. "Yeah, well unfortunately, this time, you can't call daddy and tell him to send a limo. And those stupid devil's tail logos aren't going to be much help to us here, are they?"

Devin recoiled, her face cringed as if someone had lit a match under her chin.

"Stupid little devil's tail," she clutched her chest. "Ouch. Give me a minute while I slide the dagger out of my heart."

"If I had a dagger, it might end up in your heart right now." Rosie took a deep breath, placed the back of her hand against her forehead and closed her eyes. "I'm sorry, I'm just so, so…"

"Frustrated? Angry? I get it and I don't blame you." Devin continued to paddle them back toward shore.

A bolt of lightning flickered, lighting the sky with a blue strobe. Seconds later a boom of thunder vibrated the air, and they both jumped. As if the atmosphere had been electrified, the hair on Rosie's arm rose. A chill snaked up her spine and along the back of her neck. The thunder acted like a starter's gun at the beginning of a race and immediately following it came the rain. The first few drops pitter-pattered the deck in a slow rhythm.

"Let's find some shelter and get out of the rain until I figure out what to do next," Devin said as she lifted the padding of the bench. She yanked out the blanket they'd used earlier and handed it to Rosie. Next, she removed two large towels. They were dirty and wrinkled. She tossed them at Rosie's feet.

Rosie picked up the towels using only her fingertips and held them away from her body. "These are gross," she said as she studied the stains and holes. Devin continued to rummage through the storage space. "What are you looking for?"

"Anything that'll keep us dry."

"Don't you have a tarp on this boat?"

"A tarp? I don't know…"

"What do you mean, you don't know? You don't know what you keep on your boat?

"It's not my boat."

"It's not your boat?" Rosie dropped the towels.

"The key was in the ignition. I figured we'd just borrow it for a couple of hours."

"You stole a boat?" Rosie wiped her hands on her dress and scratched at her temples.

"Relax Rosie. Everything is going to be ok. Hey look. Fireworks. They must be left over from the Fourth." Devin pulled a few sparklers and a rocket from the bottom of the storage compartment. The cellophane wrapping on all of them was yellowed with age.

"The Fourth from what year? 1776?" Rosie asked. "And what are we going to do with sparklers? Sit on the beach, cook s'mores and sing kumbaya?"

"Not the sparklers, the rocket. Maybe if we shoot it off, someone will see it."

"It's not a flare. Do you think sending up a firework rocket will signal that we need help?"

"Not normally, no, but coming from this island, it might. It's the only idea I have. Do you have another?"

Rosie glanced to her right then left, scanning the turbulent sea while trying to keep her balance as the boat rocked side-to-side. "Can you tell if it still works? It looks kinda old. Are there any matches?"

"Hmm. Matches?" Devin moved things around in the storage area and pulled out a first aid kit. It also was yellowed with age and the writing on the cover was faded. She struggled to open it. When the lid finally popped open, the sparse contents flipped out onto the floor of the boat. She picked up a pair of scissors and a packet of aspirin. A ball of twine and a small bottle rolled under the Captain's chair and she got on her hands and knees to retrieve them. "It's a bottle of mercury," she said.

"Mercury?" Rosie felt her nose wrinkle in an involuntary display of disgust. "I thought people stopped using that like in the 60s. Any matches?" she asked.

Devin shook her head.

A small metal container had fallen between the cushions of the bench. Devin reached in for it.

"Darn. What good's a rocket with no matches or a lighter?" Rosie said.

Devin snapped open the metal container. Inside were three wooden matches.

"Bingo! We have matches." She snapped the container closed and put it and the ball of twine in her pocket.

The rain had moved beyond a random sprinkle and now splattered them with regular frequency.

"Let's go sit under the trees and stay dry," Devin picked up two oars that lay on the floor of the boat, her backpack and the other end of the rope that was tied to the boat.

"Come on. Grab the blanket and towels. Let's go!" she said as she scampered over the back of the boat.

Rosie grabbed her bag, flip-flops, towels and blanket and followed Devin. After making sure the boat was securely tied to a tree, they jogged past the beach and toward the woods.

## SHIT JUST GOT REAL

When Devin and Rosie reached the woods, a thick layer of large leaves and vines crisscrossing overhead blocked most of the rain. Only a few random drops made it through and fell on them. Rosie placed her bag down, shook the blanket, and was about to lay it on the ground when Devin spoke.

"May I make a suggestion?"

Rosie paused. "Sure. What?"

"Why don't we sit on the towels and drape the blanket over our heads, sort of like a tent. It'll keep us dry and we'll be more comfortable."

Rosie studied the blanket, then the branches overhead.

"You know," Devin continued. "Sort of like camping."

Rosie returned the suggestion with a blank face.

"Let me guess. You've never been camping."

Rosie didn't answer. She simply tightened her lips.

"Here, let me show you." Devin pulled the ball of twine and knife from her pocket and cut four short pieces from the thin rope. First, she took the blanket from Rosie and scrunching up each of the four corners, circled the twine around each edge to make a knob. Next, she secured the ends of two of the pieces of rope to trees positioned several feet from each other. She moved quickly and with confident efficiency. She then stuck an oar into the sand one at a time, banging each in deeper into the ground with a large rock. Finally, she tied each of the other two corners of the blanket to an oar, creating a ceiling that slanted downward and hovered over the towels.

"This should do until the storm passes," Devin took a step back and admired what she'd just created.

"Let me guess," Rosie surveyed the lean-to. "You also starred on 'Survivor'."

"Nah." Devin stooped down and crawled under the overhanging blanket and evened out the towels. "Nothing but basic camping skills."

They each sat on a towel and peered out toward the water, watching as the wind and waves rocked the boat.

"At least we won't have to worry about freezing to death," Devin said. "This time of year, the temperature only drops to mid-70s at night here.

Rosie shot her a side-ways glance. "Is that supposed to make me feel better?" A mosquito hovered in front of her eyes and she swiped at it.

"Oh, come on. Lighten up. No one is hurt. You'll survive this."

"That remains to be seen. I may have a heart attack any minute." Suddenly a thought occurred to her, and she stared at Devin. "Do you know CPR?"

Devin shook her head.

"Oh, great," Rosie's hands flew in the air. "So I could save you but if anything happens to me, I'm screwed."

"Nothing's going to happen to you." Devin gently pushed an elbow into Rosie's ribs. "Stop worrying. Besides, there are worse things than being stranded on a deserted island with a fun, good-looking dyke like me."

"Humph," Rosie puffed. "I'll take alone in my dry, unhaunted hotel room any day. Hurry up and light the rocket will you, so we can get rescued and get out of here. This place is disturbing."

Her eyes repeatedly scanned the various dolls hanging from the surrounding trees. One, outfitted in a dirty, Victorian-style, lace dress, hung from a matted mass of hair. Its bright blue eyes were frozen open and appeared to be staring directly at them. Another, a baby doll with curly blonde hair, pursed red lips and dressed in a pair of onesie pajamas, hung upside down by a bare foot tangled in a vine. Several dolls hung poised on high branches and many more clung to low bushes. A bride and groom doll lay side-by-side on the ground partially hidden under a bush. A swarm of maggots crawled over them. The shimmering movement of the miniature worms gave the impression the dolls stirred beneath them.

The sight made Rosie feel as if something crawled on her skin. She found herself wiping imaginary offenders from her arms even though when she looked, clearly there was nothing there. "How do you think all these dolls got here?" she asked.

A doll lay in the sand not far from them. It was naked. The body was face down, but the head was twisted one-hundred and eighty degrees so it peered upward. The face was covered in a dingy web of cracks and chipped paint. It had large, dark eyes and like many of the other dolls, appeared to be staring in their direction.

"Devin, I think the eyes on that doll just moved," Rosie said.

"Oh right, and next it's going to ask if it can have some of our chips," Devin chuckled.

"No. I'm serious. Its eyes were looking up before, toward the sky. Now they're staring right at us."

"Impossible," Devin scoffed. "You're letting your imagination run wild. And if they did move, probably the wind blew them."

"I can't stand all these stupid dolls. I feel like they're watching us. Don't you feel like they're all staring at us? That one is too close. Will you move it, get it away?"

"Which one?"

"The one that's laying on the ground. Right there. Please. Throw it into the forest or something."

Devin sauntered to the doll, bent over, picked it up and brushed the sand off it. It had green eyes that stared up at Devin and when she tipped the head down, the eyes clicked close.

"See? The eyes are normal doll eyes," she said. The doll wore a pair of blue overalls. One of the straps was broken, and it hung unattached. The bottom of the pants was tattered. It was missing an arm and there was a huge hole where half its head should've been. Dirty black streaks covered its face, body, and clothes. It resembled a war victim. Devin swung it side-to-side by the arm. Each time she swayed it, its eyes and mouth clicked open then would snap closed.

Devin spoke in a high-pitched, mocking voice. "Hello, Rosie. My name is Driselda, and not only am I a haunted doll, I can also talk. If you throw me into the woods, I'll crawl out to haunt you, but I'll also bore you to death by talking to you non-stop. And I can sing, listen… Oh baby, baby, you're a doll…"

Rosie tried not to laugh but couldn't hold the giggle in.

Devin approached the blanket, peered inside her backpack, and pulled out her camera. She knelt down next to

Rosie and took a selfie, holding the doll up by the hair between them.

"Quit it. That's gross and disgusting. The germs. Ug. Please, just get rid of it." Rosie cowered from the decrepit toy that hung from Devin's hand. "I implore you."

"Well, since you implored nicely." Devin walked away from Rosie and faced the woods. She swung the doll in a large circle over her head several times as a cowboy would swing a lasso. When she released it, the doll flew high into the air and somersaulted as it soared until stopping with a loud clunk when it hit a tree. The sound of snapping branches continued for a few seconds as it tumbled to the ground, then all was quiet other than the soft patter of rain.

Devin returned to the blanket.

"Let's shoot the rocket and pray we get rescued and off this revolting island," Rosie said.

"Revolting? This is paradise. People pay huge money to be able to spend time on a deserted tropical island. You're getting it for free." Devin studied the sky. "I think we should wait until the storm passes. I'm afraid if we shoot the rocket up now, the rain will put it out before it gets high enough for someone to see it."

"Aren't they made to go high fast? Faster than rain could put it out?"

"I have no idea. I've never used one before. But I don't want to take that chance since we only have one rocket, do you?"

Rosie pulled her knees toward her chest and rested her chin on them. She wrapped her arms around her shins and gently rocked side-to-side.

"I don't think the storm will take long to pass by," Devin said. "Typically, they only last about an hour. Then we can set off the rocket from the beach and hopefully be rescued."

"Hopefully is the magic word there, isn't it?"

"No, the magic word is, hungry?"

Rosie shook her head.

Devin raised the wine bottle.

"Might as well," Rosie held the two plastic glasses while Devin poured the wine.

They sat in silence for a while, with nothing but the sound of rain gently falling on the leaves above them. Occasionally, a bolt of lightning pulsed through the air, followed closely by a ground-shaking grumble of thunder.

Rosie broke the silence with a scream that sounded more like a high-pitched chirp.

"Ah! What's that?!" she yelped.

"What's what?" Devin's head pivoted as she searched for what had provoked Rosie.

"That!" Rosie's arm extended toward some nearby shrubs. "Something is moving. Under that bush."

Devin jumped up and squatted to peer down under the wild green growth.

"This?" She held a long thin snake by the tail. It wiggled wildly in the air. "This is just a little ol' green snake. This little fellow won't hurt you. He eats insects mostly."

Rosie crossed her hands in front of her chest. "How can you touch it? Please, get rid of it. Put it down somewhere far away. I'm petrified of snakes. Please, do something with it."

Devin wrapped the snake around her hand and cooed to it as she walked back to where she'd picked it up. She bent over to place it on the ground but Rosie interrupted her.

"Oh no. Not there. That's too close. It could slither our way. Get it farther away from me." Her hands fluttered, shooing Devin away.

Devin trotted several yards down the beach and tenderly placed the snake on the ground. "There you go little snaky. Slither away and have a nice life." She watched it disappear before returning to the lean-to. Once beneath the blanket roof, she shook the rain off her hair toward Rosie, who cowered from the spray.

"Let's play a game to pass the time," Devin said.

"I don't feel like playing a stupid game." Something crawled along the top of her ear. She let out a shriek and slapped at the side of her head.

"Oh come on. Don't be a poop."

"What game? Hide and seek? Duck, duck goose?"

"No, truth or dare. Come on, it'll be fun."

"I don't even know how to play."

"It's easy. You pick truth or dare, and you have to either answer a question or do what you are dared to do."

"That doesn't sound like much fun."

"Come on. It'll keep your mind off the dolls."

Rosie's eyes flipped back to a doll that dangled from a tree in front of them. The head was only half attached and tilted in an odd, distorted angle. "You can be sure I won't pick dare, so I pick truth."

"Ok, so why was your mother so protective of you?"

Rosie released a long sigh. She played with her glass of wine before answering.

"My brother. I had an older brother. He was two when I was born. He'd been born ill. Very ill. I don't know what he had exactly. All I was told was that he was not a healthy baby. He didn't make it to his fifth birthday. So, I think my mother was overprotective of me because of that. She wanted to do everything in her power to make sure I didn't get hurt or sick."

"I'm sorry to hear about your brother."

"Yeah, I don't remember him of course. But I wish things would've been different. It would've been nice to have grown up with a brother. A healthy one. So that's what the tattoo is." She held up her ankle. "See? It's a little angel. I got it for my brother. And what about you? Any brothers or sisters?"

Devin didn't answer immediately.

Although it was early evening and typically would still be quite light out, the cloud-covered sky blocked the sun. The air was gray and shadowy.

A bolt of lightning pierced the air and thunder boomed. They both cringed and their shoulders raised up towards their ears as they waited for the thunder to stop growling. When it stopped, Devin took a sip of her wine. Before she spoke she turned, made eye contact with Rosie and cleared her throat.

"There's something I want to tell you. You may find this strange. I've never told anyone before. But I've been thinking for some time that I want to. I want to tell someone. And for some reason I can't explain, I trust you. Maybe it's because you lost a brother. I feel you'll understand. Is it ok if I tell you?"

Rosie nodded and shrugged. "Sure. Yeah, I guess."

"I, ah, also had a brother. Fred. He was named after my dad. Something terrible happened when he was four."

"Oh, Devin."

"We were at a circus. I was six. My mom had gone into one of those trinket stores to get something. She told us to sit on a bench and wait for her. This was back when my mom used to do stuff with us, before, well, before. So, anyway, as soon as she disappeared from sight, I told my brother to follow me. I wanted to run around the back of the petting zoo and see if I could get on one of the ponies. I'd been in 'The Littlest Cowgirl' the year before and thought I was a real cowgirl. So, we ran around the back of the carnival where all the trailers are. He followed me, of course. His cute little chubby legs waddled as fast as he could to keep up with me and he squealed with glee."

She paused, picked up a handful of sand and allowed it to slip through her fingers before continuing.

"So, we're back behind the trailers where all the carnies camp out. It's dusk, so they're standing around fires that burned in those big, rusty drums. It's right around Halloween so there's a chill in the air. I remember they warmed their hands near the fire. They had frying pans balanced on metal rods over the flames. You could smell meat cooking, well burning actually. And there was a lot of brown bottles and loud laughter. It was the kind of laughter that drunk men make though I didn't know that at the time of course. And me and my brother, we were silly with joy, laughing and running. I thought it was wonderful."

"Suddenly, we ran around a corner and there it was. A clown. A very tall and scary clown. He was peeing. I'll never forget it. He turned his head and glared at us with the most haunting look. When he smiled, those huge red lips spread wide across his face. He had blue eyes and high eyebrows. And large, pointy teeth. There was something about those teeth against those red lips." She shuddered.

"Imagine a cobra giving you a death stare just before striking. That's what it was like. The sight of him standing there peeing, and that smile. And to me, at that age, he looked to be ten feet tall. I screamed, turned, ran and when I ran, I knocked Fred down. He started crying, but I kept running."

"Sometimes, I swear I can still hear him crying." She paused and lowered her voice to barely a whisper. "I left my brother."

She rubbed her temple.

"What happened to him?" Rosie asked. Her voice was soft.

Devin shook her head. "They found his body, but never…" She cleared her throat.

"Oh Devin. I'm so sorry." Rosie covered her mouth with the tips of her fingers.

The corners of Devin's lips arched downward. "So, I ran

back to my mom, and as I was running, I kept looking back over my shoulder. I tripped and fell. Split my chin open. See?"

She tilted her head back and exposed a scar that ran along the bottom of her chin.

"So, when I got back to my mom, of course, she was hysterical because we'd been missing. And I come running back, crying, with blood pouring out of my face. You can imagine."

"This is terrible. What happened?"

"I lied. I didn't want to get in trouble and admit that I'd talked Fred into going with me. So I said two men dressed in black came and grabbed him. Two men in black capes wearing black masks. What was I thinking? I've often asked myself that. Maybe I was thinking about Batman, I don't remember. All I know is I didn't want that clown coming anywhere near me. I pointed in the opposite direction and told her I'd chased them but the men pushed me down and that was how I'd hurt my chin. I said I'd been able to escape but couldn't save Fred. That they had carried him away. So instead of being discovered to be the coward I really was, everyone thought I was a hero for trying to save my little brother."

"Oh Devin. I'm so sorry." Rosie rested a hand on Devin's knee.

"I'm ashamed of course. And the guilt. Not a day goes by I don't regret not being honest and doing the right thing. If I'd only told the truth, they might've been able to save him."

"You've carried this around for almost twenty years? How horrible for you."

"Yeah. My mom, well she sorta flipped out, mentally, know what I mean? Can't say I blame her. She blamed herself. Turned to pills and booze. She was never the same. And my dad. Well, my dad never actually said it, but I always felt he blamed me. It's as if he knew, somehow, he knew. He was never the same toward me. That's why when he gave me this camera, it meant something."

"Why?"

"I mean, I always got whatever I wanted. All the toys, the trips, whatever, he never said no, but he never gave me anything that made me feel he cared. This," she said as she patted the camera, "is special, for many reasons. First, he knows it's my dream to be a movie producer, like he is. I think I want to make him proud of me. And this camera, it's not even in production yet. This is a beta version. It's not scheduled to be produced for two years. The company gave it to him to test out. And he gave it to me. That means a lot."

"I can see why you'd feel that way. Why did you choose now, and me, to talk about it?"

"I dunno. It could be because I turned twenty-five last week, and that got me thinking. I've been alive for a quarter of a century. I mean, we can never count on how much time we have left of course, but let's say I live to be a hundred. Well, I'm guessing the last twenty-five-years won't be so great. So I actually have two more, twenty-five-year segments left."

"It doesn't sound like much when you put it that way," Rosie said.

"I know, right? So I was thinking, I don't want to live the rest of my life living a lie. Pretending I didn't do something horrible that I did."

"But you were only a kid. You were traumatized. I think you need to let it go and not beat yourself up about it."

"You may be right. But I also want to, somehow, and I'm not sure how to accomplish this, but somehow, do something good to make up for it. If it's even possible. But I at least have to try."

"Why tell me? Now?"

"It's hard to say. You got lucky, I guess." She smiled with one side of her face and a single dimple popped onto her cheek. It was a fleeting display though as she quickly grew serious. "I can't say for sure. There's this sudden, pressing need inside me to change. To become a better person so that during the next twenty-five years, I can make a difference in the world. It feels like the right time, the right place and with the right person. For some reason, I trust you. You have that honest way about you. I don't think you'll run to the paparazzi as soon as we get back and sell my story to the first celebrity gossip magazine."

"Nah, I wouldn't do that," Rosie said. "But I might hire an attorney to sue you for kidnapping and psychological damages."

Devin gave her a gentle push. "Try it and I'll show up in court with Driselda and the rest of her buddies from here."

Rosie shivered. "Oh good gravy, don't do that." She glanced at some of the dolls. Her tone grew serious. "Do you think that's why you're such a daredevil? Are you trying to prove you're not afraid of anything?"

"My shrink thinks so. After what happened, I promised myself I'd never be afraid again. And I've never told another lie since. So yeah, maybe I am trying to compensate." A half-hearted smile raised her cheeks. "But at least you won't ever have to worry about me lying to you."

"No, only made up stories about lost boats and keys."

"Oh, come on. That doesn't count. I was goofing around."

"Well, no more goofing this trip. Deal?"

"Deal."

"Ok, now my turn for truth or dare. I know you'd do anything I dared you to, so I pick truth."

"That's not how it works. I get to pick if I want truth or dare."

"Too bad, I'm changing the rules."

"I see I'm not the only bossy one on this island. I kinda like that. Ok, shoot."

"Why did you choose me to talk to on the boat?"

"Why wouldn't I choose you?"

"I don't know. I mean, you could've picked any woman there to talk to, and you picked me. I want to know why."

"Why not?"

"That's not a good enough answer."

"Hmm... not a good enough answer the lady says. Ok, let me think. You were so... so..."

"Lonely? Desperate?" Rosie interjected.

Devin shook her head. "No, your self-image is all wrong. You're nothing like that. You looked, hmm, how do I say it? Kind. Honest. Trustworthy. Those sorts of things."

Rosie sensed her cheeks were flushed as a warmth immediately spread up from her neck. She avoided Devin's gaze and Devin continued.

"Let me see if I can explain it. I felt like you'd be fun to get to know. I've had plenty of girlfriends that were sexy—"

"Oh, soooo, you're saying I reminded you of a Girl Scout and I'm not sexy?"

Devin slapped her forehead with her palm. "No. That's not what I meant. Oh boy, am I screwing this up." She studied Rosie's face. "Ok, for example, you have a certain confidence about you. You have your own style. You're not trying to be trendy or fashionable. You just are... you. Does that make sense?"

"Yeah, you basically said I'm not sexy and have a terrible sense of fashion."

Devin tilted her head. "That's not what I meant."

"Yeah. ok. Let's forget that question. It was a stupid question, anyway. I'm asking another one instead."

"You can't do that–switch questions."

"Yes, I can. You marooned me on this island. I get one do-over."

Devin chuckled. "Fair enough. Shoot."

"Why no girlfriend?"

Devin was drawing smiley faces in the sand with a stick. "I want dare."

"Too bad," Rosie said.

"Hmm, let me see if I understand the question. Why don't I have a girlfriend, is that the question?"

Rosie giggled. "Yes."

"By the way, now I get an extra one."

"Extra what?"

"Question."

"Fine. Go on."

"Let's see if I can explain this. I did have one, a girlfriend. We broke up a couple months ago. Remember when I told you I was in Key West to figure out some life stuff?"

"Yes."

"Well, that's part of it. The girlfriend situation. I mean, I've always had plenty of girlfriends, not at the same time, of course. I mean, one at a time. But it's always been easy for me to find a girlfriend. Not so easy to keep them, however."

"Why?"

"Why? Hmm… I guess if I could figure that out, then I wouldn't have a problem, now would I?"

She opened the bag of chips and handed it to Rosie, who reached in and took a handful.

"Every time I've had a girlfriend, after, oh about a year, either I find they're too boring for me, or they accuse me of being too wild."

"Fine pair we are. I'm too boring and you're too wild."

"Well, that's what they keep telling me, so I guess it might be true. That's what happened with the last one. Tiffany. She wanted to settle down, raise a family. She didn't want to travel, make movies, and do all the fun things I like to do."

"Wait. She wouldn't strap on a parachute and leap joyfully out of a moving aircraft 10,000 feet in the air with you?

"Ha! No way would she do that."

"No wonder you broke up with her. I mean a girl's gotta expect that her girlfriend is willing to risk her life for you, right? How about the alligator wrestling? Would she at least do that?"

"Very funny. I'm not that bad," Devin said.

"You have to admit, you are a bit of an extreme risk-taker. Do you think you'll ever want to settle down?"

"Yes. I do. That's part of my problem. I want to settle down. Live a normal life, whatever normal is. I realize life is not about jumping out of airplanes, surfing the biggest waves, cliff diving. I mean, doing those things are fun, but at some point, I want to put all the daredevil stuff behind me. Share my life with someone who loves me." She patted her heart. "Me. Not my life. Not because of my dad or my movies. Someone who really loves me. And we raise a family together. Kids, dogs, white picket fence, the whole nine yards. If you'd asked me five years ago, I'd said, 'no way'. But I feel different now. Maybe I'm growing up. Finally. I dunno."

She bit into a chip. "And you? Did you ever want to get married and settle down? You seem like the type."

"Is this truth question number two?"

Devin laughed. "Yep."

"Yeah, I've thought about it. Finding the right woman to be in a good, loving, long-term relationship with. But I guess I never believed it was possible, so I gave up looking. I accepted the fact that I'll live the rest of my life alone, with Itchy. And when he goes, I'll rescue another Itchy."

"Don't you have any dreams? Isn't there anything you really want?"

"Is that question number three?"

"Yes, but who's counting? Give me your glass, goofy," Devin said and poured more wine into each glass.

"Yes, there is something I really want," Rosie said. "Two things actually. I want to write books. Books for children. Books that can help change their lives. Help them to become more confident, kinder and wiser. Books I wish I'd had when I was a kid."

"You seem like you're kind and wise to me."

"Thanks, I guess I am. But I mean, confident and bold. Sorta like you. But also, kind and wise."

"Are you saying I'm not kind or wise?"

"Yes, I mean no. I mean, often, people that are bold and confident are lacking wisdom and empathy. And the ones that are kind and caring lack confidence. It's hard to explain. I think children should be taught how to have all those things, the whole package. It seems like a lot of parents don't have a grasp on some of those issues themselves. How can they possibly teach their kids about something they themselves don't understand? The kids grow up having one or two of those qualities but lacking the others. And on it goes. A propagating cycle."

"That sounds like a great idea. Why haven't you written the book already?"

"Oh, I don't know. I guess I'm afraid."

"Afraid? Afraid of what?"

"Afraid I'll fail. Afraid people will make fun of me. My mother's voice echoing inside my head. 'You can't do that. You won't succeed.' So, I never tried." She laughed. "I guess it's kind of funny, isn't it? I want to write a book about confidence but I'm too chicken to write it."

"You should write it. You'd be great at it."

"Thanks, maybe I will. Who knows? If I'm lucky, some of your bravery will rub off on me."

"And what's the second thing you really want?"

"This is going to sound silly. I want to find someone who loves me."

"That's not silly."

"No. I mean, really loves me. Loves me more than they love themselves. As in puts my needs and wants ahead of theirs, not always of course, but at least sometimes. Not that I need someone who would die for me though that'd be nice." She let out a quiet chuckle. "I guess I'm…" She turned her head and looked out to sea. "I'm tired of feeling like I'm disposable."

"Did your past girlfriends make you feel that way?"

Rosie nodded. "Yeah, I guess they did. You know, I never thought about it that way, until now, but it was always all about them. What they wanted. What they needed. I'm not sure why. I guess I'm partly to blame for allowing it. And I didn't realize it when I was in the relationship, of course. I don't think you ever do. But after this last time, for example, when she broke up with me and left. Just like that." She snapped her fingers. "Like it was easy for her. Tossed me away like last week's stale pizza. I was crushed, hurt, all that. It wasn't until later that I realized she actually never truly loved me. All she talked about was herself. I never felt she cared about my thoughts, my feelings. I felt disposable." Rosie knew her bottom lip trembled, but she couldn't stop it. "Does that make any sense? Am I being silly?"

Devin was quiet. When she spoke, her voice was low and slow.

"Yeah, yeah it does make sense and no, you're not being silly. I'm ashamed to admit it, but I think I've been like that. Like the kind of woman you dated. I didn't mean to be, of course. I mean, I didn't do it on purpose. But I was always so busy doing the things I wanted to do, that I wasn't always as kind or attentive as I should've been. I guess that's called being selfish. Now that I think about it and look back on it, it's pretty ugly. It's not as if I meant to be self-centered. It's just that it was so, so—"

"Easy?" Rosie asked.

"Yeah, I guess. Easy," Devin tipped her wine glass toward Rosie. "See, it's destiny that we were to meet today. I mean, I came here to reflect on my life. To try to figure out why I had these nagging thoughts that in spite of having everything I could ever want, I still wasn't satisfied. There was always this feeling lurking, that there was more. But I could never figure out what was missing. I think I'm starting to get an idea of what it is. And you, maybe you'll figure out what was missing in your past so you can find it in the future."

"Hey. I have a good idea." Devin's face lit up. "Why don't we collaborate? You write the book. And I'll make a movie out of it."

"Do you think we could really do that?"

"Of course we could. You write that damn book and send it to me. I'll take it from there."

Rosie's bottom lip had stopped quivering, replaced by a smile that felt as if it blossomed from her heart. She dabbed at her nose with a napkin. "And what about you?" she asked. "You were going to tell me about your dream, but we were interrupted by the storm. So tell me. What's your dream?"

"Is this question number three?"

Rosie blew a flatulent noise through her lips with her tongue.

"Well," Devin said, "like you, I have two dreams. I already told you that one of my dreams is to produce my own movies. But movies that mean something. Films that move people, make them think. Make them feel. I have this idea, I don't know how to explain it exactly, but I have this theory that I want to share with the world."

"What theory?"

"Well, it's not a theory exactly. It's more like a... ok, so don't laugh. It's about our spirits." As she spoke, her voice gathered momentum and increased in speed. "It's my belief that we live on, spiritually, after we die. That we don't really die. I mean, our bodies do, of course, but we don't." She patted her heart. "Who we really are, spiritually, doesn't die."

"Where do you think we go?"

"We go here," she waved her arm through the air.

Rosie's eyes tracked Devin's hand. "You mean like ghosts?"

"Yes, and no. Not like a 'BOO' kind of ghost, but as a spiritual being. Call it a ghost if you want."

"Do you think they're all good or do you believe in evil spirits?" As Rosie asked, her eyes scanned the trees, momentarily landing on each doll that hung from the branches.

"I think they're good. I think evil is a human-only trait."

"So you want to make a movie about that. Where our spirits go after we die?"

Devin nodded. "That's why I'm here, in Key West. I'm scoping out possible sites for shoots. That's why I wanted to come here." She pointed with a finger toward the ground.

"Here? You mean this island?"

Devin nodded. "It'll make a great location for a concept I've been toying with. I'm hoping it'll comfort people like my parents and your family. People who have lost a loved one. And this camera–"

"Darn. Hold on Devin. I really have to pee," Rosie said. "Give me two minutes. I want to hear your idea but I can't hold it anymore. I'll be right back. Pass me one of those napkins."

Devin handed Rosie a napkin.

"Save my place," Rosie said as she stood, took a deep breath and studied several of the nearby dolls. She headed toward a thin trail that disappeared into the woods, away from most of the dolls.

She'd only walked a few steps from the beach when she saw something in the middle of the path that stopped her.

"Devin," she yelled, "come here."

Devin walked up behind her. "Yes?"

"What's that?" Rosie asked. Her arm was extended, and she was pointing at something.

Devin peeked over Rosie's shoulder to see what had captured her attention.

"It looks like poop," Devin said matter-of-factly.

"Devin. What could possibly be on this island that's large enough to leave a poop that big?"

Devin pressed a fingertip to her lips. "A cow?"

"A cow?" Rosie crossed her arms. "You're not serious. You expect me to believe there are cows on this island? I mean come on. That's a large poop. Do you think there are wolves, bears, or alligators on this island?"

"Nah. The island's not big enough to support a population of wolves or bears. And you won't catch a gator here. They don't like salt water. It's probably a chimp. Or, someone else had a picnic here and they had to go."

"That is gross to the extreme," Rosie's face contorted.

"I agree. I can't believe I let you talk me into coming to this island. What was I thinking?" An impish smile played on Devin's lips.

"Oh, why you. There's no way..." Something caught Rosie's attention. She stopped talking and bent forward toward the pile of excrement to get a closer look. "Oh my God, look." She stood straight, pulled her head back and away, covered her mouth with her palm, and pointed down.

Devin bent over, stooping closer to the dark mass on the ground. Four tiny fingers stuck out from the heap of brown turd.

"It's a part of a doll's hand," Devin said.

"Yes." Rosie backed away from it. "And I know you're not going to believe me, but I swear I just saw it move."

"You're spooked and starting to see things. Here," Devin said, "I'll take care of it for you." She took a few steps to the side of the path, lifted a large rock and struggled to carry it back, gently placing it on top of the poop. "There, out of sight, out of mind. Now go pee and forget about it."

Rosie shuffled around the rock, keeping a suspicious eye on it, then followed the narrow path deeper into the forest. Branches hung low and heavy with wet leaves. Cautiously, she'd spread them apart and duck or weave through them. Occasionally, using a stick, she'd delicately move a spider web out of the way and stoop low to pass under it.

When she came upon a clearing near a large tree, she glanced around to make certain that nobody or nothing was watching. Other than two dolls that hung nearby, she was alone. She squatted with her back to the tree. As the urine flowed from her, she closed her eyes and breathed a sigh of relief. When she'd finished, she tried to avoid looking up into the trees, but the disturbing sensation that the dolls were watching her was too strong. Her gaze lifted and jumped from one doll then to the other.

One doll hung upside down, its legs tangled in the vines. Its dress flipped downward and covered half its face. Its arms reached toward the ground as if pleading for someone to help it. The other doll was dressed in a black wedding gown, complete with a dark lace veil covering its face. It sat on a large branch of a tree resting against the trunk.

Repeatedly she told herself, *'they're just toys'.* But the feeling of eyes staring down at her, and the thought that there may be more hidden that she couldn't see, caused her skin to prickle and her heart rate to increase. A sensation of light moisture accumulated on the back of her neck.

She glanced toward the sky. The rain had let up and the worst of the thunderstorm had passed, but the light of day had thinned. The large nearly round moon had risen above the horizon. Hopefully they could shoot off the rocket now and a nearby boat would see it, rescue them, and get them off this dreadful island.

Rosie turned to face the path to return to where she'd left Devin, but something in the middle of the path stopped her in her tracks and she froze. She didn't blink. She didn't breathe. She didn't move. For a brief time, she wondered if even her heart had stopped beating.

In the middle of the path, the path she'd just walked down, was...

*A doll.*

It stood, motionless, staring at her. The doll wore a pair of blue overalls that had a broken strap and were tattered at the bottom. It had only one arm and half its head was missing. Its face was covered with cracks and chipped paint. Large, green eyes stared back at her. Unmistakably, it was the same doll that Devin had thrown into the woods earlier.

Pressure on her chest reminded her to breathe. A mixture of thoughts and emotions whizzed through her brain. She planted her hands on her hips, tilted her head and cried out. "Damn it Devin. We had a deal."

There was no answer.

"Devin?" she raised her voice.

"What?" came the response from the direction by the beach where they'd been sitting.

"That's not funny," she yelled back. She soothed herself by rubbing her hands up and down her arms while glancing upward at the dolls that hung overhead. In addition to the two that she'd seen earlier, she now saw a third that she hadn't noticed before.

"What's not funny?" Devin's voice wafted through the forest.

"The do..." The word froze in her throat as her gaze returned to the path. Her mouth hung open and she blinked.

The doll was gone.

## WTH?

First Rosie screamed.

Then, she ran.

She sprinted down the trail as quickly as her flip-flopped feet would allow, swatting at branches that hovered in front of her. At one point a spider web wrapped and clung to her face and her screams intensified as she peeled the sticky threads off herself. By the time she burst into the clearing where she'd left Devin, she was hysterical.

Devin scrambled to her feet. She trotted to meet Rosie. "What's the matter?"

Rosie spoke through gasps of breath. She bent forward resting her hands on her knees for support. "Devin. Tell me you played a prank on me and put that doll in the path."

Devin's eyebrows furrowed down. "What doll? What path? What are you talking about?"

Rosie pointed to the woods behind her "The path I just went down to pee. Please, tell me you were playing a trick on me and put it there to scare me. I won't be mad." She clutched the front of Devin's shirt. "Tell me!" Her voice trembled.

Devin studied Rosie's face, leaned closer, and peeled a line of spiderweb from her hair. She shook her hand in an attempt to release it from her finger but ended up wiping it on her shirt. "No, Rosie. I wouldn't do that. I promised you, no more goofing around."

"Swear on your brother's soul you're telling me the truth." Rosie repeatedly spun and checked the woods behind her.

Devin gripped Rosie's shoulders and squared her so they faced each other. She narrowed her eyes. "I swear. I told you. I wouldn't lie to you. Now, tell me what happened."

"Devin," Rosie kept glancing over her shoulder. "There was a doll, that same doll you threw into the woods, Desperelda, or whatever you called her. That doll was standing in the middle of the path." Her shoulders still heaved, and she wrapped her arms tightly around herself.

Devin stared at Rosie, then glared toward the path. "Impossible. I threw it in the opposite direction."

Rosie shook her head, opened her mouth, but no words came out. She closed her mouth.

"Rosie, look at me." Devin took hold of Rosie's chin and forced her to make eye contact. "There's no way. Someone is trying to scare us. Calm down and take a deep breath."

Rosie groaned while trying to breathe. Her speech was reduced to short, gasping sentences. "Devin. It was. The same. Doll." She didn't want to cry but she was a bundle of frayed nerves that were about to explode.

"Wait here," Devin turned and marched toward the woods.

"Devin. No. Don't go. Don't leave me here alone," Rosie pleaded.

"I'm getting to the bottom of this. Here," Devin returned to their makeshift tent, reached into the zippered pouch of her backpack and took out the small red knife. She flipped out the largest blade and handed the handle of the knife to Rosie. She then jogged into the foliage and disappeared.

Rosie sat beneath the blanket, her arms wrapped tightly around her knees, clutching the knife in one hand, holding her bag to her chest and waited. She trembled.

The last rays of daylight were thin and whispers of night had crept in. It'd stopped raining, and the air was moist with dense humidity. Each tree cast its own eerie shadow that menacingly swayed like large, ghostly fingers playing across the landscape. The clouds, still drifting lazily in front of what was left of the sun, caused the colors on the island to be muted into dull shades of a greenish gray.

With the passing of the storm, the island was abuzz with sounds. A mixed variety of chirps, tweets, coos, chattering and other animal babbling drifted from the forest. Occasionally, a loud screech cut through the air and Rosie would twitch. In another environment, the sounds might have been pleasant, but here, now, the noises made her feel as if hundreds of invisible insects crawled on her. She continued to rub her arms as if that would wipe the sensation away. Occasionally, she heard what sounded like a long, low moan off in the distance.

*It must be the wind through the rocks above,* she thought as she glanced upward toward the mixture of jagged stone and forest peaks that towered above her.

Her attention was caught by a particular sound and it caused her to stiffen. She held her breath in order to better hear it. Mixed within the medley of noises that permeated the forest, she thought she heard the word, *'mama'*. There it was again. Soft and distant but distinct, she heard, *'ma-ma'.* Two syllables. She was positive that she'd heard it. She wasn't imagining things.

*Maybe it's a mockingbird,* she thought. *Either that or a doll's voice box is stuck.*

Nearby, a small branch cracked. She jumped, let out a low whimper and shuttered.

"Devin," she rocked as she talked to herself. "Please come back."

She glanced at her phone. The battery indicator was red. It was 7:05. She figured they only had about an hour to get off this disturbing island before sunset.

Something moving quickly through the forest stunned her. She stopped breathing, stared at the group of moving branches and gripped the knife tighter, holding it out in front of her. Taking a deep inhale, she waited.

Devin bolted from the path.

"Devin," she exhaled the word.

"Ha," Devin said. "You look funny holding out that little knife. I suppose if something attacked you, you could tickle it with that blade."

Rosie glanced down at the knife, flipped the blade back into position and slipped it into the side pocket of her dress.

"Well?" she asked. "Did you see anything?"

Devin plopped beside her, brushing the spattering of rain drops and twigs off her shoulders. "Nothing," she said. "Are your glasses ok? I mean, did the lens pop out, or did you put it in backward or something?"

Rosie thrust out her lower jaw and she spoke through gritted teeth. "My. Glasses. Are. Fine."

Devin shook her head. "Maybe a chimp put the doll there. They can be pretty mischievous."

"I think I'd heard if a chimp had scampered through the forest, don't you? I mean, I don't think it tip-toed behind me and quietly placed the doll there, then snatched it away without making a sound."

Devin shrugged. "Well then, there's only one other solution. You must be hallucinating."

"Hallucinating? What?" Rosie said. "No way. Devin. I

know what I saw. I saw a doll. And it wasn't just any doll. It was *that* doll."

Devin reached for Rosie. Her hand rubbed her shoulder. "Calm down. It's ok. It happens. When people get highly stressed, they begin to imagine things. They see things that aren't there. It's their imagination. It's not your fault. You're scared. I get it."

A blaze of anger grew inside Rosie the likes of which she'd never felt before. "Devin. I swear, I'll use your very own knife to stab you."

"It's all right. Forgettaboutit. Let's shoot off the rocket. The worst of the storm has passed. It'll be dark soon. The rocket should show up nicely now. Someone is sure to see it and come to our rescue, ok?"

Rosie nodded, removed her glasses and rubbed her eyes.

They walked to the edge of the beach, Devin in front, Rosie clinging to the back of Devin's shirt, keeping a vigilant eye to the right, left, and behind them. They stopped near where they had tied up the boat which still rocked rhythmically with the waves.

Devin removed the rocket from the cellophane wrapping and read the instructions. "It seems simple enough. All we have to do is simply light it, hold it, and it shoots up."

"Be careful," Rosie said. "People blow their hands off with those things."

Devin took the match box out of her pocket. She opened it and as she was taking a match out, the box flipped out of her hand and the matches fell onto the wet sand.

"Damn," she cursed as she dove, scooped them up and blew the damp sand off them.

"Did they get wet?" Rosie asked.

Devin studied them. "I think they're ok. We'll find out soon enough."

Devin struck one of the matches against the side of the match container. Nothing happened.

She was about to strike it a second time when Rosie tugged on her sleeve. "Devin?" Her voice was thin, weak.

"What?" Devin snapped as she concentrated on lighting the rocket.

"Devin." Rosie repeated the word and gave another, rougher, sleeve tug.

"What?!" Devin's voice had an edge of impatience to it. She paused before trying to light the match again to look at Rosie.

A familiar sensation flooded Rosie. The same feeling had occurred when she was a kid and was on a whirly twirl ride at the carnival. She was light headed and felt as if she'd either faint or throw up. Her gaze remained fixated toward the boat.

Devin turned to see what had captured Rosie's attention.

Standing in the shallow water, beside the boat was a doll. It was dressed in a black scuba outfit, complete with mask, fins and snorkel. Its two tiny hands were held high up above its head.

Each hand clutched a spark plug.

# TIME TO MEET THE NATIVES

Rosie swallowed hard. "Now try telling me I'm hallucinating."

"What the hell? There's no way." Devin muttered. "Here, hold these." She pushed the rocket and match toward Rosie who shifted her bag onto her shoulder and clutched the rocket against her chest. Devin took off running down the beach toward the boat, grains of sand flipped from behind her feet with each step.

The scuba diver turned and plunged, disappeared under the water, taking the two spark plugs with him.

"Damn," Devin stopped short of the water. As she walked back toward Rosie, she repeatedly glanced over her shoulder toward the boat.

"I still don't believe it." Her head shook side-to-side.

"How could you not believe it? You saw it with your own eyes," Rosie said.

"Looks can be deceiving. Trust me. I've seen weirder things on my father's sets. Someone is playing tricks on us." She studied the surrounding trees. "Someone is trying to spook us."

Rosie's gaze followed Devin's as they both surveyed the trees and vines that towered over them and the thick underbrush that graced the forest floor.

"They're doing a good job. Devin, I seriously doubt if this is a Hollywood set. I think this island is haunted and we—"

A sudden look that had appeared on Devin's face stopped her mid-sentence. Devin stood motionless, her face blank and expressionless as she stared at something behind Rosie. Slowly, Rosie twisted and looked over her shoulder to see what had caused Devin to stop in her tracks.

Behind her, high above, a doll climbed down a tree. Its tiny arms and legs moved sluggishly and methodically as it inched its way down the bark. Once in a while, it'd stop, turn its head in their direction, and smile before resuming its descent. It was dressed in a red and black checkered flannel shirt, blue jeans and white sneakers. Its eyes were completely black.

The sound of something crashing through the forest caused Rosie and Devin to turn their attention in time to see a doll tumble to the ground from a branch above. It landed on its back, and wiggled in the sand, its arms and legs pointing upward, like a turtle struggling to flip over.

Rosie screeched, "Devin. They're coming alive! Do something."

Devin's voice lowered, and she spoke through clenched teeth. "Coming alive my ass. They're not alive Rosie. Someone is operating them remotely. Watch this." She grabbed one of the oars, untied it from the blanket, and approached the fallen doll. She swung the oar and connected with the doll, sending the toy's head flying through the air. The body, without a head, continued to struggle while the head wobbled on the beach nearby. The eyes repeatedly blinked.

Devin swung the oar again at the body and it shattered

into pieces. An arm flew in one direction while a leg tumbled in another. The body, with one arm and one leg still attached, landed several feet from them. Each of the sections of the doll continued to squirm independently.

Devin ran to the torso and reached for it.

"Don't touch it!" Rosie yelled.

"I'll show you that it's a robot," Devin said. Her cheeks were flushed pink as she bent down and picked up the doll by the remaining sole arm. While she walked back toward Rosie, she peered inside the body through the hole where the head had been attached. "You need to see this so you can stop—"

She didn't finish the sentence but brought the doll closer to her eyes. Abruptly, she stood motionless as her mouth flopped open. The doll twisted in her hands. As if she'd been holding a cobra, she released a high-pitched scream and threw the torso into the water. All color drained from her face. Her skin turned an odd shade of washed-out pale.

"What?" Rosie asked. "What did you see?"

Devin's head shook. Her eyes were large. "Nothing."

"Nothing?"

"Nothing. I expected computer chips, batteries, wires, speakers, you know, the normal robot stuff, but it was empty with literally, spiderwebs. Just as you'd expect the insides of an old doll that's been hanging around a forest to look."

Her eyebrows furrowed low. She reached for her camera, aimed it toward each of the body parts, and snapped the shutter. Repeatedly, she reviewed the images on the camera, then the doll parts.

"What?" Rosie asked. "How can that be? And will you stop taking stupid pictures?"

Devin pressed the camera to her cheek and the view finder to her eye. The shutter kept snapping. "I didn't get to finish explaining to you about my theory. I suspect this camera, if I can figure out how to make the correct adjustments, will prove my hypothesis about spirits."

"What do you mean? That you'll be able to take pictures of ghosts?"

"Yes. Ghosts or spirits."

"Oh Devin, I'm way to creeped out to hear about this now."

"Come here. Look at this picture I took of you earlier." Rosie approached her and Devin tilted the camera's LCD screen toward her.

"Yeah, so? Me sitting on a blanket in the forest. What's so special about it?" Rosie asked.

"See what happens when I make this adjustment and zoom in?" Devin turned a knob on the camera.

"I see a green haze around me now," Rosie said. "What is that?"

"Right. That's the type of energy field you're emitting. Proving you are biomaterial that's alive. I get no such haze in the photos of the dolls. Look." She pressed a button and photos rotated. A variety of doll images flashed before her. "See? That proves there's no living material present. Meaning, the only other logical explanation is they're robots."

"But what about spiritual? I mean like a ghostly presence? Your camera can't capture that, can it?"

"I think it can. My theory is there's a spiritual presence that floats in a sort of space between alive and dead. It's neither. And that presence emits traces of left over biomaterial that can be detected with a sophisticated-enough measuring device. Like this camera. I just haven't had it long enough to figure out how to adjust it properly."

"But you see none of that with the dolls, right?

"Right."

Rosie exhaled an audible sigh. "But when you looked inside the doll, you didn't see anything that would normally be in a robot, right? I mean there were no wires, circuit boards?"

"Right."

"So, that means whatever is happening doesn't have a logical explanation."

"Correct."

"Which means there must be an illogical explanation."

"One would think," Devin said.

Rosie groaned and clutched her stomach. "Devin. I know you think this is a fun and exciting adventure, but I'm a simple girl. I make pottery. I knit. I'm not made to deal with voodoo spirits and haunted dolls. I'm more than a little freaked out right now and am trying my hardest to keep my shit together." Her eyes scanned the dark forest, pausing when a thought occurred to her.

"Devin. Jimbo was right. It is real. I wonder what the other secrets are that he didn't tell us?"

"It can't be real Rosie. Think about it. They have to either be robots or alive."

"What if they're neither?"

"Well, if they are neither, then my theory is correct. I just need to figure out how to prove it. Here, hold this for a minute. I have an idea." She handed Rosie her camera and with the agility of a mountain goat, scaled to the peak of a six-foot boulder. When she reached the top, she said, "Ok, give it back to me." She reached down toward Rosie for the camera.

Rosie handed the camera up to Devin but, as if in slow motion, she saw her hand let go of it before Devin had time to grab it. She watched in horror as the camera bounced onto the rock, then hit several more rocks as it tumbled toward a puddle of seawater below.

"No!" Devin screamed. "Grab it!"

Rosie dove and scooped the camera just prior to it plummeting into the water.

"My camera!" Devin's voice sounded injured. "Give it to me."

Rosie lifted and handed it to Devin, presenting it as carefully as if it were the Queen's jewels.

Devin inspected the exterior, rubbed some scuff marks, then peered through the lens, pushing buttons and moving levers.

"Is it ok? Did I break it?" Rosie babbled. "Devin, I'm so sorry. If it's broken, I promise, I'll buy you another. I don't care how much it costs. I'll take out a loan. I'm so sorry. I didn't—"

The site of Devin's face stopped her cold. It was a face that stared at death.

"Oh shit. It's broken, isn't it?" Rosie nervously twisted one hand inside the other.

Devin shook her head. "No, it's not broken. It's, it's actually working," she said, her voice hesitant. "Some sort of adjustment happened from the tumble. Now I can see them. There's a purple haze around them."

"What do you mean them? The dolls? A purple haze? What does that mean Devin?"

The doll that had been crawling down the tree had almost made it to the bottom. Devin scampered down the rock, placed her camera into the knapsack and laid it on the sand. She grabbed the oar and bolted toward the doll that still clung to the tree. With the oar lifted over her head, she emitted a scream like a martial artist before they break a board and swung the wooden paddle toward the doll. It flew off the tree and landed on its back in the water. Frantically, its tiny arms and legs fluttered, but it was unable to make progress and sank, leaving a trail of bubbles.

Rosie ran behind Devin and clung to her shirt. A rustling

low in the bushes caught their attention. A doll, dressed as a nurse with a dirty, ripped dress and missing an ear, crawled toward them. Devin took a step in its direction but before she could go after it, several others appeared at the edge of the forest. One doll had only a single leg, and it hopped on its remaining limb. One, dressed as a hobo, was armless. A chubby baby doll with no legs, maneuvered through the sand as a military person would crawl under barbed wire, using its arms only, dragging its torso. Some dolls walked, others crawled. Dirt, grime, stains, spiderwebs and wiggling insects covered them all as they crept out of the forest.

"Rosie, run!" Devin screamed. She grabbed her backpack and the oar and took off running away from the sandy beach toward the rocky coast with Rosie close behind.

They'd put some distance between themselves and the beach, when Rosie slipped on the slimy seaweed and fell onto the coral.

"Ow. Damn it. Stop Devin!" she said as she inspected the blood that oozed from her knee. "I can't go any more. I can't run in these flip-flops."

They both frequently flashed quick looks behind them, toward the direction of the beach.

"Do you still think they're being operated remotely?" Rosie asked.

"I don't know what to believe," Devin said. "It doesn't make any sense. I didn't see any mechanisms but, the purple…" Her voice trailed off. "Give me the rocket. I'll shoot it and let's pray someone sees it."

"The rocket?" Rosie felt her face go blank. Her already elevated heart rate leapt to a higher level.

"The rocket. I gave you the rocket and the match." Devin's words had a sharp edge to them.

Rosie turned her palms over and stared at them. They

were empty. Her bag still hung from her shoulder. "I don't. I don't…" she mumbled.

"What did you do with it?" Devin gripped Rosie by the shoulder.

"I don't. I don't…" Rosie tried but couldn't finish speaking as she let her bag slip from her shoulder. Frantically, she searched through it. Her sweatshirt lay on top. She snatched it and tossed it onto the sand. She grabbed the yarn and half-finished blanket, yanked them out and clutched them above her head while her other hand searched the bottom of the bag. When she allowed her hand and the knitting to drop back into the bag, her face and spirit also fell. Her head shook back and forth as she stared unblinking into Devin's eyes.

"Oh God. You dropped it on the beach, didn't you?" Devin gripped at her skull as she answered her own question. "You did. I have to go back and get it."

"No. You can't leave me." Rosie recognized the panic in her own voice but couldn't calm it.

"Then we have to go together."

"No. I can't go back there."

"Rosie." Devin inhaled deeply through her nose and exhaled through her mouth before speaking. She lowered her voice and spoke calmly. "We need that rocket. Either I go get it. Or you go. Or we both go. But we need to get it. Pick one."

Rosie glanced up at the trees. Branches were crackling as several dolls overhead climbed down. "Ok, let's go," she said.

# ROCKET MAN

Slowly, they made their way back along the shoreline toward the beach. When they reached where the sand met the rocky coast, they hid behind the thick brush and peered at the boat. White light of the moon peeked out from behind scattered clouds, easily allowing them to see the vessel. It rocked gently, lifting and dropping with the rhythm of the ocean waves.

And... It was covered with dolls. Dolls scoured the boat. And as if they were searching for something, things were being tossed overboard. Discarded items, buoys, life jackets, seat cushions, floated in the water. The way the dolls swarmed the boat reminded Rosie of a National Geographic movie when maggots flocked over a decaying body. The sight caused a sudden rush through her as if the blood in her veins had been replaced with icy red slushies.

"Oh fuck. Devin," she whispered. "What are we going to do?"

Devin's face reflected a look of shock. "I didn't take you to be the swearing kind."

Rosie felt the pressure in her head building like a

steaming pot that's about to blow a cover. She guessed that the veins in her forehead and neck would be bulging. They always did when she was stressed or angry and now she was both. She grit her teeth and spoke through them. Only her lips moved. "I'm not. But I figure being stuck on a *fucking* haunted island with *fucking* dolls that come *fucking* alive is a *fucking* good time to start. Don't you think?" She inhaled deeply in an attempt to calm herself, then quietly stated, "Ok, what's Plan B?"

A robot doll made of a shiny, silver metallic material stood on the stern of the boat. Most of the dolls were one to two feet high but he towered over them by a foot. His head rotated a full hundred and eighty degrees and he faced them. Moments ticked by as he stood motionless, as if analyzing the situation, before he moved again. Methodically, he climbed to the rope that attached the boat to the tree and hand over hand, like a highly skilled, military special ops soldier, made his way over the water back to the beach. He landed on the sand with the grace of a ninja and proceeded to walk in their direction. He ambled toward them with a limp.

Several of the smaller dolls stopped what they were doing and followed the silver robot. None, however, performed the same maneuver of using the rope. A long driftwood tree had been placed as a bridge between the boat and the beach, and they walked or crawled along the dried log. Occasionally, one would fall off and it would either sink or drift away with the waves.

"Devin. What is that?" Rosie pointed at the silvery figure. "It looks like a human—"

They spoke at the same time.

"Rocket ship?"

"Submarine?"

"Torpedo?"

"Let's go," Devin tugged on Rosie's arm. "We can't go back to the boat."

"What do we do? Where do we go?"

"I'm not sure, but we can't go that way."

They turned and cautiously made their way back over the rocks along the shore. Rosie slipped often and when she did, she'd fall into a murky, seaweedy puddle. Each time they looked back, they caught sight of the miniature robot that continued to follow them. Its progress was slow but steady as it climbed, effortlessly hoisting itself up and over each rock, then leaping down to the next.

"I'm going to kill that little bastard," Devin wrapped both hands around the handle of the oar, gripping it tightly.

"No, leave it alone." The toe thong of one of Rosie's flip-flops had popped out and she was trying to push it back into the hole. "Let's keep going. It won't be able to catch us."

"Go where? Run around the island all night until the sun comes up? You'll never make it in those flip-flops. Here. Take my sneakers." Devin reached down and began to untie her sneakers.

"I can't wear those. They'll never fit me. They're huge. They're like clown shoes." As soon as she said it, Rosie gasped and covered her mouth with the tips of her fingers.

A pained look flashed across Devin's face. She stopped untying the laces.

"Oh, Devin. I'm sorry. Really, I'm sorry. It just slipped out. But seriously, I'm a size six and a half, what are those like twelve?"

"Ten," Devin's voice was soft and she refocused her attention on loosening and removing her sneakers.

A scraping noise caused them both to glance back. The silver robot had made progress toward them. The rest of the dolls were left far behind but he was able to climb and jump over rocks with greater speed.

"Here," Devin slipped out of her sneakers. "You can't walk in those. Put these on. Lace them up tight. It'll be better than those flip-flops."

"But you can't run around barefoot," Rosie protested but slipped her foot into one of the sneakers and tugged firmly at the laces.

"I'm not barefoot. My socks will help protect my feet. Besides, I'm a surfer and skateboarder. I practically live bare-foot." She glanced back at the robot and clenched her teeth. "I'm gonna get that one."

She allowed her backpack to slip to the ground, regripped the oar, and crept back in the direction they'd just come from. A large tree had fallen and stuck out toward the water. She hid behind it and waited. Rosie watched from a distance.

When the silvery doll walked by her, Devin released an ear-piercing scream and swung the oar. The oar split into fragments. Devin shrieked, dropped what remained of the paddle and pressed her hands to her chest. The doll didn't budge but simply turned its attention to her, rotated, changed directions, and proceeded to head in her direction.

"Holy shit," she screamed and ran back toward Rosie, rubbing and shaking her hands. Her palms were flushed red. "Come on, let's go. Hitting that thing was like hitting a baseball bat against a Sequoia tree."

As they made their way along the coastline, the robot kept a steady pace behind them. Several other dolls appeared out of the woods and followed as well. They were slow, but their progress was steady and unyielding.

After a while, Rosie grabbed Devin's arm. "Stop," she said. "I have to rest. I can't go on like this all night. Running in these sneakers is like trying to run wearing snorkel fins. What are we going to do?"

"Look, up there." A rock wall ascended overhead and

Devin pointed to the top of it. "There are some sort of caves. We could scale this wall and hide in there until sunrise."

"And if we go into a cave and the dolls follow us there, then what do you suppose happens?"

"We're trapped in a cave," Devin's voice deflated. "Not such a great idea I guess, huh?"

The number of dolls following them along the coast had grown. It was dusk now and other than scattered moonlight that sparkled across the water, they were surrounded by a combination of shadowy grays and dim blacks.

They were down low on the coast, near the water. Above them rose cliffs that were scattered with trees and caves. Above and behind that looked to be thick with forest. The scuffled sound of movement from within the forest had grown more intense.

"It sounds like there's hundreds of them," Rosie said. "Why do you think they're following us? What do they want?"

"I have no idea," said Devin. "But I really don't want to find out, do you?"

Rosie shook her head and peered behind them. Several dolls were making their way over the rocks and seaweed. The larger silver robot had been able to keep a steady distance in front of the others.

"Come on, let's keep going," Devin said. "That way," she pointed along the rugged coast.

They made their way along the shoreline, following a trail that inched its way upward, forcing them to climb over large boulders. They stumbled often and when they fell, the sharp coral often cut their skin. Both had scraped and bloodied palms. Devin's jean protected her knees somewhat, but Rosie's were scraped.

They were climbing over a large boulder when Rosie

slipped, tumbled and crash landed on her back on the rocks below.

"Are you ok?" Devin yelled down from the top of the rock.

Rosie groaned, grimaced, and reached slowly for her glasses that lay beside her in a small tidal pool. "Yeah. I think so. I landed on my knitting. That cushioned my fall a little."

Devin scampered down to help her. "You're lucky you weren't impaled by one of those needles. Here, take my hand, I'll help you."

Rosie fiddled with her glasses and lens. "Damn it," she huffed.

"What's the matter?" Devin asked.

"My glasses, the frame is cracked and the lens won't stay in." She replaced the glasses on her head. The left side tilted downward. The right side was missing a lens. She rubbed her lower back and started to stand but fell back into the shallow pool of seawater. "My ankle Devin. I think I sprained it."

Devin grabbed her firmly by an arm and helped steady her as she teetered, then finally stood. "Can you put weight on it?"

Rosie tried taking a step with the injured foot and winced. "Only a little. It really hurts."

The clinking sound of metal scraping over rock grew louder.

"Come on," Devin draped Rosie's arm around her shoulder and helped her to limp forward.

It was slow going as Rosie groaned and Devin huffed while they hobbled over the wet, seaweed-draped rocks. They turned a corner and were suddenly faced with a steep cliff that plummeted downward to crashing waves below.

"Shit," Devin said.

Both their gazes first lowered toward the agitated water then lifted up to the cliff that towered above them. Rosie watched Devin as she assessed their situation and frantically tried to come up with a plan, just as she was. When Devin's contemplation lingered on the steep path that led to the water below, Rosie said, "I won't make it."

Devin scanned their surroundings. "Ok, give me a minute. I'll—"

Rosie gripped Devin's arm. "Shush. What was that?"

"What was what?"

Rosie held her breath on an inhale.

"Psst." They both heard it and searched for the source.

"Ladies. Psst. Up here." It was a forced whisper.

They looked up.

At the mouth of a cave, motioning wildly for them to climb up, were two, small, nun dolls.

## TRUST US

The nuns' frantic gestures increased in intensity. "Come on. Hurry," they chanted while their short, little arms waved excitedly. "Before they turn the corner and see you."

Rosie and Devin stood frozen, exchanging glances. A silent conversation passed between them.

"Oh, for the good and mighty Lord and our Savior, Jesus Christ and all that is holy, you can trust us. We're nuns," one of them whispered in a husky, rushed voice.

Faced with the sound of approaching dolls from one side and the cliff down to turbulent water below on the other, Rosie and Devin made their choice, faced the steep, rocky cliff and prepared to climb.

Rosie tried to scramble up the cliff first but struggled with her ankle. Devin grabbed a piece of driftwood and handed it to Rosie to use as a cane and followed behind, helping to guide her toward the entrance of the cave. Several times, Rosie had to pull herself upward with little more than her fingertips gripping onto a thin crack in the rock. Devin held onto the bottom of her good foot and pushed, helping to propel her upward.

The nuns urged and encouraged them. "Hurry. Hurry. They're coming. You're doing great. You're almost here."

When they made it to the cave, and crawled over the ledge, Rosie's arms vibrated from exhaustion. Both women collapsed onto their knees, breathing heavy for several minutes.

"Hurry. Follow us," one of the nuns said and ran ahead. Her short legs waddled as fast as they could. Rosie and Devin rose slowly, their chests still heaving from the exertion. Devin ducked under one of Rosie's arms and helped her limp after the nuns by taking some of the weight off her ankle. Rosie hobbled by delicately touching the ground with her bad foot and leaning on the driftwood cane and Devin.

They were in a dark, dank cavern. Wide cracks between the large coral boulders that formed the ceiling allowed for a limited amount of light to creep in, creating eerie, shadowy shapes that danced along the sides of the walls.

When they'd traveled a distance from the entrance, one of the nuns said, "We can rest here for a while if you want. It'll take them a while to climb the cliff."

They were in a circular enclosure that had several paths leading out in different directions. The air was stuffy, stale.

Rosie immediately crumbled and lowered herself on a rock ledge. She lifted her bad leg up, tenderly placing it on the rock in a horizontal position. Devin shrugged her back-pack off, placed it beside Rosie and walked the circumference of the enclosure, investigating each of the exits. She reached out and touched the side of the cave, rolled what she'd felt between a thumb and forefinger, then brought it to her nose and smelled it. She winced then wiped whatever it was on her jeans.

The nun who'd spoke was the larger and heavier of the two. She had a jovial face, flushed with pink cheeks. The other nun was petite, thin, pale, and wore glasses. Both were dressed in identical, typical nun garb: a long, ground-length, black tunic. Over each of their heads, hung a black veil. A tight, white coif encircled their faces and necks. Hanging from their necks were a necklaces decorated with a large crosses. Rope belts cinched their waists and a set of rosary beads draped down the side of each of their hips from the belt. The skin that was exposed on their faces and hands was a light pink and had the shiny look of plastic to it. When they moved or spoke, they were stiff and animated.

The smaller of the two dolls clapped her hands. Her voice was childlike.

"It's so good to see people again. It's been so long since we've seen any. Alive that is," she quickly added.

"What happened to you two? Why are you here?" The more matronly and mature nun asked.

"Our boat wouldn't start," Rosie explained. She pulled her bag closer to her.

"A doll dressed in scuba gear took the spark plugs," Devin said. She was surveying their surroundings, eyeing the walls and ceiling.

The dolls exchanged glances. They nodded and spoke in knowing unison. "Scuba Joe."

"By the way, I'm Sister Dorothy and this is Sister Martha," the larger, rotund doll introduced them.

"I'm Rosie and this is Devin," Rosie said. "Thank you for saving us."

The nun dolls were about the same height as most of the other dolls that they'd seen, except for the larger, silver one.

Rosie scanned the interior of the cave. It was cool, but since the humidity was so high, it was not a refreshing coolness. It was the kind of dampness that made her shiver. Droplets crawled down the sides of the walls.

Other than a few random rocks and twigs, the floor of the cave was empty. In the corner of the cave was a pile of what looked like abandoned trash. Things that might have washed ashore such as pieces of lobster traps and buoys, ropes, plastic bottles, broken beach chairs, the top of a cooler, a few yellow, crinkled magazines and books. The rest of the area was empty except for small black shapes that hung along the edge of the ceiling. Their darkness contrasted against the mossy, green-gray coral.

Rosie pointed at the clumps of furry blobs with folded, shiny black wings. "Are those what I think they are?"

"Bats." Sister Martha nodded. "They won't bother you. They eat insects, mostly."

"Well they haven't been doing a very good job," Rosie wrapped her arms tightly across her chest. The damp chill had got to her and she looked in her bag for her sweatshirt. It wasn't there.

"Damn. I left my sweatshirt back there," she said as she rubbed her arms.

"So, what the hell's going on here on this island?" Devin had checked out all the exits and now stood in front of the nuns, her hands gripping her hips.

"Hell is a good word to describe it," Sister Dorothy said.

"Worse than hell," Sister Martha added. "I'm sure you've heard about the curse."

"Yes, but I can't believe it's real." One of the bats shifted and fluttered its wings. Devin eyed it with suspicion.

"Oh, it's real alright. We didn't think it was real either and now look at us." Sister Martha glanced down at herself.

"But how—" Devin began but was interrupted by Sister Dorothy.

"I understand it's hard to believe, but some things cannot be explained. As you must have faith in the almighty God above and our good Lord and savior, Jesus Christ, you must also acknowledge there are wicked forces on this planet whose intentions are evil."

Sister Martha raised her tiny hands, cupped her mouth, contorted her face into a sneer, and whispered. "From the devil."

"Yes, from the devil," Sister Dorothy echoed.

"How did you become dolls?" Rosie asked.

"We came here, just like you did." Sister Dorothy's hands were clasped behind her back and she paced as she explained. "About fifty years ago. Came to have a nice picnic one afternoon. Rowed here from Key West. There weren't as many dolls here back then. A few but not this many."

"What happened?" Devin asked.

"A sudden storm came up, as they tend to do here, and our boat drifted away. We were stranded. Just like you are. We thought we'd be rescued in the morning when a fishing boat went by, but while we slept, something wicked happened." Sister Dorothy was speaking but both nuns nodded in agreement.

"Very wicked," Sister Martha chimed.

"Someone put a curse on you?" Rosie grimaced and she reached to rub her swollen ankle.

Both dolls shook their heads side-to-side. Sister Dorothy stopped pacing and spoke. "Not a curse."

"But I thought that was how a human's soul got trapped in a doll. If someone put a curse on them?" Now it was Devin who paced back and forth. She strolled in front of the nuns. Repeatedly, she ran her fingers through her hair. The white locks now stuck out in ruffled, random directions.

"That's one way," Sister Dorothy indicated the number one with a teeny finger, "but that's not the only way."

Sister Martha elbowed her friend. "Don't tell them the secret Sister."

Rosie stopped caressing her ankle and looked up.

"What secret?"

Sister Martha's eyes grew wide behind her round spectacles. "Why the secret of Doll Island, of course."

## DOLL ISLAND HOLDS MANY SECRETS

Devin and Rosie exchanged glances.

"The secret of Doll Island?" they repeated simultaneously.

"Yes," Sister Martha answered in the affirmative but her head shaking indicated a negative. "The island has a secret and we're forbidden to share it."

Sister Dorothy tossed her a serious look. "Oh, come on, Sister. What's the worst that could happen if I tell them? I get cursed and my soul stuck in the body of a doll for eternity? Too late. That's already happened."

Sister Martha lifted the crucifix from around her neck, kissed it, then tapped it to her forehead, chest, then once to each shoulder.

"The secret is, there's another way your soul can be stolen and enslaved into the body of a doll," Sister Dorothy explained. "And that is, if a doll kisses you, they can suck your soul out, allowing their soul to enter your body."

As the concept sunk in, Rosie felt her face contort with disgust. By the look of horror on Devin's face, she was thinking the same thing.

"You mean, trade places, as in, trade souls?" Devin's face twisted as if she were in physical pain.

"Precisely," Sister Dorothy gave a firm solitary nod along with the word.

Sister Martha simply silently bobbed her head up and down in agreement.

"Why would anyone kiss a doll?" Rosie's head felt as if it were going to explode. She massaged her temples. The throbbing in her ankle was painful but it didn't compare to the pulsating pressure inside her skull.

"You don't," Sister Martha answered. "The dolls attack you to do it."

"Is that what happened to you?"

"Yes, that's what happened to us," Sister Dorothy said. "We had no idea a doll could suck your soul out and trade places with you. We'd heard the myth that someone could curse you and your soul would end up in a doll's body. Of course, we didn't believe it–"

"Until night fall." Sister Martha had a habit of finishing her friend's sentences.

"Yes, until night fall. When we saw the dolls come to life and they began chasing us."

"Were you nuns back then?" Devin asked.

"Hell, no," Sister Dorothy blurted.

Sister Martha elbowed her. "Sister! Mind your mouth."

"Oops, forgive me." Sister Dorothy's miniature pink hand covered her mouth. "I mean, no, we weren't nuns. We were teachers. I taught math and Sister Martha taught English."

Sister Martha chimed in. "We lived in Boston. We were spinsters."

"So what happened?" Devin had stopped pacing and now stood, gripping an elbow with one hand and chewing the corner of a thumb of the other.

Sister Dorothy continued. "Well, we were stranded on the

island, just like you are. And when darkness fell, the dolls began chasing us. We were terrified, of course. We had no idea why they chased us, but we ran. And eventually they trapped us, and two of them, nun dolls, well, made the change. It was quite frightening."

"Quite frightening," Sister Martha mumbled but it didn't break Sister Dorothy's stride in explaining.

"Yes, at first it was quite upsetting, but over the years, we've gotten used to it. We decided it must have been the will of our good, almighty Lord God for us to serve him and do his will to help people like you. So, we took a vow to help anyone in any way we can to escape the fate of what happened to us."

Sister Martha mimicked. "We took a vow."

"We're the only dolls on the island that won't try to make the change with you."

Devin and Rosie exchanged glances.

"Is that what you call it, when they swap souls, 'making the change'?" Devin had stopped nibbling at her thumbnail and now rubbed her chin as she scrutinized the nuns.

The heads of both nuns jiggled up and down as they repeated the words, "Making the change."

"How long have you been on the island?"

"Fifty-two years."

Rosie spoke up. "So, what do we do now? How do we make it through the night, so we can be rescued in the morning?"

Sister Dorothy picked up a twig and drew a ragged rectangular shape in the sandy floor of the cave.

"This is the island. We're here." She drew a small 'x' on the bottom right hand corner of the shape. "We need to get you here." She scratched another small 'x' in the sand at the top left hand corner of the rectangle. "To the other side of the island. There's the original ceremonial circle where the

Shaman first performed the ritual over two hundred years ago on Ria and Naomi. If we can get you to the circle, it's a sacred zone. No dolls are able to enter it or they'll erupt in flames and their souls will forever be damned in hell. At least here, they have a chance of returning to human form. You'll be safe there, in the sacred circle."

"Well, ok then. Let's go," Devin reached for her knapsack, glanced down at Rosie's ankle then back toward the nuns. "How far is it?"

"It's about four miles from here," Sister Dorothy drew a line from one 'x' to the other, "to here. You should be able to walk it in an hour but with her bad foot, it'll take twice that long at least."

Devin squatted on her heels so her face was level with Rosie's. She rested a hand on one of Rosie's knees. Her thumb moved in a gentle, massaging way. "Will you be able to make it?"

As cold as she was, Rosie felt a surge of heat flash through her body from where Devin's skin touched hers.

She stared into the captivating eyes that studied her and said, "I'll make it," and swung her leg over the side of the ledge that she'd been sitting on. A sharp pain shot up her leg and she sipped in a deep inhale through clenched teeth.

"We'll show you the way," Sister Martha said. "If you carry us, it'll go much faster."

The sound of something scraping against rock caused them to pause. The nuns each tilted their head slightly and exchanged a knowing glance.

"I recognize that sound. That's Double Ds' bad leg, scraping," Sister Martha waddled back toward an opening on the side of the cave and peered down the cliff. When she returned to the group, she said, "They're coming. And Double Ds is leading them."

Sister Dorothy gasped and a hand flew to her chest. Her face took on a look of alarm. "Double Ds is after you?"

"Who's Double Ds?" Devin asked.

"The silver one," Sister Martha answered. "Double Ds stands for 'Destructor Dude' because he destroys everything he can get his hands on. He's the angriest doll on the island." She giggled, covering her mouth with one of her petite hands.

"Yes, the silver one," Devin said. "I tried whacking him with the oar and it was like hitting a brick wall."

"That's because Double Ds is made of titanium," Sister Dorothy said.

"Titanium? Who makes a doll out of Titanium?" Rosie was standing but all her weight was on one foot with the other barely touching the ground.

"NASA," Sister Martha answered.

"NASA?!" Devin and Rosie both repeated.

"How did a doll made by NASA get on this island?" Devin asked.

"And come to be possessed?" Rosie added.

Sister Dorothy answered. "I'll tell you the story, but it'll have to be the quick version. If Double Ds is after you, you don't stand a chance unless we get moving. He's faster than the others and persistent. He won't quit."

Sister Martha poked an elbow into Sister Dorothy's ribs. "Go ahead. Tell them about Double Ds."

Sister Dorothy obliged. "Yes. Well, a few years ago, a scientist came to the island. He worked for NASA. He was having an affair with another scientist's wife, so he brought the man, her husband, here."

"And cursed him," Sister Martha joyfully added.

"Yes, and cursed him," Sister Dorothy continued. "At the time, NASA was working on a doll, a robot actually. One that was anatomically correct and indestructible."

"Anatomically correct," Sister Martha placed both hands over her mouth and giggled into them.

Sister Dorothy shot her an intimidating glance. "So, the scientist performed the Curse of the Damned on himself–"

Devin interrupted her. "Wait. On himself?"

"Yes, on himself," Sister Dorothy said.

"Why on himself? And how'd he even know how to perform the curse?" Rosie leaned on the piece of driftwood as if it were a crutch.

"I don't have all the answers and if you don't stop asking questions, Double Ds will be here soon and you can ask him yourself," Sister Dorothy snapped, which caused Sister Martha to erupt in a gleeful giggle again. Sister Dorothy continued, "So, he performed the Curse of the Damned on himself which caused his own soul to become entrapped in the robot. Once he was the robot, or doll, he made the change with the other scientist, the husband, and swapped souls with him."

"So now he was inside the body of the man whose wife he was having an affair with." It was a statement more than a question from Devin.

"Exactly. He went to live with the woman but now he's in the body of her husband. He left the other man here on the island, trapped in the robot. He's very strong."

"And very angry," Sister Martha's words mingled with a snicker.

"Sister Martha, will you stop it?" The larger nun flashed an annoyed glance in the direction of the smaller one.

"What's so funny?" Devin asked.

"Well," Sister Dorothy said, "like we told you, the robot was anatomically correct. But, before the scientist performed the curse, he broke off two pieces of the robot's anatomy. His foot—"

Rosie blurted, "So that's why he walks with a limp."

"Right," Sister Dorothy pointed to her own foot. "The scientist removed one of the feet, so there's only a stub there. That's the scraping sound you hear."

"And that's not the only place there's a stub. He removed his, you know…" Sister Martha's hand fluttered in front of her mid-section.

Sister Dorothy rolled her eyes. "Of for the love of our sweet baby Lord Jesus. You can say the word, 'penis' Sister Martha. It's not a swear word. His penis. He broke off his penis."

Sister Martha fell to the ground in a fit of laughter. "That's why he's so angry. Oh, he's terribly angry." She rolled on her back, her small black boots kicking in the air. When she finally sat up, she took off her glasses and wiped tears from her eyes.

The sound of metal scraping against the rock stopped Sister Martha's laughter and the other three from observing her odd performance. They all gazed in the direction the sound had come from. Sister Martha replaced her glasses, scampered up from the ground and tottered to the mouth of the cave. She peered over the ledge, then waddled back.

Her tone was now all business. "We better get going. He'll be up here in no time."

"We need to figure out a way to stop him." Sister Dorothy tapped her fingertips against her cheek as she thought. "We might be able to get away from the other dolls, but he won't stop until he gets you. He really wants to get back into a human body so he can get revenge on the man who stole his body and his wife. What to do, what to do?"

"There must be something that can destroy him." Rosie knew the words that were spoken had come from her mouth but she didn't recognize her own voice. It sounded both frail and frantic at the same time. She hobbled a few steps practicing moving with the assistance of the crutch. Her bad foot barely touched the ground and her good leg was getting tired.

"Not that we know of."

"I'm sorry I dropped the rocket," Rosie lowered her eyes when she spoke to Devin. "We could signal for help."

"You have a rocket?" Sister Dorothy's fingers stopped drumming against her cheek.

"Yes. A firework's rocket. Well, we had one, but I dropped it on the beach when the dolls chased us."

"Do you have matches?"

Devin and Rosie nodded.

"We can shoot him with the rocket and blow him up! Boom!" Sister Martha leapt into the air, her feet kicking high, then performed a little dance.

"No Sister, that's selfish. We can't waste the girl's rocket blowing Double Ds up just because we want to get rid of him." Sister Dorothy turned toward Rosie and Devin. "They want to use the rocket to signal for help, don't you ladies?"

Both women nodded.

"Too bad," Sister Dorothy said. "We would like to get rid of him. He irritates us all here. He's nothing but an annoyance to every female doll on the island. Thinks he's God's gift, if you know what I mean."

Sister Martha leaned toward Rosie and Devin, cupped her mouth with a hand and whispered, "Even without his…" and again fluttered her hand in front of her midsection, "you know what."

"And he rips off doll's arms, legs, heads. For no reason." Sister Dorothy made a tearing-apart motion with her hands accompanied by a menacing face.

"Except that he's angry," Sister Martha held her palms up and shrugged.

Sister Dorothy snapped her fingers. "I have an idea. Let's go back to the beach. You remain hidden in the bushes. I'll get the rocket. None of the dolls will pay any attention to me. Sister Martha and I often walk the beach and pick up debris that washes ashore. When Double Ds was left on the island, he came with a couple of things, a sword and a rope. They were left on the beach. They're over there with everything else we've collected. We save things we find. You never know when some random thing will come in handy."

"What's your idea?" Rosie asked.

"I'm not sure if this'll work, but if it does, it'll kill two birds with one stone. Help you to be rescued and rid us of Double Ds. The rope he came with is made of the same titanium material he is. It's very strong. Here's what we'll do. Somehow, we get the rope around him, tie it to the rocket and shoot them both off. If we're lucky, he'll explode with the rocket over the ocean. If it doesn't blow him to pieces, at the very least, he'll sink and hopefully won't make his way back to bother us, or you, anymore."

Devin and Rosie looked at each other.

Devin shrugged. "It's worth a try."

"Ok, let's go. Sister Martha, get the rope," Sister Dorothy commanded. "And bring his sword." Sister Martha dutifully shuffled to the corner of the cave. She retrieved a thin, silver coiled rope and placed it over her neck and shoulder. The sword was in a leather sheath and was as tall as she was. She balanced it over a shoulder and waddled back to the group with it teetering in the air, half in front and half trailing behind her.

Devin took the sword from her, pulled it from its sheath and studied it. "You call this a sword? It looks more like a steak knife."

"Don't be fooled by its size," Sister Dorothy said. "That thing will cut you in half."

Rosie tried putting more of her body weight on her foot

and cringed. A blaze of heat then cold flashed through her body and everything around her grew dim.

Devin slid the sword back into the sheath and handed it to Sister Martha. She reached for Rosie's arm. "Are you sure you're up for this?"

Rosie tugged her arm away. "I said I'll make it." She winced as she adjusted her bag over a shoulder and gripped the piece of driftwood tightly for support.

"Maybe you should ditch the bag." Devin was staring at Rosie's swollen ankle.

Rosie felt her forehead tighten. "Maybe you should ditch the camera and backpack," she snapped back.

Devin tilted her head with a nod of acknowledgment in Rosie's direction. "Fair enough. Wait. That reminds me. Before we start, let me get a shot of you two." She motioned for the nuns to come closer and slid her backpack off.

"A shot? You have a gun?" Sister Martha asked.

Rosie had already begun to hobble away when she stopped, turned, and faced Devin. "We don't have time for that."

"No. Not a gun. A movie." Devin first addressed Sister Martha then Rosie. "It'll only take a minute." She studied the camera intensely, making adjustments for the dim light.

"That's a movie camera?" Sister Dorothy stood at Devin's feet and peered upwards toward the camera. "But it's so small."

"Yep. They've made great strides in reducing the size of things like cameras and phones in the last fifty years," Devin said as she brought the camera up to her eye and began filming. "Wave and say 'hi'."

The nuns looked at each other, smiled and waved at Devin. "Hi," they spoke in unison.

"Say something," Devin instructed. Her hand motioned in circles, encouraging them.

"What do you want us to say?" Sister Martha asked.

"Anything. Introduce yourselves. Tell us a little about who you are."

"I'm Sister Dorothy, and this is Sister Martha," Sister Dorothy started but stopped abruptly. "Now what do I say?"

"Tell us the story about Double Ds." As Devin encouraged the nuns, Rosie nervously glanced over her shoulder toward the mouth of the cave where they'd entered.

Sister Martha stepped forward and began talking. "Double Ds, I mean, Destructor Dude, we call him Double Ds for short, was brought to the island by an evil man who was having an affair with Double Ds' wife. And the Curse of the Damned was cast on him, forcing his soul to be forever stuck inside a titanium robot that'd been made by NASA. With um. No privates." She pointed to her mid-section with one hand while covering her mouth to hide a laugh with the other.

The sound of metal scraping against rock echoed inside the cave.

"Oh for Heaven's sake." Sister Dorothy glanced in the direction of the sound then shuffled off after Rosie. "Enough of this. Unless you want Double Ds to suck out your souls, we better get going."

Devin stopped filming and replaced the camera into the knapsack. After hoisting it onto her back, she scooped up Sister Martha, ran after Sister Dorothy, lifted her and placed a nun on each shoulder. "Let's go."

Sister Dorothy pointed toward the back of the cave. "I'll show you a shortcut through the woods that'll take us straight to the beach. Let's destroy Double Ds."

# CAN DOUBLE DS BE DESTROYED?

The path through the cave twisted downward in a gradual slope. As humid as the island had been during the thunderstorm, the air inside the cave was even thicker with moisture due to the lack of ventilation. Although thin beams of light crept through spaces between the giant boulders allowing the four travelers to see shadows and shapes, the going was tedious. The dampness created a perfect growth environment for the green moss that covered the ground and walls which made walking treacherous. Devin took the lead with the nuns on her shoulders while Rosie hobbled behind.

At one point Devin lost her footing, slipped and fell. Rosie's gaze was fixated on the ground as she carefully scrutinized where each foot would be placed next when she heard, "Ouch! Damn it."

When she looked up, she saw Devin seated on the ground with the two nuns still straddling her shoulders, clinging to her hair.

"Are you ok?" Rosie asked as she limped toward the other three.

"Yes," Devin rose, swiping the mud and moss from her bottom. "Gross. My butt's all wet."

"It's disgusting in here." Rosie crinkled her nose. "It smells like a mold factory. We're going to end up with some sort of a lung infection."

"We're almost out," Sister Dorothy pointed ahead. "Just a little further, that way. Shh," she instructed, placing a finger against her lips. The group fell silent.

Other than an occasional drip of water, there was no sound.

"Do you think we've lost them?" Rosie whispered.

Sister Dorothy shrugged. "Maybe. But I–"

Then they all heard it. The sound of metal scraping against stone.

"Nope," she said and they resumed making their way through the cave.

Soon the path split. "That way," Sister Dorothy pointed to the left.

They scurried along and after turning a corner, were greeted by a large exit of the cave. Cautiously, they stepped out into the night. Air that had previously felt clammy was now oddly refreshing. Determining the coast was clear, they ventured out of the cave and onto a ledge that overlooked the beach below. Rosie and Devin crept to the edge of the cliff and peered down.

"Look! There's the boat," Rosie indicated below using her driftwood cane. Devin, with the nuns still on her shoulders, hustled toward her to take a look.

The beach and boat were still covered with dolls. From high up, they looked like ants crawling over a discarded sandwich from a summer's picnic.

"Where did you drop the rocket?" Sister Dorothy asked.

"Over there," Rosie pointed. "By that big boulder was the last time I remember having it."

"Ok," Sister Dorothy said. "Put us down. We're going to get that rocket. We'll be right back."

"We?" Sister Martha's tiny eyebrows drifted high onto her forehead as Devin lifted the nuns off her shoulders and placed them on the ground.

"Yes we. Come on." Sister Dorothy straightened her habit. Sister Martha lay the sword down and wiggled out from the titanium rope she'd wrapped around her neck and shoulder. She placed the rope on the ground beside the sword.

"But what do we do if Double Ds gets here before you get back?" Rosie asked.

The nuns had begun to make their way down the side of the cliff. Sister Martha stopped long enough to say, "I recommend you run."

# PLAN? WHAT PLAN?

R osie and Devin placed their bag and backpack down,
dropped to their bellies, slid to the edge of the cliff
and peered over. They watched as the nuns tediously made
their way down the cliff and waddled onto the beach. Dozens
of dolls walked or crawled along the sandy coastline. The
two dark forms easily mingled among the mass of moving
figures, attracting no attention.

For a while, there was no conversation between them.
Both were mesmerized by the activity below.

Rosie spoke first. "So, you trust them?"

Devin answered without breaking her attention on the
beach and boat. "Who? The nuns?"

"Yeah, the nuns. Do you trust them?"

"I guess. What choice do we have? They seem legit."

"Can you believe this is happening to us?" Rosie's ankle
throbbed and despite the warm summer night air, she still
felt chilled from having been in the cave. She wished she
hadn't lost her sweatshirt. "Is this a bad dream? If it is, will
you please wake me up?"

Devin reached for her knapsack, took out her camera and

began recording the scene below. "If it's a dream, when I wake up, I hope I don't forget it. It's going to make the most amazing movie."

Rosie glared at her. "Movie? Is that all you can think about? Making a movie? We're in danger of having our souls sucked out. I'm terrified that I'll spend eternity in the body of a damn doll and you're planning a movie?"

Devin momentarily stopped filming. "Are you kidding? If this is really happening, and it certainly seems like it is, I have footage of it right here." She patted her camera. "This proves my spiritual theory. This is going to be the movie of the century. My father will be so proud."

"Devin, I can't believe–" Devin interrupted her by placing a hand on her shoulder.

"Don't worry Rosie. I won't let anything happen to you." She flashed a quick grin then continued to film.

The three-quarter moon alternated between shining bright and dimming as clouds passed in front of it. Large silver-gray shadows drifted over the activity as clouds floated in front of the moon. The sight was eerily creepy. The thought occurred to Rosie that had she been watching this scene in a movie, she would've turned it off.

Rosie tracked the nuns as they made their way toward the huge boulder where she last remembered holding the rocket. The two tiny figures circled the rock, searching, until the larger of the nuns stopped and motioned for the other to join her. They both bent over and lifted a dark shape that was taller than they were. Their movements were awkward and the smaller nun struggled to keep her end up. But after several drops and repositioning, they managed to carry it away from the beach and toward the cliff they'd just descended.

"They got it," whispered Devin.

From deep inside the cave came the sound of metal scraping against stone. "Oh shit," she said.

"Please hurry," Rosie prayed out loud.

As the moments ticked by, the sound of Double Ds' scuffing grew louder as did the grunting of the two nuns as they climbed the cliff with the rocket.

Devin stopped filming and replaced her camera. "Come on, let's help them," she said.

In an attempt to stay out of sight from the dolls below, Devin and Rosie crawled along the edge of the overhang toward the bushes. When the nuns reached the top of the cliff, Devin and Rosie greeted them.

"Here, take it," Sister Dorothy groaned as she pressed the nose of the rocket up toward the women.

Devin grabbed the rocket and handed it to Rosie. She then reached a hand toward each nun to assist with their final climb to the top. One by one, they curled their own small, chubby fingers around one of her larger extended fingers and she hoisted them up.

Devin examined the rocket. "It looks ok."

"Do you still have the other matches?" Rosie asked.

Devin reached into her pocket and pulled out the tiny match box. "Let's pray this works."

Both nuns made the sign of the cross, folded their hands in prayer position, closed their eyes, and moved their lips to a silent chant.

"No, I didn't mean…" Devin said. "Oh, never mind."

The scraping of Double Ds' leg grew louder.

"Quick," Rosie heard her own voice squeak. "What's the plan?"

"Yeah, what's the plan?" Sister Martha repeated.

"One of you acts as a decoy and one of you throws the rope around Double Ds." Sister Dorothy explained. "Make sure you get it around his arms, so he can't use his hands, otherwise, he'll bust out of it. Then we'll tie one end of it to the rocket. You light the rocket and—"

"BOOM!" Sister Martha yelled and jumped into the air.

"Shh," the other three reprimanded.

Sister Martha wobbled off to get the titanium rope where she'd laid it down.

"Throw a rope around him? Do you mean like a lasso?" Rosie asked.

"Yes, like a lasso," Sister Dorothy nodded.

Rosie turned toward Devin. "You need to do that."

"Me?" One of Devin's hands flew to her chest and she took a step back. "I can't throw a lasso."

"You lassoed a calf that time."

"I was five years old and three stage hands held it down."

"Well I certainly can't throw one," Rosie tried to straighten her glasses but no matter what she did, they sat crooked on her face. "Not that I want to be the decoy."

"Ok," Devin held out a hand. "Give me the rope." She handed her camera to Sister Martha. "Here."

"What do I do with this?" Sister Martha clutched the camera and held it with straight arms away from her body as if it were a ticking bomb. It was about half as big as she was.

"Look through here," Devin tapped the view finder, "and press this button," she pointed to a round, red button. "That'll start filming. When you want to stop, you hit it again. I want to get this on film." As she spoke, she wrapped the rope into several large loops, allowing it to hang from her hand, then tied a slip-knot and tested it to make sure it moved easily.

"What do I have to do to be a decoy?" Rosie asked looking first to Devin then to Sister Dorothy. Sister Dorothy's response was a blank look and two raised palms. Devin opened her mouth to answer but the words froze as Double Ds stepped out from the shadows of the mouth of the cave. He stood stationary with only his head rotating, as if analyzing his situation. Moonlight reflected off his titanium body making him look like something from another planet in a sci-fi movie.

"You'll think of something!" Sister Martha yelled before she and Sister Dorothy scuttled and cowered behind Devin's legs.

# ROPE 'EM UP LITTLEST COWGIRL

Double Ds scrutinized the area as he attempted to get his bearings. His head paused momentarily as his gaze fixated on Devin, then he began walking in her direction. He'd step with his good leg, then drag the other footless stump. The leg with the foot fell silently but the other scraped each time it dragged across the rocky floor of the cliff, sounding like a nail across a blackboard.

Devin took a step back toward the edge of the cliff. Double Ds continued moving in her direction.

"Hey! Dickless," Rosie yelled. She stood to the side of the entrance of the cave and Double Ds had not seen her. With the insult, he turned, first his head, then his body rotated to change directions. He then headed her way.

"That's right. You heard me. You want a piece of me?" she taunted. "Well then. Come on. Come and get it."

Rosie inched her way back, drawing Double Ds away from Devin and the nuns.

Devin swung the titanium rope over her head. The circle hovered above her, looking like a large glistening angel's halo in the moonlight.

Rosie's body had grown electric with fright but she kept chattering. "Come on Dude. Show me what you got." She had backed herself almost to the edge of the cliff. Double Ds methodically made his way toward her. His silver arms were raised up and reached forward, zombie-like.

"Devin?" Rosie mumbled, her eyes flitting between Double Ds and Devin.

The rope circled above Devin's head one final time then she released it, sending it flying in Double Ds' direction. The silver circle flew through the air and hit the robot on the back sending both him and the rope to the ground.

"Shit!" Devin and the nuns all spat the same word. Devin snapped the lasso back to her, re-gripped the rope below the knot and began circling it again over her head.

It took Double Ds a few seconds to stand. Once upright, he took several more moments to acclimate and regain his balance.

Rosie took another step back. Her foot was now only inches from the edge of the cliff. She stared over the ledge to the tumbling waves that washed over the large rocks below, glanced at Double Ds, then focused on Devin.

"Devin!" she pleaded.

Double Ds had begun walking again and was only a few steps from her. She inched side-ways. He followed her maneuver.

"Hey titanium Twinkie," Devin yelled.

Double Ds stopped. His head rotated in Devin's direction.

Devin released the rope again. This time the center of the loop fell over his head. She yanked it hard and the circle enclosed around his arms, zipping closed tightly around him. She tugged firmly another time, and he was dragged across the coral ground toward her.

Rosie took two giant steps forward and bent over, resting her hands on her knees. When she stood, she pressed her palms to her chest and took several deep breaths. Her lungs felt as if she was the one that had been roped and it was her chest that was being squeezed.

"You did it!" Sister Martha leapt in the air as she held the camera to her eye and continued to film.

"Holy Mother Mary, you did it," Sister Dorothy made the sign of the cross.

Double Ds lay on his back and wiggled side-to-side but was unable to get up. Devin efficiently wrapped the rope several times around his torso, finishing the entrapment by securing it with a tight knot. When she'd finished, she jumped up and away as if she'd just roped a calf in a rodeo competition.

"Amazing. I did it." She dusted the dirt off both palms by rubbing her hands together and glanced around. "Who has the rocket?"

The nuns picked up the rocket and hustled it to Devin. She reached into her pocket, pulled out the matchbox and retrieved a match.

"Let's pray this works," she said as she ran the rope down from Double Ds' body and secured it around his good ankle.

Both nuns crossed themselves, closed their eyes and chanted silent prayers.

Devin held Double Ds upside down from one end of the rope and she wrapped the other end securely to the rocket. He wiggled like a fish that had just been reeled in and hung on display.

"Ok, here we go." She handed the match box to Rosie who placed it inside her bag.

"Pray this works." The nuns crossed themselves as Devin lit the match and placed the flame against the end of the rocket's wick.

## ROCKET'S RED GLARE

The flame caught onto the fuse with a small display of sparks and slowly inched its way up the thin, yellowed rope.

"Get back," Devin ordered as she stood at the end of the overhanging cliff and pointed the rocket toward the water.

She covered her eyes with her elbow and waited, occasionally peeking as the flame sizzled and crept up the wick.

A loud 'whoosh' pierced the night air as the rocket took off, leaving behind a thin trail of gray smoke. It soared toward the moon for a couple of seconds, a comet-like bright light spurting flashing sparks of red, white and blue. Silhouetted against the moonlight was a black human shaped robot that trailed behind the rocket. But soon the weight of Double Ds lowered the arc and the rocket's trajectory dropped. At first it'd been pointing toward the sky. But seconds later, the nose dropped and it headed lower, toward the horizon. Finally, it made a sharp downward turn and plunged, sputtering into the black sea water.

Within moments it was over and the night air fell silent.

The four standing on the cliff exchanged glances.

Sister Martha lowered the camera. "Well, at least he's gone."

Devin reached and took the camera from the nun. "Did you get it all on film?"

Sister Martha nodded.

Rosie stood, staring out toward where the rocket had disappeared. She felt as if her heart had sunk with it. She turned her head toward Devin. "Do you think anyone saw it?"

Devin's head swung back and forth. She looked down at the nuns. "How do we get to the other side of the island and to the ceremonial circle?"

A rock tumbled, and their attention jolted toward the entrance of the cave. Dozens of dolls walked and crawled from out of the black hole that was the entrance while several more climbed down from the cliffs. Two made their way over the ledge from the rocks below.

## CALL HER GULLIVER

"Rosie, run!" Devin yelled.

Rosie grabbed her bag and took a step toward the path the nuns had used to climb to the beach.

"No. You can't go that way," Sister Dorothy hustled in front of her, blocking her escape. "Take us with you. We'll show you where to go."

Rosie grabbed both nuns and stuffed them into her bag.

"That way. Toward the coconut trees!" Sister Dorothy pointed toward two huge coconut trees that towered over the others and leaned into each other, creating an archway. Rosie hobbled in their direction.

She glanced over her shoulder. Devin had picked up the titanium sword and bravely faced the legion of dolls that steadily progressed toward her. The sword looked like a carving knife in her hands, but she swung it threateningly toward the toys that advanced.

"Devin, come!" Rosie hollered.

"You go. I'll give you a head start and will catch up," Devin yelled back.

Before entering the woods, Rosie paused to glance back

at Devin. The nuns peered out from inside the bag. Devin was swinging the sword at the cluster of dolls that quickly closed in on her. The first doll she swung at was dressed as a witch. The sword swished through the air and sliced the top of its head off. The scalp with long scraggly auburn hair along with the black pointy hat, flew several feet and landed in the dirt. The second whoosh of the blade cut the doll just above the knees. It landed on its two stumps and tried to walk but kept tipping over.

Another doll, a soldier, ran at Devin with a bayoneted rifle. Devin swung and severed its neck. The head rolled off the edge of the cliff. The doll continued to run wildly in a circle, bumping into the other dolls.

Heads, hands, arms and parts of torsos flew through the air as Devin swung ferociously with the titanium blade. Soon, however, she was encircled by dolls.

"Rosie. Go!" One of the nuns ordered.

Rosie turned and took a few steps into the forest.

"She's not going to make it I'm afraid," the other said.

Rosie stopped and peered down at the two small faces that looked up at her. "What are we going to do? We can't just leave her."

"I'm afraid there's not much we can do," Sister Dorothy's head rotated side-to-side.

"She's a goner," Sister Martha muttered. "You'd best save yourself." The three of them watched in horror as Devin fought for her life.

# THE AWAKENING OF A VIKING
## WARRIOR PRINCESS

"There must be some way to stop them." Rosie was frantic. Her pulse beat fast and hard. It was as if each heart beat were a war drum thumping in her ears. She searched her surroundings for something she could use as a weapon. "Are they afraid of anything?"

Both nuns shook their heads, then Sister Dorothy held up one miniature finger. "Sister?"

"Yes, Sister," answered Sister Martha.

"Fire?"

Sister Martha's eyes popped wide and she nodded vigorously.

"Oh yes. Fire."

"Do you have any matches left?" Sister Dorothy looked up toward Rosie.

"Yes. We have one match left."

"Perfect," Sister Dorothy slapped her hands together. "Here's what we'll do. We'll make a torch. Then you run in and rescue her by keeping all the dolls away from her with the fire."

"Dolls don't like fire," Sister Martha said. "We burn."

"Why do I have to run into a circle of haunted dolls?" Rosie said. "Why can't one of you do it? You're one of them."

Sister Dorothy's hands waved in front of her face. "Oh, they'd attack us. We're not big enough to overtake them all."

"Tear us limb from limb," Sister Martha recoiled deeper into the bag.

"Damn it," Rosie huffed. "Ok, it's our only hope. But what is dry enough to make a torch? Everything on the island is damp."

"Use this," Sister Martha pulled up Rosie's knitting from inside the bag.

"My blanket?" Her shoulders dropped. "Ok. Hurry. Get out. Help me." She put her bag on the ground and the nuns scampered out, pulling the knitted blanket behind them. Rosie slid the needles from her knitting and dropped them back in the bag.

"Help me find a stick large enough for a torch," she instructed and the nuns scattered under the bushes. Rosie searched but most of the branches were mere twigs, not large enough.

"I found one!" Sister Martha yelled as she dragged a thick branch from beneath the bushes.

Rosie kept eyeing Devin as she wielded the blade and sliced at the many attacking dolls. So far, she was holding her own, but the onslaught of dolls coming at her was increasing.

"Where are they all coming from?" Rosie said as she wrapped one end of the branch with the knitted blanket, tying it tightly with a long strand of yarn.

"Oh, there's lots of dolls on this island." Sister Dorothy was wringing her hands while Sister Martha held the crucifix and prayed.

Devin had dropped the sword and was swatting dolls off her legs. She'd grab one by the hair and toss it over the cliff, then reach down to wrestle the grip of another off. When she'd pry its hands from her, she'd rip the head from the body and toss them in different directions. It reminded Rosie of a person trying to keep a swarm of bees off themselves.

Rosie reached into her bag and took out the tiny match box. "This is our last match. Pray this works."

The nuns crossed themselves. Their lips moved in silent prayer.

Rosie lit the match and held the flame to the end of a piece of yarn. The knit blanket quickly burst into a ball of orange flames.

She thrust the flaming torch high over her head. The muscles in her jaw tightened. Inhaling deeply, she filled her lungs. As she took her first step in Devin's direction, she was amazed that the pain she'd previously felt in her ankle was gone. She felt electric and alive in a way she'd never felt before. When she opened her mouth to exhale, a screech unlike anything she'd ever heard come from a human body before bellowed out. She knew the sound was coming from her yet it sounded completely foreign, as if an alien creature were issuing a war cry. When the roar ended, she screamed, "Die all you plastic fuckers!"

# NOW WHAT?

W hen Rosie bolted out of the forest with flame held high and shrieking threats, she saw Devin and the group of dolls momentarily pause and stare at her. Instinctively, she knew that along with a blazing torch, she carried the crazed look of a woman possessed and intent on killing. It gave her a sense of power unlike anything she'd ever experienced in her life. And in those few moments between when she left the safety of the edge of the woods and attacked the first doll, she was conscious that this must be what warriors feel in the heat of battle. For the first time since she could remember, there was no fear, only an all-encompassing sense of rage and power that seemed to take over every molecule of her body.

The first doll she swung at was naked and had long blonde hair. It gripped tightly onto the back of Devin's pants. Rosie swiped at it with the flaming torch and sent it flying, its hair on fire.

The second doll she attacked clung to Devin's ankle and was climbing up her leg. She lit its dress on fire and it released its grip and fell to the sand. The fire distorted its features as it lay melting on the ground. Its arms, legs and face twisted into charred blobs as flames consumed it.

Two dolls had attached themselves to Devin's arms and she wrestled to dislodge them. Once they were off, she threw them to the ground and Rosie set them on fire. A doll dressed as a nurse hung from Devin's backpack and was climbing toward her neck. Rosie swung the torch at it but she missed the doll and smacked Devin's shoulder with the flame, catching her shirt on fire.

"Ah! Shit!" Devin screamed, dropped to the ground and rolled in the sand. The fire went out and the doll let go. Rosie lit the nurse on fire.

"I'm sorry Devin. I'm sorry," she muttered as she continued to swipe at the masses of dolls that had formed a circle that quickly closed in on them.

"You're doing great," Devin yelled. "Don't stop!"

Rosie swiped the flame toward as many dolls as she could, but they kept coming. Dolls approached them from every direction and more kept emerging from the woods and climbing over the cliff.

"Where are they coming from? Devin, there's too many of them!"

She had just lit two dolls on fire that were dressed in sailor outfits when she felt it. A weight tugging on her braid. She swung around but couldn't see what was on her back.

"Devin," she screamed. "Get it off me!"

Devin struggled to walk with several dolls clinging to her legs. She made it to the titanium sword and chopped the heads and hands off several of them while continuing to fight her way toward Rosie.

When she reached Rosie, she grabbed the doll that had a firm grip on the braid. It was a Pinocchio doll.

"Get it off me!" Rosie shrieked.

Devin tried to open the tiny hands, but they were entrenched in the braided hair.

"Hold still," Devin demanded. Rosie stopped moving except for involuntary trembles.

Devin held the Pinocchio doll by the long nose and pulled it away from Rosie's body. With a swift downward swipe of the sword, the dolls hands were severed. She held up the handless body, sliced off the head, tossed the torso onto the sand and the head over the cliff.

Rosie pulled her braid to the front of her shoulder and peered down at the two small hands that clung to her braid. They were still moving.

A squeal pierced the air as frantically, she untangled one hand, then the other from her hair and lit them both on fire.

Many of the dolls had retreated into the woods, opening a clearing in the circle.

"Devin, let's go!" Rosie yelled but when she turned to look at Devin what she saw horrified her. Devin's arms were weighed down by several dolls that had swarmed her. Several had attached themselves to her clothes and now climbed toward her head. One doll, dressed as a pirate, clung to her neck and was moving toward her mouth.

"Nooooo!" The word that emitted from Rosie's throat sounded to her own ears to be a combination of an elephant bellow and cannon boom. She raced toward Devin, but she reached her too late. The doll's lips had brushed Devin's.

Rosie grabbed the pirate by the legs and yanked it. The doll's hands had been gripping each side of Devin's face. When Rosie pulled it off, four long, red, scratch marks decorated each of Devin's cheeks. Rosie lit the pirate's beard on fire and tossed it.

She then swiped the flame at the dolls that clung to Devin's arms, legs and back. They released their grip as they tried to protect themselves from the fire.

"Come on!" Rosie grabbed Devin's hand and led her through the break in the wall of dolls toward where the nuns stood watching at the edge of the forest. As they escaped, she swiped the fire toward dolls along the way, lighting several of their hair and clothes on fire.

Devin grabbed the Sisters and cradled each against her armpits as if they were footballs and dashed into the forest. Rosie, still clutching the torch, scooped up her bag and was on Devin's heels.

When they'd escaped a fair distance, they stopped running. Devin lowered the two nuns and both she and Rosie fell to the ground, holding their sides, puffing and gulping air, while they tried to catch their breath.

"Whew," said Sister Dorothy. "That was close."

"Too close," Devin ran her fingers along her lips.

Sister Dorothy waddled toward Devin. "He got you, didn't he?"

Devin's fingertips remained on her lips when she nodded. "I think so. Am I? Will I?"

"Do you mean will you be changed over into a doll?"

Devin nodded.

"I don't think it had enough time to make the change."

Rosie scrutinized Devin. Other than being dirty and frazzled, she looked the same. "How long does it take to make to, you know, make the change?" she asked.

"Depends, but usually you need a connection of at least five to ten seconds for the soul transfer to occur," Sister Dorothy said. "It didn't seem as if the pirate connected long enough."

"How will I know?" Devin kept wiping her lips on her sleeve.

"Oh, believe me. You'll know. There'll be no doubt," Sister Dorothy said.

"You start to feel funny," Sister Martha's face scrunched as if she smelled something bad.

"Funny? Funny in what way?" Rosie asked.

"Funny, like tingly. First your lips get itchy, at the spot where the soul transfer occurred. Then, you get a little dizzy and your whole body tingles. And you start to forget everything as your soul leaves this body and is transferred into the dolls. It's like you're in a fog. You know what's going on but you don't. It's a very strange sensation."

Devin and Rosie remained seated on the ground. The nuns climbed on a nearby rock and sat. They watched and waited. The air around them was eerily quiet.

"How long does it take," Devin asked, "until it happens?"

Sister Dorothy shrugged. "There's no law about it. It just happens."

"Do you feel any different?" Rosie asked Devin.

Devin shook her head. "I don't think so."

They waited a couple more minutes.

"How about now?" Rosie asked. "Are your lips itchy?"

Devin tenderly touched her lips. Her head swung side-to-side.

She stood, paced and they waited. Rosie and the nuns studied Devin's every move as Devin repeatedly rubbed her face an hair, and felt her lips.

"How about now?" Rosie still clung to the flaming torch. "Any different?"

Devin's face grew somber. Her voice became unusually low as she stared at Rosie and the nuns with narrowed eyes and muttered, "Who are you?"

"Devin!" Rosie whimpered. She felt as if her heart would burst out of her ribcage. She jumped up and clutched at her own chest.

"Just kidding!" Devin's enormous smile popped across her face.

Rosie crumbled and buried her face into the hand that wasn't holding the torch. Devin grabbed her but Rosie pushed her away. She turned her back to Devin and wiped her eyes with her fingertips. "You're the biggest jerk."

Devin twisted her neck and peered at the burnt spot on her shoulder. "That's what you get for trying to light me on fire."

"I'm sorry," Rosie spun around. "But with only one lens, everything is distorted."

Devin placed a hand on Rosie's shoulder and rubbed it. "I'm only joking. It's going to take more than a pirate to suck out my soul. But, thank you. I do appreciate you saving me."

"For a moment there, I thought you were a goner," Sister Martha still sat on the rock next to Sister Dorothy. Her feet were swinging and the knocking of the heel of her boot against the rock made a rhythmic tapping sound.

Devin's upper lip curled into a sneer. "I'd like to burn every last one of them."

"You can't blame them for wanting to get out of the doll bodies and return to being human again. They didn't ask to be born a doll." Sister Martha spoke while continuing to tap her boot against the rock.

Devin shot her a look but didn't respond. She spoke to Rosie, "Anyway, thanks."

Rosie simply nodded.

"You didn't tell me about the hidden Viking Warrior Princess lurking inside you," Devin tenderly moved a lock of hair that hung in Rosie's face and curled it behind one of her ears.

Rosie sniffled and swiped at her nose with a knuckle. "I have no idea where she came from, but don't count on her resurfacing anytime soon. She was a one-shot wonder." She turned toward the nuns. "Ok, now where do we go?"

Sister Dorothy slid down off the rock. "We best get you to

the site of the ceremonial circle on the other side of the island. That's the only place you'll be safe."

"Sounds good to me. Let's go." Devin readjusted her backpack. "Which way?"

"That way," Sister Dorothy said, and pointed toward a trail that veered off to the left.

"Sister?" Sister Martha bolted upright and stood on the rock. A concerned look flooded her face as her gaze flirted between the trail and Sister Dorothy.

"Yes, Sister?" Sister Dorothy replied.

Sister Martha's voice was weak. "Through C-Alley?"

"It's the only way," Sister Dorothy answered in a matter-of-fact tone. "They'll never make it through the forest or around the waterfront. There's too many of them."

"But—"

Sister Dorothy closed her eyes and flashed the palm of one of her shiny, plastic hands in her friend's direction. "There's no but's. It's the only way."

"What's C-Alley?" Devin interrupted the discussion.

Sister Martha's eyes were wider than normal. She scampered down the side of the rock, stood at Devin's feet and stared up at her.

"Crocodile Alley."

# LIFE IS ABOUT CHOICES

"Crocodile Alley?" The words were slow to leave Rosie's mouth. "Devin? I thought you said there were no crocodiles on this island?"

"I said there were no alligators on this island."

"They're the same thing." Rosie heard her voice crack and swallowed hard. Her gaze drifted to the ground around them, searching for any sign of movement.

"Oh no," Sister Martha's arms spread wide. "Crocodiles are much bigger and more aggressive. And their noses—"

Sister Dorothy shoved her. "Will you shut up?"

"Ok, everyone calm down," Devin's hands patted the air. "Tell us what our options are and we'll decide."

Sister Dorothy shrugged and folded her arms across her ample bosom. "As I already said, I don't think you'll make it going around the waterfront or through the forest. There are too many of them. They'd all give anything to get out of a plastic body and back into warm, living, breathing skin. They'll stop at nothing to change places with you. Your only hope is to go through Crocodile Alley. If you can make it through there, it's only a short distance to the sacred ceremonial circle. There's not many dolls on that side of the island. Most won't risk going through croc alley to get to it. You'll be safe inside the sacred circle until the cruise ship comes by in the morning."

Devin and Rosie swapped looks of skepticism.

"What do you think?" Devin asked.

"It sounds like we don't have much of a choice." Rosie blew gently on the quickly dying torch in an attempt to flare up the diminished flame.

Devin crossed her arms. "Let me see if I understand this correctly. Either go through the woods and along the waterfront in which case we need to battle tons of dolls that want to suck the souls out of us. Or, we go through an alley filled with crocs who'd like to have us for dinner. And not in the polite way. Is that right?"

"Correct," Sister Dorothy confirmed.

"And why aren't there any dolls in C-Alley?" Devin asked.

"'Cause the crocs'll eat 'em," Sister Martha slapped her hands together in a chomping motion.

"Why would crocs eat dolls?" Rosie had wrapped more yarn around the torch and it sprung back to life. "It doesn't make any sense."

"Try explaining that to the crocs. They'll eat anything that moves," Sister Dorothy said. "We've lost many dear friends, may their souls rest in eternal peace."

She and Sister Martha crossed themselves.

Sister Martha whispered, "Sometimes we find pieces of them in the croc-poo."

Devin and Rosie made quick eye contact.

"How many people have made it through croc alley?" Rosie asked.

The nuns checked with each other and shook their heads.

"None, that we know of."

"I thought you took a vow to help save people from what happened to you."

"We did," Sister Dorothy spoke, and Sister Martha nodded in agreement.

"How many people have you led through croc alley and helped escape from the island?"

"None. Only because none of them would go through croc alley. They all chose to take their chances through the forest.

"You mean…" Devin's voice trailed off.

The nuns shook their heads and made the sign of the cross.

"We tried," Sister Martha said.

Devin and Rosie exchanged glances again. They both tightened their lips and nodded in agreement to the silent conversation.

"Ok," Devin inhaled deeply then released it slowly.

"Take us to croc alley."

# C-ALLEY

"That way." Sister Dorothy lifted a tiny finger. She pointed toward a narrow path that twisted down a steep incline. It disappeared from view through a thin gap between several large boulders. The entrance was covered by an overgrowth of vines and branches and would easily have been missed if it'd not been pointed out.

"Where does it go?" Rosie asked.

"It goes underground," Sister Dorothy said. "You'd be wise to beef up that torch a bit unless you want to be caught in an underground tunnel with a bunch of crocodiles and no light."

Rosie looked into her bag. "I still have some yarn left."

"We'll need something more than that." Devin studied the trees that surrounded them and pulled off several large, dead leaves. "These will burn better and longer." She began weaving them into short, tight ropes. "Here," she said and handed several leaves to Rosie. "Weave the ends together to make longer strands, like this."

"Where did you learn how to do this?" Rosie asked as she followed Devin's lead and wove the leaves into strips.

The worst of the storm had passed and the nearly full

moon provided plenty of light with only an occasional cloud darkening the landscape,

"One of my dad's shows is a reality survival show." Devin held up a string of woven leaves and studied her handiwork. "We'll wrap some around the torch and keep the rest in your bag in case we need them later."

When Rosie's bag was nearly filled with the twined leaves, she zipped it shut, put her arm through the rope handles and pulled it onto her shoulder. Devin adjusted her backpack, picked up the nuns and placed them on her shoulders.

"Let's go," she said, and they started down the path. Squeezing through the narrow opening between the large rocks, they left the forest behind and entered a coral-encased world. As they descended, the trail quickly grew narrow and steep. With each step, the night sky disappeared until soon they were completely surrounded by rock. Unlike the other cave they'd passed through that had allowed for a small amount of light and air to enter, this enclosure plunged them into seemingly airtight darkness.

"Pew." Sister Martha's tiny nose crinkled. Shadows from the flame danced across her face. "It stinks down here. It smells like croc breath."

"How do you know what croc breath smells like?" Sister Dorothy asked.

"It smells like this. Like rancid death."

"Ugh." Rosie swiveled the flame to get a look at their surroundings. The floor, ceiling and walls were all made of large, porous, coral stones. In the distance, she heard the sound of dripping water. Beyond the few feet of light that the fire provided was complete blackness. There was an odd odor to the air. A rank mixture of mold and an ammonia-like stench of urine burned the inside of her nostrils. She covered her nose with her free hand. "It does smell down here. And it's so cold and damp. No wonder no one wanted to take this path." Her voice echoed.

"We're walking down toward the water table so there's a lot of moisture," Sister Dorothy explained. "Soon you'll see water on both sides of the path. That's where the crocs hang out. Keep your torch handy. It's the only thing that'll keep them away from us. Watch your step."

The four made their way along the stoned path, each taking short, cautious steps. Devin led the group with the nuns on her shoulders and held the torch. Rosie shuffled directly behind, clinging to the back of Devin's shirt. The path they walked on was raised only inches over the surrounding moist earth. As they made progress, the level of water slowly increased from simply damp ground to what appeared to be an indoor pond. They moved in silence with the only sound an occasional echo from the distant drops of water.

"How much further?" Rosie finally asked. She'd worked hard to keep her anxiety under control but the combination of darkness, smell and thought of nearby crocodiles had taken its toll. She was about at the end of her rope and either had to get out of there and back into fresh air, or she'd snap.

"I'm not sure," Sister Dorothy said. "We've never been down here. Only heard about it."

Devin stopped short and Rosie bumped into the back of her. "Then how do we know we're on the right path?"

"We don't." Sister Dorothy's voice had a matter-of-fact tone to it.

They continued walking. The path narrowed and took a sharp left turn. They had to slide their backs along the wall to avoid stepping in water and inched forward sideways.

"Gross," Rosie moaned as the bare skin of her back scraped against the cold, slimy wall. She was trembling uncontrollably, whether from fear or dampness, she didn't know.

Devin held the torch down low, pointed toward the black wetness on the ground that surrounded them.

"Keep an eye out for greenish golden eyes," Sister Dorothy said. "If you see some, that's not a good thing. We'll know we're on the right path when we come to—"

"Holy shit!" Devin uttered. "What's that?"

In front of them was a large, gray, torpedo shaped object with the words, "U.S. NAVY" emblazoned on the side.

"When we come to the sub," Sister Dorothy finished her sentence.

## ANOTHER ISLAND SECRET

"A sub?" Devin said. "What's it doing here?"

"Who do you think made these underground tunnels? The crocs? During the war, the Navy used to hide their subs down here."

"Why is this one still here?" Rosie asked as they gazed at the monstrous structure before them.

"There was an accident," Sister Dorothy explained. "They were testing or transporting some type of radioactive material. I'm not positive about all the details but something happened and poisonous material leaked out. The entire area was contaminated. Killed everyone down here instantly. The Navy determined it was too dangerous to remove the bodies. Lied to their families, said the sub sank. So they left it here with the bodies of the poor souls still at their stations as they were at the moment of their deaths."

"No way. This is outstanding." Devin hustled up the ramp that led to the sub. She placed the nuns down on the metal guardrail. They clung to the rail and nervously looked to their right and left. Devin bounced up the plank and peered into a small round port window.

"She's right Rosie. I can see skeletons sitting in chairs at the controls. They still have their uniforms on. This is insane. Come here and take a look." She swung her backpack off as Rosie limped up the plank.

"You're insane if you're thinking of taking pictures," Rosie said when she reached the top.

Devin handed her the torch. "Of course I'm taking pictures." She removed her camera and began adjusting the controls. "Are you kidding me? This is amazing."

"You can take photos in the dark?" Sister Martha asked. She clung tightly to the guard rail they were perched on. Both she and Sister Dorothy kept a guarded watch on their surroundings.

"Yes, with this camera I can. The special night vision feature captures subtle rays of light and energy." She was busy snapping photos, turning her body, to get a variety of angles of shots inside the sub. Several times she stopped to adjust the controls on the camera.

"Devin." Rosie tried to avoid looking but repeatedly stole glances inside the sub at the skeletons. "Let's go. Stop with the stupid photo shoot, will you? I'm trying really hard not to panic but I'm getting claustrophobic. I mean, we're in an underground tunnel, and not only are there soul-sucking dolls after us, not to mention crocodiles, but now skeletons. I'm afraid this—"

"Ok, ok. I get it. Put away your Worry Wilma voice. We're going to be fine." Devin tried the handle of the door to the sub but it didn't budge. She stared down at the camera and scrolled through the images she'd just taken. "Holy shit! Take a look at this."

She turned the camera's LCD screen toward Rosie. The image was of a skeleton dressed in a Navy uniform. It sat perched in front of a row of controls and monitors. A combination of a green and lavender haze surrounded it.

Rosie had difficulty speaking. "Devin!"

"Exactly," Devin's voice was squeaky high with exhilaration. "Just give me a couple more minutes. We're going to get off this island and I'm going to make the best movie." She spun around snapping shots of the area surrounding the sub, including pictures of Rosie, the nuns and the footpath and ramp they'd just walked on. "This will make the most incredib–"

Her chatter stopped abruptly and she lowered the camera away from her face. Where previously her skin had an attractive orange glow to it, reflecting the fire's light, it now turned an ashy, pasty white. Her eyes widened and she didn't blink as she stared at Rosie with a haunted look.

"What?" Rosie demanded.

Devin held up the camera so Rosie could see the shot she'd just taken. It was a photo of the path they'd walked over. The thin trail, walls and ceiling were various shades of gray. To the right and left of the path was water, which showed as black in the image. However, beneath the water, invisible to the human eye but showing up clearly on film, were hundreds of illuminated, lime-green, long, oval shaped eyes.

# WHEN GREEN EYES AREN'T LOVELY

"**H**oly…" Rosie's voice trailed off.

"What?" Sister Martha was still sitting on the railing but tugged at Rosie's braid.

Devin turned the LCD screen of the camera toward the nuns.

"Are those green things what I think they are?" Sister Dorothy asked.

Devin nodded.

The nuns crossed themselves.

"Nobody panic." Devin replaced the camera back into her knapsack.

"Too late," Rosie muttered.

Devin's head swiveled as she searched the area. "How do we get out of here?"

"Follow the trail." Sister Dorothy indicated in the direction the nose of the submarine faced. "This path should take us directly to the edge of the island where the ceremonial circle is. Once we get out of the tunnel, I was told it's not very far."

"Devin," Rosie's voice trembled. The tip of a finger pointed toward the path they'd walked on moments before.

Several crocodiles had climbed up from the water and now waddled in their direction. Their noses and tails swayed side-to-side as their short, stocky legs took methodical steps to close the distance between them. The croc in front, the largest one, opened its mouth wide and hissed. Lines of spittle connected the top and bottom rows of neatly lined, extremely large, and pointy, white teeth.

Rosie's heartbeat quickened. A tightness gripped her throat. Her muscles felt hard and heavy like stone and she froze in place. She was hypnotized by the eyes that were headed her way. "I can't breathe," she managed to murmur.

"Yes you can. Let's go," Devin ordered. She gathered the two nuns and pushed Rosie, breaking the spell she was in. "Stay on the path and keep the flame down low in front of you."

A line of crocs followed them, steadily shuffling nose to tail, along the narrow path. The dark water that flanked them was eerily still. Occasionally a large set of nostrils snorted through the water followed by a pair of greenish eyes breaking the surface. When the crocs following them got too close, Devin would run back, threaten them with the torch and they'd retreat.

Sister Martha began chanting quietly, "Yea though I walk through the valley of death—"

"Will you shut up," Sister Dorothy snapped and slapped the back of her head.

The group made their way through the tunnel until finally reaching an opening. Once again they were out in the salty sea air. The storm had drifted completely away and the black sky was decorated by twinkling stars. The moon's bright light glowed, unimpeded by clouds. Long, thin shadows created from the branches of trees that danced soundlessly around them reminded Rosie of scary shadows in cartoons that would reach up and grab people. The air was eerily still and silent, as if the world had been put on mute. Rosie's trembles had grown worse to the point that her arms and legs shook uncontrollably.

"Thank God," she said as she plopped down on the ground beside the path. "I've never been so happy to see the moon."

"Let us pray to our good Lord and Savior Jesus Christ for guiding us through something so wicked." Sister Dorothy crossed herself. "Amen"

"Amen," Sister Martha echoed.

Devin sat beside Rosie. As Rosie laid back and rested her forearm over her eyes, Devin kept a watchful eye on the entrance for any lingering crocs. None dare venture beyond the safety of the moist cavern.

"What time do you think it is?" Rosie asked not bothering to open her eyes.

Devin glanced at the moon. "It must be midnight at least."

"Please tell me we're almost there." The words escaped Rosie's mouth accompanied by an exhausted sigh.

"Yes, I believe we are," Sister Dorothy said. "Of course, I've never been there, but I've been told when you come out of the tunnel, to turn right. It's only about a mile through the brush. We should see it when we hit the beach."

"I'm dying of thirst," Rosie said. "I'd kill for some water."

"I don't have any water, but we still have a little wine left. Here, hold this." Devin handed the torch to Rosie. Rosie sat up and held the torch.

Devin reached into her bag, pulled out the wine bottle and yanked out the cork.

"Wine?" Sister Martha clapped her hands and danced a jig. "Oh, we love wine. It's been so long."

Devin gave the bottle to Rosie. She took a swig then

handed it back. Devin then held it to Sister Dorothy's lips then Sister Martha's.

"I'd forgotten how good that tastes," Sister Dorothy said. "Fifty-two years is a long time to go without wine."

Sister Martha smacked her lips. "Can I have another sip please? Just a tiny one." She held her miniature doll fingers up to indicate about a half inch.

"Sister!" Sister Dorothy chided. "You be careful. You never could handle your wine very well."

"Oh come on. One little sip isn't going to hurt anything." Sister Martha held both arms up like a child asking to be picked up.

Devin held the bottle to the nun's lips and held it while she drank. She and Rosie then took a couple more sips and finished the wine. Devin placed the empty bottle on the ground beside her.

Rosie stared at the discarded bottle then at Devin. "You're not going to leave that there, are you?"

A look of confusion flashed across Devin's face. She glanced at the bottle then back at Rosie.

Rosie dipped her head and lifted her eyes. "Littering?"

"Tell me you're not serious," Devin chuckled "If you"–

"Oh, fine. Forget it." Rosie rubbed her ankle. "Let's do this. I can make another mile." But when she stood, she winced.

"I might make a suggestion," Sister Dorothy said.

"And that would be?" Devin asked.

"There's not as many, but there're still some dolls on this side of the island and they'll be looking for you."

"Ok, go on."

"Well, one of the ways they can tell it's a human and not a doll walking through the jungle is because of your size. If they see something moving through the bush that's tall, they'll assume it's a person."

"And what do you suggest we do about that?" Rosie was walking, testing out her ankle and flapping her arm that wasn't holding the torch in an attempt to warm up. "Fly above the trees?"

"I suggest you crawl," Sister Dorothy said.

"Crawl? A mile? Through that jungle?" Rosie's eyebrows popped up and her mouth flopped open. She stared at the nun that had just made the ridiculous suggestion.

Both nuns nodded.

Rosie looked at Devin. "Devin, I can't crawl for a mile. I can walk a mile, but crawl? Spiders? Snakes?"

"I think she's right Rosie," Devin said. "She's been right about everything so far."

Again, both nuns nodded.

Rosie sighed. She looked down toward the ground, then back toward the nuns, then at Devin.

"Ok, fine. But I'm not going first." She handed the torch to Devin.

"Which way?" Devin asked.

Sister Dorothy pointed out what looked like a low trail that disappeared through the bottom of the thick overgrown, tangled growth of the forest. It was no more than three feet high.

Devin got on her hands and knees. Sister Dorothy climbed up the side of her jeans and walked on her back. Straddling her neck, she wedged herself between Devin's head and knapsack. Rosie put an arm through each rope of the bag's handle and wore it like a backpack. She followed Devin's lead and got down on her hands and knees. Sister Martha climbed onto her shoulders and straddled her neck, holding onto Rosie's braid like a horse's rein.

They crawled into the forest.

## JUST WHEN YOU THOUGHT...

The crawling was painfully slow. Not only did it frazzle Rosie's nerves but also her knees, shins, and the palms of her hands. Devin would stop, move ahead a couple of feet, then stop again.

Finally, Rosie couldn't take it anymore.

She tapped Devin on the butt.

"Why are you going so slow?" she whispered in a forced, hoarse voice.

Devin rotated her head to toss a whisper back over her shoulder using a matching abrasive expression. "You try crawling while holding a torch with one hand and wiping away spiders, ants, scorpions and other creatures I don't even recognize, to try to make the path better for the person crawling behind you."

"Oh. Ok," Rosie said, "take your time then." She faced Devin's rear end and couldn't help but admire the large and athletic derrière that was perched inches from her face. Her thoughts drifted to what it would look like without the baggy jeans when—something cold and wet dribbled down her neck. Cautiously, she dabbed at it with her fingertips. It was red and the first thought that jumped to her mind was that she was bleeding. But on further examination of the liquid, it was evident that the sticky substance was thinner and lighter colored than blood.

She smelled it.

It smelled like wine.

"Hey!" she whispered to Sister Martha, rotating her neck as far as she could. "Did you just pee on me?"

She couldn't see the nun that sat perched on her shoulders but heard a muffled giggle. "Sorry. It's the wine. It goes right through me."

Rosie hung her head.

They started crawling again.

"Oh good gravy," Rosie said to Sister Martha. "Why didn't you—"

Her sentence was cut short when her face smooshed against the back of Devin's bottom.

"What the heck Devin?" Rosie snapped. "Next time, could you give me a—"

She looked forward and immediately spotted what had caused Devin to stop so abruptly.

Inches from Devin's face was a pair of very large, bulbously round, candy-cane red shoes.

## NO TIME TO CLOWN AROUND

Rosie saw Devin's head lift up at the same time hers did.

The first thing she noticed were the oversized red shoes. Her gaze drifted from there up to the billowing polka-dotted pants, past the three round, white fluffy buttons that decorated his chest, to his pasty white painted face. His smile was wide, framed by a two-inch, red-lipsticked border. He had an equally red round ball painted for a nose. High arched eyebrows gave him a look of fixed surprise. His blue eyes screamed of complete wickedness. And the wide smile and pointy teeth that peered down at them reeked of evil.

He towered above them and from their perspective on the ground, he looked to be twelve feet tall.

Devin leapt up first like a jack-in-the-box that'd been sprung. The noise she uttered was a combination of an unearthly scream and cry. She swiped at the clown with the torch. He jumped back away from the flame. Then she took off like a sprinter who has exploded out of the starting blocks after the gun has gone off. Rosie saw the blur that she recognized to be Devin and Sister Dorothy flash past her.

The image was a fuzzy flash but the fear in both their eyes was unmistakable.

If she'd been on water, it looked as if Devin would've been able to run across the very top of it.

Rosie sprang up and with Sister Martha clutching her braid, followed Devin in the direction they'd just come, away from the clown.

Devin pushed through branches like a receiver running through a defensive line toward the goal, not caring that the boughs swished back and slapped at Rosie. For the most part, Rosie was able to duck under the attacking swooshes of wide leaves but occasionally one caught her across the face.

"Ouch. Damn it, Devin. Stop. He's not following us," she pleaded.

"Are you sure?" Devin slowed enough to investigate and to loosen the grip Sister Dorothy had on her neck.

Rosie and Devin both panted violently.

"What the fuck was that?" Devin asked Sister Dorothy.

"That's Clownie," Sister Martha said between pants. Even though she'd not been running, she was out of breath from working hard to hold on. "He's the meanest on the island."

"I thought you said Double Ds was the meanest?" Devin said.

"No. He was the angriest. Clownie is the meanest. He enjoys hurting things."

"Is he a doll?" Rosie asked.

"Oh he's a doll alright. Just a big one," Sister Dorothy said.

Devin's face was as white as the clown's. Her gaze did not deviate from the path they'd just run down. "Rosie, I can't. I can't…"

Rosie put a hand on Devin's shoulder. "I know. I under-stand Devin."

"It's him. It's the same one." Devin's face contorted in a

pained expression. Her arm shook as she pointed. "I'm positive."

"It can't be Devin. That was almost twenty years ago and across the country. It can't be the same clown."

Devin lowered her forehead to meet the palms of her hand. "My brother," she said. "I can't go back that way," she said and waved a hand in the direction they'd run from. "I'd rather face the crocodiles again."

"The crocs will have caught your scent. They'll all be out looking for you now. There's no way we'll make it back through there," Sister Dorothy said.

Devin searched frantically to the right then left. "There must be another way. We have to find another way." She squatted down and brought her face closer to the nuns. She grabbed Sister Dorothy by the arms and gave her a gentle shake. "How do we get to the ceremonial circle a different way?" There was a frenzied edge to her voice that Rosie hadn't heard before.

The nuns shook their heads.

"I'm sorry. There is no other way." Sister Dorothy peeled Devin's hands off her arms.

"Impossible," Devin stood. "I'll find another way." She scoured the tops of the trees.

"Devin." Rosie placed a hand on her shoulder. "Listen. Calm down for a minute. Let's think this through. If we—"

She stopped talking when a clown suddenly appeared from the woods a few feet from them.

Devin, still gripping the torch, turned and took off. Rosie scooped up the nuns and her bag, and chased the torch that moved quickly through the night away from her.

## BOO

Devin charged through the forest as swiftly as she was able to with bare feet. Rosie kept up the best she could with a bad foot and oversized sneakers. With the thick growth and dim light, it was difficult to see ahead but Devin crashed through branches and brush as if the devil himself was chasing her. And perhaps he was.

"Hurry!" The nuns chanted encouragement.

"I'm going as fast as I can," Rosie huffed between breaths.

They'd been running for about ten minutes when she pleaded, "Devin. Please. Stop."

Devin turned and peered at Rosie then over Rosie's shoulder. "Is he still chasing us?"

"I, I don't think so," Rosie muttered while swallowing gulps of air. "What are we going to do?" She'd put the dolls down and leaned against a tree. She pressed her back against the rough bark and held her side. Her lungs ached.

The two nuns exchanged glances then each raised open palms and shrugged.

Devin paced nervously. She still held the torch but the fire had dwindled to a small flicker. She stared over Rosie's shoulder down the path they'd just crashed through. "Give me some of those leaves for the fire."

Rosie reached into her bag and handed a fist full of the braided leaves to Devin, who wrapped them around the top of the torch. The fire flamed back to life.

"There has to be some way we can out maneuver, avoid, or trick him. We're so close to the ceremonial circle. Think. Think." She talked more to herself than the others. One hand clutched the torch, the other scratched the back of her head.

"If there's a solution," Sister Dorothy said, "we don't know what it is. He pretty much gets his way on the island. He's bigger and meaner than the others and simply takes what he wants."

"How long has he been here?" Rosie asked.

"Oh, about twenty-years," Sister Dorothy said.

"Why hasn't he made the change with anyone already?" Devin stood before the path, vigilantly watching for any sign of movement.

"First," Sister Dorothy explained, "you have to realize, we don't get a lot of people on the island at night anymore. It's not like the old days when people would wander here unsuspecting, thinking it's a nice, tropical island. Those days are pretty much over. Our reputation has spread far and wide. People avoid the island after sunset as if it were a leper colony. Or worse. If a doll could make the change with one of you here tonight, it'd be like hitting the lottery."

"How do you know about the lottery?" Devin asked.

"We get a lot of papers, magazines and books wash up. We read a lot," Sister Martha said.

"And some say Clownie is picky about the body he'll change with. He refuses to get stuck in a body that's old or ugly, so he's been patient. I can't say for sure that's true, but that's what some say."

From somewhere deep in the forest, a maniacal laugh

pierced the night air and the conversation stopped. A chill flashed through Rosie's body. The trembles that she'd had when they came out of the cave were gone. She was over-heated now and sweating from the running. But the laugh caused a different type of chill to snake through her body. This one started at the base of her neck and flashed down her spine to her toes. She glanced down at the goosebumps that had erupted on her arms.

"You can't out run him," Sister Dorothy said. "Well, you might be able to." She lifted a tiny doll finger toward Devin. "But you," she pointed to Rosie's swollen ankle. "If he wants you, he'll catch you."

"Oh Devin," Rosie groaned and held her stomach.

Devin turned her back from the path she'd been studying to face Rosie.

"Rosie," she said. "I won't let anything happen to you. I promise. I'll think of—"

She stopped talking with her jaw suspended in the open position with her gaze fixated over Rosie's shoulder.

Rosie slowly took a step away from the tree and turned her head to see what had captured Devin's attention.

Clownie's pale white face, blue eyes and sinful smile stuck out from the back side of the tree at an odd angle.

The tiny hairs on the backs of Rosie's arms rose to atten-tion as the clown's large red lips curled back and a single, quietly whispered word slithered through his spiky teeth.

"Boo."

# DEAL OR NO DEAL?

Devin shuffled back. The nuns scampered and took cover behind her legs, clinging to her jeans. Rosie hobbled backward but kept herself between the clown and Devin.

"What do you want?" she asked, her voice defiant.

The clown stepped out from behind the tree.

"Be careful," one of the nuns said. "I wouldn't trust him. He's evil."

"Stay back," Devin demanded. She thrust the tip of the flaming torch toward him.

Clownie retreated, holding his white-gloved palms up facing them. His hands and fingers moved furiously. As his wrists swiped the air, his fingers pointed and curled, and his hands would occasionally touch or slap his body and head in short bursts. His facial features matched his intense gestures in animated movements.

Rosie responded by moving her hands similarly, matching the speed and intensity of his actions.

She swung her head around toward Devin and explained, "He's signing," then returned her attention toward the clown.

Rosie heard Devin from behind her. "What's he saying?"

She answered her without taking her eyes off Clownie. "He says he's happy to finally meet someone who knows sign language. He used to be a personal clown to a rich family's little girl who was deaf."

"We always wondered why he made those funny movements with his hands," one of the nuns said. "We thought he had some type of disorder."

"Ask him why he's life-sized and not a small, doll size," Devin said.

Rosie's fingers flashed in front of her face and the clown responded.

"He says the family made a life-sized doll of him."

"Find out how he got on the island? Why was he cursed? Who cursed him?"

Again, Rosie flashed hand signals and the clown answered.

"He said he doesn't feel that's necessary to discuss."

"Don't trust him," Sister Dorothy said. "He's evil to the core. He's constantly pulling body parts off dolls and animals for no reason. We think he gets pleasure out of seeing others suffer. That's how he gets his jollies. He's the devil incarnate in a doll."

"What does he want?" Devin asked. She still cowered several steps behind Rosie.

Rosie motioned and after Clownie answered, she said, "Oh God."

"What?" Devin and the nuns asked simultaneously.

Rosie went numb. She felt as if all the blood and bones had drained from her body in an instant and that nothing remained but mush. Turning her back to the clown, she faced Devin and took a few wobbly steps closer to her.

She hesitated, not sure how to say the words that needed to be said. Finally, she spoke.

"He said he wants to make a deal."

"What kind of deal?" Rosie watched as Devin's eyes, thick with concern, searched her own.

"He'll make sure one of us leaves the island safely in return for the other giving up our soul to him. Otherwise, he says," she swallowed hard, "we'll both be changed over by morning."

## DEAL DENIED

Devin and Rosie stared into each other's eyes as if they were talking, but no words were exchanged. The interaction only lasted a few seconds but it seemed to Rosie like an eternity. The sound of her own breathing and heartbeat pulsated loudly in her ears.

Finally Devin shook her head and spoke.

"Tell him no fucking way. Tell him—"

Clownie clapped and Rosie turned back to face him. His hands moved with lively motions.

Rosie twisted her head toward Devin. "He says you can tell him yourself. He's mute, not deaf."

"If he's mute, how could he say 'boo'?" Devin asked.

Clownie motioned with his hands and shrugged.

"He says he can only laugh and say 'boo'," Rosie said. "He's not sure why. That's how he was after he was changed."

"No deal," Devin shouted at the clown. Her face was red and the veins in her neck were enlarged and protruding. Her voice had a penetrating edge to it. "We're both leaving this fucking island. Alive. With our own souls."

Clownie's hands made a few movements then he turned and walked back into the woods.

"What did he say?" Devin asked as they watched his back disappear into the greenery.

"He said fine, have it your way. He said he'll be back with his clown brigade."

"Clown brigade?" Devin looked down at the nuns.

"He's accumulated about a hundred clown dolls over the years. They'll do whatever he says. They're like his army. In return for joining his ranks, they're protected from his wicked wrath," Sister Dorothy explained.

"There's a lot of them," Sister Martha said. "And they're mean."

# THE LESSER OF TWO EVILS

"We need to make it to the Sacred Circle." Devin squatted to be closer to the nuns. "Please think. Isn't there another way?"

The nuns exchanged glances and suddenly, Sister Martha's face exploded in a look of shock.

"Oh no. I won't do it," she crossed her stubby arms in front of her chest, closed her eyes and turned her back to the group.

"It's the only other way Sister." Sister Dorothy gently laid a hand on her shoulder. "We took a vow."

Sister Martha's head continued to swivel. "I don't care. I won't do it. I agreed to croc alley but I won't do that."

"Do what?" Rosie asked.

"Well," Sister Dorothy took a deep breath. "There is one other way to get there." She pointed to the right.

"Ok, great. Let's go then. What are we waiting for?" Devin asked.

"That part of the island is marshy. You know, slimy water," Sister Dorothy explained.

"Yuck," Rosie felt her mouth contort with the word 'slimy'.

"Ok, so we get wet," Devin said.

"Well…There are things that like to live in marshy areas," Sister Dorothy explained,

Sister Martha blurted, "Snakes."

"Snakes? Oh no. Devin." Rosie took a step back and away from the group. "I can't do snakes."

"Agreed," Sister Martha waddled to stand beside her. "And there's lots of snakes."

"There's no way I'm going into a marsh where there's snakes Devin," Rosie said. "I'll take my chances with a doll, a crocodile or a clown, but not snakes."

"How do all these animals survive on this island?" Devin asked.

"They eat each other," Sister Dorothy said.

"And dolls," Sister Martha added.

"Ok, let's think this through," Devin was pacing again. "We need to get to the sacred circle. In that direction is a clown with an army of a hundred dolls. In this direction is a swampy marsh with snakes. Anyone got any ideas how we get out of this?"

No one spoke.

## BAD OR WORSE, PICK ONE

Minutes crawled by.

Devin broke the silence. "We have to do something."

"How about we build a raft and paddle back to Key West?" Sister Martha suggested.

"We don't have time to build a raft," Devin said.

"And we can't paddle all the way back to Key West," Rosie said, quickly adding, "sharks. Ugh."

Sister Martha shrugged. "Well, that's the only idea I have."

"Ok," Devin spoke to the nuns. "Let's talk about the snakes. What kind?"

"All kinds." Sister Dorothy counted them off one at a time on her fingers. "Rattlers, pythons, boa constrictors."

"What? No cobras?" Rosie bobbed her head.

"No cobras," Sister Martha shook her head. "They're not indigenous to this area, but there was that one time—"

"Sister," Sister Dorothy interrupted her. "She was being facetious."

"Oh," Sister Martha's mouth downturned into a pout. "Well, I was going to tell you about Anna."

"Who's Anna?" Devin asked.

"The anaconda. She's not indigenous to this area either but she seems to get along nicely here. She's about twenty-five feet long and must weigh five hundred pounds."

"Holy smokes," Devin said. "What the heck could she possibly eat to get to be so huge?"

"Pretty much anything she wants," Sister Dorothy said. "Mostly chimps and crocs we think."

"And dolls," Sister Martha added.

Devin's face twisted as she grimaced while looking up and away. Suddenly her eyes and mouth widened and she yelled, "Rosie! Watch out!"

Rosie glanced up in time to see a doll falling from a branch high above. It was a male ventriloquist's puppet doll dressed in a formal black tuxedo. Its eyes stared with an exaggeratedly round gaze and they flipped from right to left. The lower jaw snapped open and shut like that of a holiday nutcracker, making a smacking sound as it chomped while tumbling through the air. When it landed on Rosie's chest, the force knocked her to the ground. Instinctively, she clutched at it and tried to pry it off, but its tiny fingers had a grip on her collar bones. Rosie screamed. Devin threw herself at the doll, snapped its head off and tossed the head into the bushes. Next she wrestled the hands off Rosie's collar bones, breaking one finger at a time to pry it off. Once the doll was no longer attached to Rosie, Devin ripped each arm and leg off and flung them in different directions, finally hurling the body as if it were a grenade deep into the forest.

Rosie lay on the ground rubbing her collar bones.

Devin squatted beside her. "Are you ok?"

"I'm not sure." Rosie huffed in an attempt to catch her breath. Devin tenderly touched her fingertips to where the doll had clenched Rosie's skin.

"They're just scratches," she said.

"Oh Devin." Rosie gripped Devin's forearm. "That was so close."

Devin nodded. "I know. Too close."

"There'll be more," Sister Dorothy said. "If one found you, the others won't be far behind."

"We can't stay here," Devin said, then stood and wildly searched up, down and around the surrounding area. "We have to get to the circle. Let's take a vote. Either we face the clowns or the snakes. Who votes for the clowns?"

Rosie and the nuns raised their hands.

Devin made eye contact with each of them. She said, "Good luck," turned and strode in the direction of the swamp.

"Wait," all three shouted.

"You can't leave us," Rosie said.

"I'm not facing a legion of clowns Rosie." Devin's head shook. "I can't."

"Ok. Well then, what's your plan if we go that way?" she pointed toward the marsh.

Devin eyed the direction of the swamp. "I'm guessing the snakes that pose the most threat prefer the water. A five-hundred pound anaconda can move efficiently in the water but not so much on land."

"So fine, what are we supposed to do? Fly over them?"

"You've got the right idea. I'm thinking if we can stay above them, we might make it."

"Above them? How do we get above them?"

Devin pointed up. "The trees."

Rosie and the nuns followed where her finger pointed to.

Rosie's lower jaw fell open. "Are you suggesting we swing through the trees like Tarzan? Because if you are, you're crazier than I thought."

"No Rosie. The trees are dense enough, look." She pointed upward. "The branches are huge. We can easily stand on them. And they're close enough, we can jump from tree to tree, or if we need to…" She glanced around searching for something. A piece of driftwood, part of a long, flat plank, lay on the beach, tangled in a cluster of fishing ropes. She ran to it and using her pocket knife, freed it from the entanglement. She dashed back to Rosie with the board balanced on her shoulder. "This can act as a bridge."

Rosie shook her head. "Devin, you, Miss Athletic, may be able to scamper around a forest like a trained circus trapeze chimp but I'm afraid of heights. If you think you're going to get me up there," she pointed toward the trees, "and using a rotting piece of driftwood to—"

"Rosie." Devin wrapped a hand around the back of Rosie's neck and gazed, unblinking into her eyes. "You can do this."

Rosie stared deep into the orbs and their magical medley of colors. She wanted to believe the woman that stood before her. A part of her wanted to say, 'Yes Devin. I trust and believe you'. But another part of her, a very complex matrix of lifelong fears muddled her brain. The anxiety section of her mind was on full alert with every warning buzzer she'd ever experienced, going off and sounding a full alert.

Sounds of shuffles and breaking of small branches came simultaneously from several directions. From somewhere in the darkness, a high-pitched squeaky voice repeated the animated word, *'mama.'* The four of them turned toward the direction the sound came from but saw nothing.

"Rosie. You. Can. Do. This," Devin repeated.

Rosie swallowed then gave a single, slow nod.

"Ok. Let's go."

# MOM ALWAYS SAID, KEEP YOUR FEET ON THE GROUND

The first tree they climbed was a thick coconut tree that had fallen and leaned upward at a forty-five degree angle against another tree. Devin easily scampered up it, dragging with her the piece of driftwood, which she wedged through the branches of the first tree and through a large 'Y' of a massive adjoining Banyan tree. She scurried back down, brought the nuns up, placed them on the branch, then returned for Rosie.

"You ready for this?" Her gaze was so intense, Rosie felt as if some of Devin's courage was being transferred into her.

Rosie took a deep breath and began climbing by using a combination of crawling and hugging the tree. She was about half way up when she looked down and said, "Devin. I can't do this."

Devin was behind her. "You can do this Rosie. Just don't look down."

Rosie lifted her eyes, focused her attention forward and continued to climb. When she reached the 'Y' she sat with her arms tightly encircling the trunk. Her eyes were closed.

"I can't look down."

"That's ok," Devin's voice was calming. "You don't have to look down. Just watch me."

Rosie peeked the eye open that had the lens and kept her gaze fixated on Devin.

Devin placed the plank from the tree they were on to the next one, testing it to make sure it was secure.

"Look," she said as she stood on the plank and bounced up and down to show its sturdiness, "it's only a couple feet away."

"Devin I can't make it all the way over the marsh. There's no way. It's too far. I can't—"

"Shush, shush." Devin crossed the plank back to her and squatted so their faces were only inches apart. "Have you ever heard the old saying, something about a journey of a thousand miles begins with one step? That's all you have to think about, the next step. You did the first step. You climbed the tree. Now, this next move is easy. Look. It's only two steps and you'll be on the other side."

Rosie looked at Devin, then the driftwood and the next tree.

She opened her mouth and the words, "I can't–" came out but one of Devin's fingers placed gently on her lips stopped the other words from escaping.

"If that board was on the ground, could you walk across it?" Devin was nodding,

Rosie matched the nod.

"Good. I thought so. I want you to pretend it's on the ground. Here, watch me." Devin placed her right foot on the bridge, took a small leap, and landed on a flat, wide branch of the next tree with her left foot. She smiled, extended her arms, flashed an animated, "ta-da!" then returned to Rosie and the nuns.

"I'll take the nuns over, then be back for you, ok? Give me your bag."

Rosie kept one hand clutching the tree she was pressed against and used the other hand to pass Devin her bag.

Devin scooped up the nuns, brought them to the second tree and gently placed them down. Both nuns clung to the tree and each other. She then returned for Rosie. She helped Rosie to stand and held onto her hips from behind as Rosie inched forward.

"It's worse if you go slow," Devin said. "Trust me. Just take a leap and you'll be there."

Rosie froze. "I can't."

"Here," Devin guided Rosie back. "Let me go first. All you have to do is take a tiny jump and I'll catch you." She dashed over the plank and stood on the other side of the short bridge, her arms extended.

Rosie wiped her palms against her dress. She heard Devin's voice but her eyes were glued to the plank that she was supposed to step on.

"Come on. Pretend you're on the ground. I'll catch you, promise."

Rosie peeked down. Below them was a mixture of black and green swamp water. She thought about turning around and climbing back down the tree but the thought of snakes and clowns and haunted dolls flooded her brain. She started to sway.

"Rosie!" Devin's voice was firm, strong. "Look at me," she demanded.

Rosie's gaze left the water below and stared into Devin's eyes. Those wonderful eyes that were perched above the mouth that was talking and encouraging her.

"Now don't look down. And breathe. Keep looking at me. I want you to take one step my way then jump into my arms. I'll catch you," Devin commanded.

Rosie didn't move.

"Rosie. I *will* catch you." Devin's voice was more authoritative this time.

Rosie took a deep breath, held it, and leapt in Devin's direction. When Devin's arms wrapped around her, she exhaled, closed her eyes and squeezed her tightly.

"I was so afraid," Rosie mouthed the words more than speaking them.

"I know, but you did it," Devin wiped some hair away from Rosie's cheeks. "You did it. I told you, you could do it." She rubbed Rosie's arms. "We're going to get through this," she whispered and kissed her forehead.

They separated, and Rosie sat next to the nuns. Devin glanced around, surveying their options. "Ok ladies, next," she said. "There." She pointed to a nearby tree. "That one. You won't even need the bridge. Here, grab this vine and use it for balance as you step onto the next tree. Watch. I'll do it first."

Devin tugged on the thick vine to make sure it was secure, then stepped onto the next tree, using the vine to help with balance. Rosie easily followed, then Devin returned to get the piece of driftwood they'd used as a bridge.

They made progress this way through several trees.

"Look," Sister Dorothy said. "There's the end of the marsh." She pointed below where clearly the murky black water ended and a sandy brown color indicated solid earth.

"We're almost there," Devin said as she searched for their next move. She picked up the piece of driftwood and tried linking it to another tree, but the other trees were all too far away. The board couldn't span the distance.

"Oh no. Are we stuck?" Rosie felt her insides tighten as the familiar sensation of panic rose inside her.

"No, we're not stuck," Devin said. "But we need to climb down there," she pointed below, "to bridge across to that tree.

See it?" There was a nearby tree that was closer but it was lower than they were. "That'll be our last crossing."

"I'll go down, set the bridge then come back and get you." Devin scooted down the tree they were on with the board on her shoulder. When she reached the lowest branch, she left the driftwood then climbed back to where Rosie and the nuns were.

"Come on," she said, picking up the nuns and bringing them down to where she'd left the plank.

When she climbed back up, she said, "Rosie. This part's easy. All you have to do is climb down. I'm going first so if you have any trouble, I'll be right there to help."

Rosie hugged the tree and shimmied down. There were cuts along the insides of her thighs from where her knees gripped the bark. She prayed every inch of the way. When she finally reached the level where Devin was she sat, clinging to the tree's trunk.

"How much more?" Rosie wiped perspiration off her forehead with the back of her hand. The pit of her stomach felt like a contorted ball of nerves. Her breaths were frequent and shallow.

"We're almost there. Look." Rosie studied the tree Devin pointed to. It was farther away than any distance they'd crossed before.

"See?" Devin said. "This is the last space you have to cross. After this, we simply step onto the other tree that's fallen and it'll take us to the solid, brown earth. That's the other side of the marsh. We're practically there."

"Practically there," Rosie whispered.

Devin placed the driftwood bridge from the tree they were on to the next closest one. With a nun on each shoulder, she effortlessly pranced across like an Olympian crossing a balance beam for a gold medal performance. She scuttled across in five steps and after dropping the nuns off, scampered back.

"Devin, I can't cross this one," Rosie exhaled a puff of air. Her head swiveled. "It's more than one step and there's no vine."

"Rosie. You can do it. Look, it's not very high. The ground is right there."

"That's not the ground. That's a swamp. A swamp with snakes."

"Rosie, it's easy. It's just like walking on a curb. Didn't you ever walk on a curb as a kid?"

"Yes, but sometimes I fell off."

"But sometimes you didn't, right? It's only five steps. I'll be on the other side to catch you. Don't go slow. The faster you go, the better it is."

Reluctantly, Rosie nodded and Devin hustled across the board to the other side.

"Ok, come on," she instructed as she stood on the other side, her arms stretched forward. "I'll catch you. Just like the other times."

Rosie took a deep breath and started across.

The first step wasn't bad. And the second step wasn't too bad.

But it was the third step that got her. She was half way across, with nothing to hold on to. Devin voiced words of encouragement but she seemed miles away, as if she were in a distant, foggy dream. The words turned into a muddled blur. Rosie peeked downward and saw the shadowy water beneath her.

She began to tilt, first to the left, then the right. She waved her arms and was able to momentarily stabilize herself. Suddenly, the thought occurred to her that it'd be a good idea to sit down. As she lowered her center of gravity, her body leaned more. Again, she waved her arms, trying to steady herself, but the tilt had gathered momentum this time. Her stomach tumbled in the direction opposite her body as adrenaline flooded her and every nerve felt on fire. She screamed Devin's name.

And she fell.

## DIDN'T THINK I HAD IT IN ME

She landed on her back in the murky water, closed her mouth, squeezed her eyes tight and sank. When she opened her eyes, she lifted her head and peered upward. A dim light fluttered through muddy green water. A survival instinct kicked in and she clawed at the water with a ferocious intensity the likes of which she didn't know existed. Her legs kicked and her arms flailed as she struggled toward the light.

When she exploded up and out of the water, the first thing her brain acknowledged was Devin's voice screaming her name and yelling, "I'm coming!"

The second thing she recognized was that she was immersed in slimy water. When she stood, her feet sunk. Cool mud oozed into her sneakers and over her ankles. The water came up to her armpits and when she raised her arms, green slime hung from them. Her glasses had fallen to her chin, and with trembling hands, she replaced them onto the bridge of her nose. Mud covered the one good lens making it difficult to see.

"Are you ok?" The words entered her brain but she couldn't determine from which direction they'd come. Rosie turned, searching for land, or Devin or anything she could recognize when she made out the blurred shape of Devin's body as it hustled down the tree.

She spit out muddy water and plant matter. When she inhaled, some slime entered her throat and she both coughed and vomited at the same time in an involuntary attempt to rid herself of the foul sludge. After she'd heaved several times and coughed most of the water from her lungs, she did her best to answer.

"Yeah," she spit the word out and wiped a combination of muddy water and vomit from her chin. "I'm, uh—"

Something cool and slippery slid around her waist. An iciness instantly flooded her and when she looked down, she saw a head the size of her own floating in the water. But it wasn't a human head. It was a flat, diamond shaped head with large, black, round eyes, with skin covered in green and black spotted scales. A thin, black forked tongue repeatedly darted in and out of its mouth. Rosie's heart pounded so hard and fast, it felt it would hammer right through her chest.

"Anna!" Sister Martha's shrill voice pierced the air.

Devin had climbed down the tree and now stood at the end of the swamp. "Rosie. Don't move," she instructed.

"Devin…" Rosie whimpered.

"Don't move," Devin repeated. Her voice was calm.

The snake continued to coil around Rosie. Its body was as thick as her thighs. The combination of weight and the slow increase of pressure as it squeezed threatened to pull her down. She struggled to keep her balance and remain upright.

"Rosie, listen to me. Where's the knife?" Devin spoke slowly, deliberately.

"What knife?" Rosie's voice was quick and high-pitched.

"My red knife. Where is it?"

"In my pocket." The snake had hypnotized her and Rosie couldn't pry her eyes off its face. She realized the terror that flooded her right now was total and complete, yet the snake was beautiful in an odd way. She wondered if this is what it felt like to die, flooded by a certain peace and appreciation for the beauty in the world.

Devin's voice interrupted her thoughts, snapping her back to the moment. "I want you to slowly reach into your pocket and get the knife."

Rosie's hand shook uncontrollably. She lifted her arm, reached into her pocket, found the piece of metal and fumbled to pull it out.

"Ok. Good," Devin said. "Now, stop looking at the snake. Look at the knife and snap out the big blade. Go slow and carefully so you don't drop it."

Rosie tore her gaze away from the snake and focused on the knife. Her heart beat so forcefully, she felt it was climbing up into her throat and threatening to suffocate her.

"Devin," she spoke in short puffs, "it's getting hard to breathe."

"Don't talk. Don't exhale," Devin said. "Keep your lungs expanded. Hold your breath. Flip out the blade."

Rosie kept her attention focused on the knife, nervously watching as her unsteady hands tugged on the thin piece of silver. Both the blade and her hands were wet, and it took several attempts before it finally snapped out.

"Good," Devin said. "Now, listen carefully. I want you to slice it in the head. Slice it across the eyes as hard as you can."

"I can't," Rosie cried. Her voice quivered. "It's so beautiful."

"Rosie. You can. You have to." Devin's words were starting to muddle, as if she were drifting away.

"Do it!" came a distant command.

Rosie had stared back down at the snake again and now stood, frozen, gazing unblinking at its head. Her arm visibly shook violently. The snake grew hazy and her field of vision narrowed as the corners of her view turned gray as if someone had dimmed the lights. The pressure of the pulsing sensation in her head and neck was unbearable.

"Damn it Rosie," Devin's voiced pierced the darkness that quickly consumed her. "Do it *now*. Do it for me, please!"

As if it had a mind of its own, Rosie's arm raised then flashed downward, slicing the blade across the snake's head in a quick and determined move. Then she slashed again. And again. The thin metal sliced the scales and eyes and deep red gashes sprung open. Blood oozed out, turning the water around them blackish red.

The pressure around Rosie's middle immediately released. Her eyes registered light again and the dizziness evaporated. She took a couple deep breaths, then slowly stepped out of the circle the snake had made around her. The limp, lifeless body floated away. With her arms flailing in the air, she trudged through the muck as quickly as she could toward Devin. Her mouth opened and she tried to yell but the scream that poured from her was silent.

Devin thrashed into the muddied water toward her. They embraced, sobbing into each other's shoulders. The grip that Devin had on her was tighter than any human had ever had on Rosie in her entire life. She wanted to crawl inside Devin and stay there forever.

"Devin," she finally sputtered. Her muscles shook so violently, that her teeth chattered, making it difficult to speak. "I'm so cold."

"I know," Devin pressed Rosie's body to her own and rubbed her skin. "I got you. You're safe now."

They left the marsh and sat on solid earth. Devin cradled Rosie's face with her hands, wiping the mud and tears from her cheeks. Rosie curled into a ball and leaned into Devin while Devin cradled and comforted her.

"You're ok now. It's over," she spoke the words repeatedly, reassuringly, as she smoothed Rosie's hair and pulled out pieces of rotting debris.

They remained there until Rosie felt her heart rate return to normal.

"You alright now?" Devin helped Rosie sit up. As the fear faded, Rosie felt herself relax and she nodded.

"Good. Let's keep going, ok? Sunrise must be only a few hours away and we're not far from the circle."

Rosie nodded again and they stood. She brushed some muddy water off herself.

"Wait. Don't move," Devin said.

Rosie froze.

"Keep looking into my eyes," Devin's hands reached toward Rosie's face. Her fingertips gently brushed against Rosie's cheeks then slid down to her neck. Tenderly Devin's hands rubbed the back of Rosie's neck and between the sensation of her touch and staring into her spellbinding eyes, some of the tension Rosie had experienced faded away.

When Devin pulled her hands away, Rosie felt a light pinch on the back of her neck. Devin tossed something into the water.

"What was that?" Rosie rubbed the back of her neck.

Devin grinned. "A blood sucker."

Rosie's panic flew from zero to a hundred in a second. "Are there any more? Look. Look! Are there any more?" She searched her arms, legs, examined her shoulders, felt her face, neck, head and peered into her dress down at her breasts.

"There are no more," Devin insisted. "Calm down. You're fine." She gathered Rosie in her arms and held her tight. They stood like that, wrapped in tight embrace with Devin cradling Rosie as the moments ticked by. Their bodies pressed tightly together.

Rosie's thoughts wandered to what it would be like to be held by Devin this way at another time, another place.

"Um. Excuse me. Don't forget us," Sister Martha yelled down from the tree.

## SEND IN THE CLOWNS

The group of four continued making their way through the forest. Between the entanglement of vines, passing through thick thorny bushes, and climbing over and under fallen trees, progress was slow.

"Are you sure we're going the right way?" Rosie finally asked. Every muscle in her body ached, each step was a painful challenge.

"I'm pretty sure," Sister Dorothy answered. "I think it's not too far ahead."

"Ah, sister," Sister Martha pressed a miniature finger to her lips. "I could be wrong but I do believe it's that way." She pointed in the direction opposite the way they were headed.

"No sister, you're wrong," Sister Dorothy shook her head so strongly, her entire body swayed. "Look at the moon." Everyone glanced up and she continued. "If we go your way, we'll end up back at the cave where we started."

"Don't even tell me we're lost," Rosie said. "That'll push me right over the edge. I can't take much more of this."

"We're not lost," Sister Dorothy stamped a foot. "I know where we're going. My sense of direction is impeccable."

"Impeccable?" Sister Martha's voice raised in agitated volume. "Well then how come we got lost that time when we—"

"Shush," Devin reached down and clamped a hand over Sister Martha's mouth. "What's that?"

The sound of branches crackling caused them all to freeze.

A coconut landed beside Devin and she jumped. Everyone looked up. There was no coconut tree above them. Four heads swiveled, searching for the source of the coconut-bomb.

"Boo," a voice whispered at the same time Clownie's face appeared from behind a tree.

The group scuttled together. From out of the bushes appeared dozens of clown dolls. Some were tall and thin, some short and stocky. Some had pudgy baby faces while others wore the weathered face of an old person. There were African-American clowns, Asian clowns, sad clowns and happy clowns. Many smiled joyfully while others possessed grins of twisted evil. Many were missing body parts, hair or clothes. Most were infested with insects, bugs, spiders or maggots. All were filthy. But the one thing they had in common; they were all clowns. And there were a lot of them. They each wiggled or rocked in place as if impatiently waiting for the signal to advance.

Clownie's hands motioned swiftly.

"He wants to know if we're ready to take the deal. He says one gesture from him and they'll be all over us," Rosie said. She turned to Devin. "Devin, you can survive this. I can't. I can't go on anymore. I'm taking the deal." She lowered her eyes and turned her back to Devin.

"What?!" Devin exploded, grabbed Rosie's shoulder and spun her around. "No. No, no. You can't. I got us into this mess, I'll get us out. I'm taking the deal."

"But Devin, you have a—"

"No buts." Devin faced Clownie.

"Ok, you have a deal. But you need to give us a few minutes to say goodbye. And I need to be sure you keep your end of the deal and Rosie makes it to the circle safely. Send your tribe away. I want them gone. Far gone."

Clownie's permanent smile grew wider. He turned and faced his legion of mini-clowns. His hands made several movements and all the dolls turned. Slowly they began wobbling or crawling toward the forest. Away from Devin and Rosie.

Clownie followed them.

Devin and Rosie waited and watched as the masses of miniature plastic bodies trudged and disappeared under the bushes. When the sound of hundreds of tiny feet scraping across the forest floor could no longer be heard, Devin faced Rosie.

"Here, take these," she slipped her backpack off and handed it and the torch to Rosie. "Make sure my Dad gets the camera. And, tell him… Tell him I'm sorry. About everything. And, tell him, I loved him."

"Devin, no! This is insane. You can't do this." Tears filled Rosie's eyes and when one crept over her lower lid, she reached through the space of her glasses that was missing a lens, and wiped it away.

"Once it's…" Devin hesitated, took a deep breath and continued. "Once it's done, I want you to run that way and get into that circle." She indicated the direction with a lift of her head. "The nuns will guide you." She glanced at the nuns who nodded in agreement. "I'm sorry I got you into this." Devin pressed her palms against Rosie's cheeks and with her thumbs, wiped the tears that had spilled from her eyes. "Please try to forgive me. You know, you're a lot braver than you've ever given yourself credit for. I'm sorry it's ending this way. I would've liked to have seen if we had a chance to, I mean, I think we might've been able to make it work between us."

"Devin." The name choked in Rosie's throat.

Devin turned and faced the direction Clownie had disappeared and yelled, "Hey Clown!"

## FACING YOUR DEMON

Clownie leapt out from behind a nearby tree and landed as if posing center stage for a Broadway show.

"Boo," he whispered.

"Let's do this," Devin said. She took a couple steps toward him. He clapped his hands and wiggled his hips in a dance. She took another step in his direction then stopped, pivoted and faced Rosie.

"Can I have something to remember you by?" she asked.

"Ah, sure. Of course," Rosie said but remained standing and held her palms up.

Devin ambled back to Rosie. They stood, facing each other, neither spoke. Each silently studied the other's expression.

Devin raised both hands and gently cradled Rosie's face in her palms. Devin's touch was tender, comforting. Rosie wished she could melt into it. She tried to swing her head side-to-side but Devin held it firm.

She started to speak but the words choked in her throat, "Devin, you don't—"

"Shh," Devin placed a finger on Rosie's lips. "I do."

Rosie gazed into Devin's eyes. The beautiful mixture of bright colors that she'd stared into all day was still there but now it was muted by a thin film of moisture.

Devin moved forward, closing the gap between them. Her hands slid to the back of Rosie's head. Tenderly, she brought Rosie's face forward as she lowered her own. Rosie closed her eyes. Their lips met. First, they merged carefully, then with more intensity. Devin's lips were warm and soft. Her hands slid around the back of Rosie's head, massaging the back of her scalp while pulling her face in tighter as the kiss intensified.

The sensation was of tenderness yet at the same time electric. Rosie had never experienced a kiss that came even close to what she was feeling at that moment. Her body demanded more. She raised her hands, wrapped them tightly around Devin's back and pulled her forward, so their chests and stomachs melded together. Rosie inhaled and smelled her. Inhaled the essence of her. It was a smell that stirred a sensation that she couldn't comprehend. It reached in and shook her very core.

The kiss lasted for what seemed forever. Time stood still as Rosie allowed herself to become lost in the physical reactions the moment created inside her. Temporarily, she ignored the nightmare that was happening around them.

Devin pulled away first. She mouthed the words, "Thank you."

Rosie grabbed Devin's hands, pressed them to her own chest, and squeezed them. "Devin. You can't do this. Please, don't." Her sobs were uncontrollable now and her body shook. Tears flowed freely, chasing each other down her cheeks.

"Shh." Devin wiped her own eyes with the backs of her hand. The whites of her eyes were red. "It's ok. It's almost as if it were my destiny, know what I mean? Like it was meant to be. It's too strange to not be fate. It's my punishment for…" She looked away.

Rosie threw herself onto Devin. "No, Devin. It's not your destiny. Please. Don't do this."

"Rosie." Devin looked her square in the eyes. "I have to. One last favor. Can I have one more thing to remember you by? Your bag? Please?"

Rosie's shoulders heaved as she lifted the bag off them. She moved slowly as if it were painful to do so, and let the bag drop off her shoulder as if it had the weight of the world inside of it. Reluctantly, she handed it to Devin.

Clownie rubbed his hands together and ran his red tongue over his sharp teeth. He made a few hand signals. Devin glanced at Rosie.

"He says," Rosie had trouble speaking and the words blurted out in between sobs, "this won't hurt a bit and it'll be over before you know it. And that you'll like being in the clown body. You'll," she paused to sniffle, swallow a sob and blurted out the words, "rule the island."

The nuns stood behind Rosie, each hugging one of her calves. Their faces were somber.

Devin adjusted Rosie's bag onto her shoulder, took a giant breath, then turned to face Clownie. His arms were stretched forward as a newlywed would welcome their long absent lover. He towered over her and looked down at her as a wolf might admire a newborn sheep.

"Before we do this," she took a step in his direction, "there's something I need to understand."

Clownie lowered his arms.

"You like hurting children, don't you?" she took another step.

His smile didn't diminish, in fact, it grew larger.

"That's it, isn't it? You enjoy seeing them suffer. That's

why you're here, isn't it?" she advanced closer to the clown. "You hurt that little girl, didn't you?"

The clown's head snapped backward and he released a sinful laugh that echoed through the island, escalating in volume as it continued.

"That's why someone performed the Curse of the Damned on you. You deserved it, didn't you?"

Clownie released another evil laugh. This bellow permeated every inch of the island, filling the night air with its wickedness. As it unfurled and escalated, Rosie couldn't stop her body from trembling. It was as if pure evil had been released into the atmosphere.

Devin took a step toward the clown. "Who hurt you?" The question cut the clown's laughter short. His face grew serious.

Devin repeated the question. "When you were a small boy who hurt you?"

The ecstasy dropped from the clown's face, instead, it became drenched with sadness.

"Come here." Devin shrugged Rosie's bag off her shoulder. "I understand what you've been through. Come here. There's something I want to show you. Something you need to see."

Clownie's head tilted.

"You've been on this island for a long time," she shuffled through Rosie's bag. "Too long. Come here. You need to see this."

Clownie stepped closer so he and Devin were only inches apart. He leaned forward and peered into the bag.

In a swift motion, Devin pulled out from the bag, two knitting needles. Gripping each tightly with closed fists, she lifted her arms high over her head and lunged at the clown. The scream she emitted came from the bottom of her soul.

"Fuck you Clownie!" she yelled as she leapt and threw herself forward, sending the full weight of her body airborne. She directed the tips of the needles toward his eyes. In a swift and powerful movement, thrust the iron rods deep into the clown's eye sockets. "You'll never look at another child again!"

A roar escaped from Clownie. It was a combination of 'boo' and a laugh but there was more to it. It was a gurgled vibration of pain. He yanked out the knitting needles, and along with them came his eyes. Two round, black, empty holes remained where his eyes had been. He dropped the needles into the sand with the eyes shish-kabobbed like martini olives on the ends. He clutched at the two empty orbs on each side of his face, above his red, round nose. Stumbling wildly, blindly, he bumped into a tree and bounced back. A mixture of moans, screams and incomprehensible sounds slithered from his mouth as he continued to stagger.

Devin grabbed the torch from Rosie. "Come on. Let's go!"

## SEARCHING FOR CIRCLE

osie and Devin ran through the forest, each with a nun clutched to their chest. Devin gripped the torch in one hand and parted thick forest branches with the other, holding them until Rosie passed. Rosie's limp had gotten worse and it made the traveling slow.

Occasionally a doll would pop up in the path and rush them, but Devin would easily kick it or light it on fire and they proceeded until the beach came into view.

When they left the woods and were on the sand, they glanced left and right. There was nothing but sandy beach in both directions.

"Which way?" Devin's shoulders heaved as she spoke.

The nuns looked up and down the beach.

"I'm not sure," Sister Dorothy said. "It should be right here."

"What are we looking for exactly?" Rosie asked.

"A circle," Sister Dorothy said. "A large, black circle. It's permanently burned into the landscape. You can't miss it, or so they tell me."

"Burnt by the devil," Sister Martha piped in.

"You go that way," Devin pointed to the left. "Here, take the torch," she said as she handed the torch to Rosie. "I'll go this way. Hopefully, one of us will find it soon."

They separated and hustled in different directions. Rosie still clung to Sister Martha as she walked the beach, searching for anything that appeared like the shape of a circle. All she saw was typical sun-bleached, white sand scattered with shells, rocks, driftwood and an occasional piece of trash.

"Where is it?" she asked herself.

"I don't know," Sister Martha answered.

The rocks grew large and the beach ended. A towering rock wall extended upward, toward the jungle. Rosie stood, staring at the top of the cliff.

"Think I should climb up to get a better view?" she asked Sister Martha.

Before the nun could answer, from out of the darkness came a shout. The words filled her with excitement.

"Rosie! Come here. I found it!"

## SAFE AT LAST

R osie turned and ran in the direction of Devin's voice. When she reached her, she saw Devin standing beside Sister Dorothy on the outside edge of a large, black loop that was drawn in the sand. It was as if someone had made a fire and left the coal and ashes in the shape of a circle.

"So this is it?" Devin said as she studied the circumference.

"This is it," Sister Dorothy said. "This is where the Shaman originally cast the spell on Ria and Naomi hundreds of years ago. It's a sacred space and no dolls are allowed inside it. You'll be safe in there until the morning cruise boat comes and rescues you. You'll be able to see it from here." She pointed toward the horizon. "It'll come from that direction. The first boat leaves Key West at sunrise and will reach here about an hour later."

Devin looked at Rosie. "You ready for this?"

"Oh yes," Rosie said.

They gave each nun a hug then placed them down on the sand outside the perimeter of the circle. Rosie reached for Devin's extended hands. They joined palms and entwined fingers. Together, they stepped over the black burnt border and into the circle.

Once inside, they each breathed a sigh of relief.

"Do you feel any different?" Rosie asked.

Devin shook her head. "Me either," said Rosie.

"Don't worry. You're protected," Sister Dorothy said. "You've had a long night. Go ahead and relax. Nothing will harm you. May the good Lord bless and keep you safe for all your days." She and Sister Martha crossed themselves. "We better get going. When the first rays of sun come up, we'll be frozen until tonight and we want to make it as far as possible back toward our home."

"We can't thank you enough," Devin said. "Without you, well, I hate to think what would've happened. Is there any way we can repay you?"

"Knowing we're doing God's work is payment enough for us," Sister Dorothy said.

Sister Martha nodded and chimed, "God's work."

"May God bless and His Holy Spirit forever be with you," Sister Dorothy made the sign of the cross in the air toward Rosie and Devin. Then the nuns turned and walked toward the forest.

When they'd disappeared, Rosie plunked down onto the sand.

"It's so good to sit," she said as she rubbed her ankle and examined the cuts on her arms and legs.

"It'll be sunrise soon," Devin dropped to the ground, sat beside Rosie and examined the cuts on the bottoms of her own feet. The socks had long worn away and she'd been running throughout the island barefoot. "And we'll be rescued not long after that."

The night still surrounded them but being on the beach and out from under the trees gave them access to a star filled sky. The light of the moon shimmering across the tops of the dark waves stretched before them for miles.

"I can't wait to get off this island," Rosie said. Even though the night was still, they both continued to glance repeatedly over their shoulders.

"I know. Me too. We'll be out of here before you know it," Devin was rubbing her feet. "We probably only have about half hour until sunrise. How's your ankle?"

"It's sore. It'll be fine, I guess. Hopefully, no more running through forests."

"Well, I guess you can't say you never had an adventure, huh?"

"You mean a nightmare?"

"Just think, it's something you can tell your kids about someday."

"As if anyone is going to believe us."

"They'll believe it when they see this," Devin patted her backpack. "I have a lot of it on film don't forget. I'll make a movie. And I'll share the credit and royalties with you, of course."

"I don't care about any of that. I just want to go home and curl up with Itchy," Rosie said.

Rosie's shoulders relaxed and she closed her eyes. She hadn't realized how tired she was until that moment. She found herself nodding off and fought it. Devin slipped an arm around Rosie's shoulders and held her up.

"So, when we get off this island, if I asked you to marry me, would you?" Devin asked. "I was thinking about the honeymoon. How about Paris? No, Italy. Ok, both Paris and Italy."

Rosie's eyes were still closed when she answered. "Absolutely not."

"No to Paris and Italy? All right then Fuji? I've never been and I've heard—"

Rosie let out a tired chuckle. "Absolutely not. I won't marry you."

"What? Ok. You're right. That's rushing things a bit. How about, be my girlfriend first for a while? We can—"

"Not a chance."

"How about a date?"

"Slim chance of that."

"What percent?"

"What do you mean, what percent?"

"I mean, what percent chance is there of that happening?"

A smile crept onto Rosie's lips. "Like a ten percent chance."

"I'm good with that." Devin squeezed her grip around Rosie's shoulders.

Rosie's head started to drop and she snapped it up in an effort to stay awake.

"Lie back," Devin gently lowered Rosie onto the sand. "I'll make sure nothing happens. It'll be sunrise any minute."

Rosie allowed herself to lay back onto the soft earth. The sensation of laying still was heavenly and her thoughts drifted. She imagined what it would be like if she and Devin were in a similar situation but elsewhere. Maybe on vacation in the Caribbean, on the beach under the night sky. She was surprised when her thoughts drifted to an imaginary Devin asking her if she was hungry. Yes, she said, very, then Devin gave her that charming smile, the one she'd noticed the first time they'd met on the boat. The smile that made her tremble. In her imaginary scenario, Devin reached for Rosie's face and gently cradled her cheek before leaning in closer. Rosie's heart rate increased as Devin's face drew closer to her own. She imagined closing her eyes in preparation for a kiss.

When the kiss came, it started soft and slow. The sensation was wonderful and sensuous. Every nerve in her body was stimulated to full alert. The kiss took her breath away.

For a few moments, Rosie had slipped to a place of extreme arousal. Then she tried to breathe. When she had difficulty inhaling is when the panic crept in. She tried to breathe again but the sensation of Devin's mouth completely covering hers wouldn't allow an inhale.

Suddenly someone was singing, and in a disturbing voice they chanted words that made no sense to her.

*"Dooha bangoo bahaba mozzubee. Witchabak nosquito. Witchabak morang zee chagga!"*

In her mind, Rosie watched as Devin morphed into a doll. Her weight pressed against Rosie's chest like a vice. It was bothersome the weight, as if it were a large spider clinging to her. Fear engulfed Rosie quickly and totally. The primal urge to fight for her life shot through her veins. As if in slow motion, she imagined shoving the possessed Devin doll away from her and...

She woke from the dream and bolted up right in time to see Sister Martha flying through the air. The nun landed several feet away face down in the sand. Rosie's hands flew to her chest and she forcefully inhaled several breaths, filling her lungs with much needed air. She looked down beside her and was horrified to see Devin laying on her back with Sister Dorothy on her chest. The nun's lips were placed against Devin's.

Rosie screamed, grabbed Sister Dorothy by the leg and tossed her. The nun spiraled through the air and landed several feet away in the sand next to Sister Martha.

Devin shot upright, blinked and looked around. "What happened?" she asked.

"The nuns!" Rosie said. "They were on us."

Devin pressed her fingertips to her lips.

The nuns stood and brushed themselves off.

"What the fuck?" Devin yelled. "What about the sacred circle and your vow to God?"

In maniacal laughter, the nuns screamed, "We lied!" Their mirth pierced the still night air as they held hands and danced a jig. They then turned and shuffled toward the woods.

"Why did you wait so long to make the change? Why go through the whole night?" Devin yelled at them.

Sister Martha stopped and turned to face them. "Because, if we'd done it earlier, then Clownie or Double Ds or someone else would've changed us and then we'd still be stuck here. We had to wait—"

Sister Dorothy grabbed her by the ear and tugged. "Stop it. There's no need to be nice to them anymore. You don't have to explain anything. Come on."

They were scampering over the stump of a fallen tree when Sister Martha said, "But I kinda liked them and besides —" and suddenly, she froze. Sister Dorothy had straddled the log and was about to climb down when she froze too.

"Devin, look!" Rosie pointed toward the horizon. Yellow-orange rays peeked from the dark edge of the water.

"Do you think they were on us long enough to make the change?" Devin asked.

"I don't know," Rosie said. "Maybe the sun came up in time. I feel ok. Do you?"

Devin nodded. "I feel fine, but, I now realize what I need to do. I need to destroy this island. I can't allow this vile wickedness to continue. There's nothing but evil here."

"Devin, how are you going to destroy an island?" Rosie asked.

"Watch me." The torch had fallen into the sand and Devin picked it up. The flame was out. She blew on it and only a thin trail of gray smoke floated upward.

"Shit," she said as her eyes scoured their surroundings. "Do you have any yarn left in your bag?"

Rosie nodded, reached into her bag and handed Devin a

ball of yarn. Devin shoved the yarn into her backpack. "What else do you have in there?"

Rosie peered into the bag. "Nothing. Just my sunglasses, lip balm, hand sanitizer and a spray can of suntan lotion."

"Give me the lotion," Devin said. "And Rosie, if for any reason I don't come back, well, you know what to tell my father. And," she cradled the side of Rosie's face. "Think fondly of me when you think of me."

"Devin, don't!" Rosie pleaded. "We'll be ok. The sun is up. The dolls are frozen now. They can't get us. And the boat will be here soon. I'm not sure what you're planning but whatever it is, don't do it."

"I have to Rosie. I couldn't live with myself if I didn't at least try. I'll be back in thirty minutes. If for any reason, I'm not back with the boat comes, don't wait for me. You go and get off this island, understand?"

Rosie nodded and handed the spray can of lotion to Devin.

"Promise?"

"Promise."

"Good." Devin ran her fingers along the side of Rosie's face, leaned in and gently kissed her. She winked, then shoved the can and yarn into her backpack and took off running, disappearing into the forest.

# A GIRL'S GOTTA DO

Rosie sat alone. She hadn't realized she'd be this scared and edgy without Devin.

The nuns were still stuck on the tree trunk as if a child had left them there discarded and abandoned. The sight of them was disturbing but she didn't dare leave the circle. Even though they'd proven the safety of the circle being a sacred, safe place was a myth, it was all she had psychologically to cling to. Logically, it made no sense, but nothing about tonight made any sense. She didn't dare step over the black circumference.

The sounds of the forest waking up and coming to life stimulated all her senses. It was as if every nerve in her body was exposed and raw. A variety of bird chirps, screams, and what she presumed were monkeys' chattering, filled the air. She'd heard recordings of jungle noises before but never imagined they'd be so extreme and maddening. It sounded like someone had turned on speakers throughout the jungle and was broadcasting a mixture of ear piercing, brain numbing dissonance of noises with the intent of disturbing her.

Time dragged as she focused her gaze toward the distant horizon.

A crackling in the underbrush caused her pulse to quicken and she searched for something that would work as a weapon. There was nothing in the circle with her but her bag. Then she remembered the little red knife that was in her pocket. Her hands shook as she tried to open it and memories of the snake wafted through her mind. She banished the thoughts, instead focusing on opening the knife. The first tool she flipped out was a cork screw. She closed the eye that had no lens and focused with her good eye, this time flipping out the larger knife blade. She stood, clutching the knife in front of her and waited for whatever was going to come at her.

A monkey scampered out from beneath the bushes. It stood on its hind legs, gave her a momentary, nonchalant, curious inspection, then continued on its unhurried way along the beach.

Her heart beat furiously inside her chest and she took deep, slow breaths, hoping to slow it. For the first time, she realized how dreadfully hungry and thirsty she was. Also, she had to pee but didn't dare go without Devin nearby.

She wished she knew what time it was or how long Devin had been gone. It seemed like eternity.

Her eyes skimmed the distant line where the sea met the sky, searching for signs of human activity. There was no motion other than the repetitive waves.

The minutes ticked by with excruciating tediousness. She paced throughout the circle. Her brain was engaged full-throttle, reviewing various scenarios of what they could have or should have done differently to have avoided ending up in this situation.

Rosie had never been a particularly religious person, but she said many silent prayers to whatever spiritual entity might be listening. She promised anything if only they would both make it safely off the island.

A distant rustling deep in the forest caught her attention and the thought of Clownie coming after them caused terror to flood her.

*Maybe he wasn't affected by the sunrise like the rest of the dolls. Maybe he was able to put his eyes back in.* Her thoughts raged like a wild fire through her brain.

She glanced at the tiny blade that stuck out from her clenched fist and worried it wouldn't do much damage if Clownie was coming for her. She decided, her only hope was to run. But with her bad ankle, doubts crept in whether she'd get anywhere far or fast.

She looked at the water and considered that the option of leaving the safety of shore and swimming might be her only chance. Suddenly, thoughts of sharks, crocodiles, and snakes cluttered her brain. She quickly abandoned the possibility of a water escape. As the snapping of branches grew louder and closer, the choking feeling of panic settled on her like a weight.

She braced herself to make what could possibly be a life-saving decision.

## WE'RE GETTING OFF THIS ISLAND, ONE WAY OR ANOTHER

Rosie's gaze fixed in the direction the crashing of broken branches came from. By the sound of it, something large moved through the forest and it was moving with speed.

The blood in the veins of her neck pounded against her skin and her temples pulsated. Her body tingled with nervous anticipation. When she finally saw branches moving, she inhaled, held her breath, and prepared to scream.

Devin popped through the thick entanglement of greenery and stumbled onto the beach. Her hair, face and shirt were soaked with sweat and thin trickles of blood oozed from the thin scratches that decorated her arms and face.

"Oh Devin," Rosie sighed and ran to meet her. A tick crawled up Devin's cheek. Rosie released a squeaky groan and pinched it off. She shuttered as she vigorously shook her hand to get rid of it. She glanced over Devin's shoulder. The forest behind her was quiet, nothing had followed her. Devin's backpack was noticeably absent.

"What did you do?" she asked as she pulled twigs from Devin's hair.

"Never mind that," Devin clutched her side as she caught her breath. "Any sign of a boat?"

Rosie shook her head. "Nothing."

"That's ok. It'll be here soon."

"Where's your backpack?" Rosie asked.

"I left it at the sub."

"The sub?"

"Yes, with any luck, in half an hour, hopefully after we're off this freaking nightmare-on-earth, there'll be an explosion that'll knock this island back to hell where it belongs."

"Devin? What? How?"

"My camera has a timer. I set it and removed the covering of the flash and manipulated it so when the timer goes off, the flash will spark. I positioned it next to the opening of the suntan lotion spray can that I covered with strands of yarn. If I did it right, the spark will blow the can. I wove the twine we'd taken from the boat with your yarn, then used that as a wick to run from the can into the diesel fuel intake valve of the sub. With any luck, it'll act like a fuse and the fire will blow the tank. If it reaches the reactors on the sub, oxygen supply and any bombs that may still be on board, it should create quite an explosion. Hopefully, half the island will be blown out of the water and the rest will burn. In about thirty minutes, Doll Island should be history."

"You think that'll work?"

"I have no idea, but it's the only thing I could think of. Honestly, I give it about the same odds as you saying you'd go on a date with me and we know how that turned out."

"But your camera?"

"I had to do what I thought was right. This island can't continue to exist. I had to at least try to get rid of it."

"And what if the boat doesn't come?" Rosie turned from Devin and studied the vast blue ocean.

"It'll come," Devin said. "It comes every morning. Like clockwork."

"But what if—"

"It'll come," Devin's voice was firm and determined.

They stood in silence, scouring the horizon for a sign of movement.

## WE ALL HAVE DREAMS

"Rosie?" Devin was rubbing her lips.

"Yes?"

"Do you feel… Funny?"

"Funny? Like how funny?"

"Like my lips are itchy and tingly, a little dizzy."

"Devin that's not funny. Don't you dare—"

Devin leapt up and recoiled away from Rosie. Her eyes had a crazed look about them. She shook her head as if something bothersome had invaded the inside of her ear. Her gaze skipped around her surroundings as she surveyed Rosie and the island. She tried to walk but lost her balance, stumbled and fell.

"Who are you? Where am I?" she demanded. Her face was contorted in a way Rosie hadn't seen before.

Rosie hopped up. "Stop it. This is no time for jokes Duh… Duh." She gazed up at the trees and spun in a circle. "Where am I? Who are you?"

Suddenly Devin glanced down at her own body and began patting herself. A wide smile blossomed across her face and she ran to Rosie. She gripped Rosie by the shoulders, shook her and stared into her eyes.

"Ria. Ria. It's me Naomi. We did it. We did it. Yahoo!" She leapt up, arms and legs splayed.

Rosie looked down at her own body and slapped her chest and stomach. "Naomi? Good Lord. We did it!" She jumped high into the air and landed in Devin's arms. Devin twirled them both around. "I can't believe it. Finally, after all these years. To be out of those dreadful nun bodies."

The women clung in tight embrace and kissed while they laughed and hugged.

"And look!" Devin lowered Rosie back to the ground and pointed toward the sea. "Here comes our rescue ship. We're getting off this island."

They held hands and bounced toward the water's edge.

"Naomi," Rosie said. "I need to get some glasses. I can't see a thing."

"That's the first thing we'll do when we get to Key West. Get you some glasses."

"No, the first thing we'll do is to drink some wine."

"Yes. Wine! And bread."

"Yes, wine and bread. And sex."

"Definitely sex."

"Oh and Ria," Devin squeezed Rosie's hands. "We're going to Paris and Italy."

They jumped up and down, wiggling their hips in jubilation. They held hands and danced a jig, danced a waltz, and spun each other around.

Hand in hand, they waded into the water and waited, arms draped around each other's shoulders, as the boat approached. Soon the vessel was close enough to make out the people on board. They released their grip on each other and waved their arms frantically over their heads. When the people on the boat waved back, they clung to each other and danced.

Suddenly, from somewhere behind them on the island, came a ground shaking blast. They were blown forward and sent tumbling into the cold, salty water of the Atlantic Ocean.

EVERYONE LOVES A SURVIVOR

A ladder hung off the back of the boat and the women scampered up it and onto the safety of the boat. They were given blankets and soon surrounded by a crowd of enthralled tourists firing questions at them in rapid succession. How did they survive the night? Was the island really haunted? What did they see? Devin and Rosie answered as many questions as they could but were barely able to get a few words out when they'd be bombarded with another question.

As luck would have it, a reporter for the Key West Scoop newspaper was on board doing a story on the state of the tourism industry in Florida. She wasted no time live broadcasting the rescue.

The island had turned into a spectacular bonfire with orange and yellow flames shooting high into the sky. The tops of the tall coconut trees were consumed with fire. The scent of the burning forest saturated the air. From a distance they looked like giant lollipops of leaping flames. The reporter recorded dramatic footage of the island ablaze, zooming in on distorted dolls as they melted and fell, little balls of fire, from the trees.

The island inferno grew smaller as the boat left it behind, eventually becoming a small orange dot on the horizon, but the plume of dark smoke could be seen for miles. No one knew if anything on the island, or the island itself, would survive the blast or what had caused it.

The story of how two women survived, "The Curse of Doll Island," was promptly picked up by the AP and instantly captivated the world's attention. Not only had two women survived a night on the haunted island, but one of them was Devin Fitzroy, star of the blockbuster movie, 'Skate to My Heart', and daughter of the internationally famous Frederick Fitzroy.

Rosie and Devin had no way of knowing the insane demand the paparazzi and media was about to unleash on them. The public's hunger for every detail of their story was insatiable.

# THE END?

On the boat ride back to Key West, Ria and Naomi snuggled, entwined like a pretzel, wrapped in a large beach blanket, and took great pleasure in the warmth and nearness of each other's bodies. They sipped hot chocolate and swapped long deliberate glances and grins as they interacted with the crowd, whose attention and questions were endless. Their shivering had slowed down and the reality they'd truly been rescued and were off the island had sunk in, filling them with a giddy sense of jubilance.

Suddenly, the boat slowed and the engines stopped. The tour guide made an announcement apologizing that there would be a slight delay. Something about engine trouble but he expected to have them up and running and back to Key West in no time.

Ria placed her lips close to Naomi's ear and was about to whisper something when she heard it. Whatever words she'd intended to say were never spoken. And by the way the wide smile dropped from Naomi's face, it was obvious she'd heard it too.

The interruption came from the mouth of a little girl. She

must have been five or six. The young child repeatedly tugged on the hem of her mother's shirt and bounced up and down as she agitatedly pointed to something that drifted behind the boat. Her voice had rapidly ascended in volume and had grown from an insistent whine to an annoying high-pitched cry accompanied by stomping feet.

*"Mommy. Tell the man to stop the boat. I want the dolls!"*

Ria, Naomi and many of the other passengers followed the tip of the girl's tiny finger to see what she was so adamant about.

Floating behind the boat, bobbing up and down in the foaming wake, a log floated. It was being dragged by a rope that had become entangled in the boat's propeller.

Clinging to a section of a log were two nun dolls.

The End

# TO YOU, THE READER

~

I greatly appreciate you taking the time to read my words.
If you like this book, please leave a review. The only way I
can decide whether to commit more time to these characters
and this series is by getting feedback from you, the readers.
Your opinion matters to me. I have only so much time to
craft new stories. Help me invest that time wisely. Plus,
reviews boost my spirits and flames the fires of creativity.

**Thank you.**

**Ocean**

*Stephen King, R.L. Stine, Alfred Hitchcock, Rod Serling*
*I respect and thank you*

## AUTHOR NOTES FROM OCEAN

I struggled with what genre to call *The Curse of Doll Island*. Some would say it's a work of horror. To me, horror includes more blood and is on an entirely different level of fright than what was intended with this book. I settled on calling it a 'paranormal, suspense, thriller'. Fans of these genres, I'd love to hear if you agree.

I've always enjoyed reading about the supernatural and paranormal activity. Things that "might be", but can't be explained. Ghosts, aliens, voodoo, witches, curses and spells really fire up my imagination.

This book gave me great joy to write. There are more like it to be written in the future for sure.

If you liked this story, you might like some of my other books:

**GONE** – *A novel of suspense and romance.* "A fractured relationship is just the beginning of the unfolding nightmare, and the biggest mystery is yet to come. Caught between love and suspicion, a trip to Provincetown should have been a fresh start for Jamie and Casey, but can they really start over again, when both are swept into a world of dangerous games?

As truths unfold, personalities deceive those who don't suspect.

A thrilling story that will make you rethink your social media friends."

Gone is published by Wicked Publishing

$\approx$

**Tempted** – *When temptation knocks, should you answer?* The sequel to Gone

Jamie's relationship with Casey has been through some bumps, but hasn't everyone's? She believes all is well between them, until Casey drops a bomb, forcing them each to make a life-changing choice.

When a charismatic detective and a charming hustler, enter their lives, each with their own ulterior motives and intentions, things get more complicated as Jamie and Casey are forced to re-evaluate their relationship and life goals.

All four women are challenged to make choices and decisions that will affect the rest of their lives and each must answer the question, 'When temptation knocks, should you answer?'.

Tempted is to be published by Wicked Publishing and is due out the end of 2018

$\approx$

**Interview with a Lesbian Sasquatch** – **She's intelligent, funny, sassy and she has something to say.**

When radio host Serena Bonago received an email from someone claiming to be a lesbian Sasquatch, she brushed it off as a hoax. But when the second email arrived and convinced her that the sender was indeed a lesbian Sasquatch, she arranged for a live, on-air interview. Six months later, the world eagerly waits for answers to centuries-old questions about their social, spiritual and sexual habits and, most importantly, why, instead of avoiding mankind as has been customary, has a representative of the Sasquatch community come forward now with an urgent message.

Stay tuned as radio celebrity Harper Woolf broadcasts live from WEXG Radio, 109.2 FM studios, in the Royal Rhodium Tower Building in Manhattan.

A light-hearted, speculative fiction novella.

≈

**A Wicked Kind of Love** – *Love pulls you in different directions*, sex opens your mind to other possibilities, romance warms your heart, and the unknown keeps you guessing. Five different stories by five different authors, equals, five romances that you will fall in love with.

Several of my short stories appear in this anthology.

A Wicked Kind of Love is published by Wicked Publishing

≈

You can join my mailing list by dropping by my website

Oceanldy.com or if you have any comments, shoot me a note at oceanwrites@gmail.com I'm always happy to hear from people who've read my work and try to answer every email I receive.

If you liked the story, please write a short review for me on Amazon. I greatly appreciate any kind words, even one or two sentences goes a long way. The number of reviews an book receives greatly improves how well an book does on Amazon.

More contact info:
　Amazon: https://www.amazon.com/Ocean
　Facebook: https://www.facebook.com/oceanwrites/
　Twitter: https://twitter.com/OceanWrites
　My website: www.oceanldy.com

# THE LITTLE LEGAL BLURB

The little legal blurb